FORTY-FOUR CALIBER JUSTICE

DONALD L. ROBERTSON

CM Publishing

FORTY-FOUR CALIBER JUSTICE

Copyright © 2016 Donald L. Robertson
CM Publishing

Publisher's Note: This is a work of fiction. Names, characters, and incidents are a product of the author's imagination. Locales and public names are sometimes used for atmospheric purposes. Any resemblance to actual people, living or dead, or to businesses, companies, or events, is completely coincidental. For information contact:

Books@DonaldLRobertson.com

ISBN print: 978-0-9909139-4-8
ISBN ebook: 978-0-9909139-3-1

 Created with Vellum

COPYRIGHT

FORTY-FOUR CALIBER JUSTICE

Copyright © 2016 Donald L. Robertson
CM Publishing

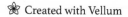 Created with Vellum

1

The sweet, putrid stench of death and burned flesh, wafting on the soft spring breeze, slammed into Clay when he topped the hill just north of home. The ranch house rested quietly in the valley below, surrounded by a sea of bluebonnets.

Clay kicked Blue in the flanks. The surprised roan, tired from three days of chasing cattle, raced down the hill, dodging the prickly pear and cedars. Like his pa had always taught him, Clay slipped the hammer thongs off both the Remington Navy revolvers as he leaned over Blue's neck. His hat blew off, but he didn't slow.

The body was hanging from a massive limb on the big, old oak next to the ranch house, the oak he used to climb and daydream among its cool branches, always soothing during the hot summers. The oak that had provided shade and respite now held a body—a body shot, hanged, and burned. Turkey buzzards, their red heads glistening in the sun, sat in the tree and on the ground.

He yanked Blue to a sliding halt and leaped from the saddle, his eyes riveted on the burned remains. Tears filled his eyes as he recognized the body. The fire had burned his pa, and the bullet hole in the side of his head had disfigured him, but he was still recognizable.

"Pa, you can't be dead, you just can't." Clay's tears streamed down his sun-browned cheeks and fell in the dust, making miniature volcanoes as they hit. His father's body swung lightly in the breeze.

Movement near the barn caught his eye. In one smooth motion, he wheeled around and palmed the Remington. Buzzards pecked and pulled at another body. The Remington bucked twice, the shots coming so fast they sounded as one. An explosion of black feathers erupted, and two buzzards became food for their kin. Clay wheeled back at the sound of wingbeats, the shots chasing the other buzzards out of the tree and into the air, where they circled slowly, patiently waiting.

He trotted over to the body at the barn. It was Slim, riddled with holes. An empty .44 Henry case lay near his body. It was a wonder Slim had managed to get off even one shot with all the bullet holes in him. Slim had been with them as long as Clay could remember. His pa and Slim had been good friends long before the war.

Ma. The thought hit him like a sledgehammer. He raced to the house, dreading what he might find.

A cool wind moaned softly through the breezeway. He opened the door into the kitchen and study. Ma must've been cooking. The fire in the stove had burned out. Flour was in a mixing bowl on the table, and the churn was nearby with a chair pulled up to it, but no Ma. Dishes and pots and pans were scattered across the kitchen. Books from the shelves in the study were lying about the room.

Clay had so many good memories here. Memories of laughter around the table with Pa and Ma and Slim, crowded together with the smell of fresh-baked biscuits, of Ma making peach preserves. Ma was so pretty. Everybody said so. At the barn dances, all the men danced with her. Pa just stood back with his confident smile. He sure loved Ma, and she him.

Clay looked into Slim's room behind the kitchen. Empty. Slim's makeshift chest had been torn open, and all of his things were strewn about the room. The mattress had been thrown back and ripped open with a knife. Ticking was everywhere. His pillow had been sliced, and feathers covered the ripped mattress.

Clay stepped out of Slim's room onto the breezeway. He glanced to the right, barely noticing the blooms of the peach trees and grapevines his ma had planted. She loved her orchard. Nothing moved behind the house except the leaves on the trees.

Three quick steps took him across the breezeway to the door into his room. He pushed it open. His room had also been torn apart. Everything lay scattered. The drawers of his bureau were on the floor, and clothes were tossed about. His bed had been sliced open, along with his pillow. These weren't Indians. This was the work of white devils. Thieves. Killers. He turned to his left and opened the door into his ma and pa's bedroom, always so neat and clean.

She lay silent on the bed. Her neck was black from bruising, where two big hands had choked the last breath of life from her. Clay's tears flowed freely, cutting little rivers through his dusty face. A sob escaped him. He grabbed a sheet from the floor where they had been scattered and covered his mother's tiny, bloody body. Her face was calm and peaceful in death, as if the ravaging and raping of her body had not reached her soul. Clay stood silent, looking at her. Gabrielle Amalina Chevalier had brought him into this world, had brought laughter and happiness into this house and made it a home. She lit up any room with her smile. Her smile was gone forever.

He had no idea how long he stood there, but, in time, the tears stopped. His soft gray eyes took a steely shade, and the promise of laughter that constantly played around the corners of his eyes and mouth disappeared. The softness of the seventeen-year-old hardened, and his heart turned cold.

"I promise you, Ma. They'll pay. Whoever did this to you will pay. I'll not rest until every one of these men is dead. I promise you that."

Clay picked up a quilt, walked out of the bedroom, and turned right onto the porch. There was gruesome work to do. He walked over to Blue, mounted him, and eased up to his pa. He wrapped the quilt around his pa and hugged him, for the last time, with a muscular arm. Reaching up with the bowie knife that Slim had given him, he sliced the rope. He hardly noticed the weight of his father. Clay laid him gently across the saddle and rode a few yards to the field of bluebonnets that his ma loved. He stepped down from the saddle and gently placed his father on the ground.

Holding Blue's reins, he walked over to Slim. Slim had grown up with Pa. They'd gone to war together. When Pa started this ranch, Slim had pitched in. Pa always said that Slim was more than a brother could ever be. They had seen the elephant together and survived. Ma had liked Slim. He was just an all-around likable guy. But crossing him could be a fatal mistake. He had been deadly with a gun, a knife, or his fists. To Clay, Slim was like an uncle. What Pa hadn't taught him, Slim had.

Clay took Blue into the corral, stripped the saddle and blanket from his back, and rubbed him down. He checked to make sure the trough was full of water and put some hay out. Blue watched him, his ears forward, as if he too felt the pain. Clay picked up the saddle and carried it into the barn. He pulled his Winchester out of the scabbard, a gift from Slim, and carried it with him.

He went to the house. He tried not to look at his ma, but then told himself: look and remember. This is what those monsters had done to his family. He picked up another quilt and went out to Slim. He wrapped Slim in the quilt and carried him to where his father lay, gently placing him on the ground.

He had grabbed the shovel when he went after Slim. He started digging. Clay was digging the third grave when he heard the horses approaching. He picked up the Winchester and waited.

Adam Hewitt rode up, followed by his oldest son, Toby, and two of his ranch hands, Bo Nelson and Luke Jones.

"Clay, what's going on?" Hewitt took in the graves and the wrapped bodies lying on the ground. "By all the things that's holy, who did this? Where's your ma?" He stepped from his horse, handing the reins to Bo.

"I don't know, Mr. Hewitt. I've been pushing cows out of the canyons. Been gone for three days. When I got back, this is what I found. They killed Slim and Pa out here. Ma's inside on the bed. She's dead too."

"They killed your ma?" Hewitt pulled his hat off and swept his hair back with a gloved hand. "Boys, get down and give Clay a hand. You're looking plumb tuckered out, Son."

The cowboys climbed down. This was hard country. Death wasn't new to them, but these folks were friends, and killing a woman in this country was about the worst sin a man could commit. Bo walked over to the bodies and turned to Clay. "You mind?"

Clay just shook his head, and Bo gently pulled the blankets back from the two men.

"Mr. Hewitt, looka here. Why, they've shot Mr. Barlow, and it looks like he was hanged and burned. What kind of low-down cusses would do such a thing? And look at Slim. My gosh, they shot him up so bad, there ain't no room for another bullet."

"Son, you mind if I take a look at your ma?"

Clay looked long at Hewitt. "I've wrapped her in a sheet. I'd be much obliged if you'd leave her covered. She was a modest woman."

Hewitt laid his hand on Clay's shoulder. "We all loved her, Son. I'll treat her with great respect."

They all heard a whimper and turned toward Toby. Tears ran freely down the boy's face.

"Toby, Son, why don't you take the horses for some water?" Hewitt said in a soft voice.

Luke watched his boss walk to the house, then picked up the shovel. "I'll finish diggin' here, if it's okay with you."

Clay nodded and walked over to the front porch. He stood there for a moment, staring into the house that had been a happy home, then slowly sat on the front porch steps. He gazed out across the hillside, where, only hours ago, he had raced down to the house, maybe for the last time. His eyes spotted his hat a short distance from the yard. He could remember the day his pa had given him that black hat. He had grown so much he could look his pa in the eyes. "You're gettin' on to being a man, Son. You need a man's hat." He remembered how Pa's face had split in that big smile. That same day, Pa had given him the set of Remington .36 Navy revolvers and the old holsters to go with them. "These are a mite old, Son, but they've done right by me for a long time. You've practiced with them quite a bit with me and Slim. You've got about the quickest hands I think I've ever seen. Just remember, never draw on another man unless you have to, and don't try to get fancy. Make the first shot count. If you have to shoot, put that bullet in the third button, and don't stop shootin' until the threat's gone."

A smile ghosted across Clay's face as he remembered how excited he had been. Slim was standing there with a big ole grin on his face. "You deserve 'em, boy. You're right good with those irons. Just remember, don't be loose with 'em. Last thing you want to do is kill a man. Ain't somethin' you can forget once you done it. It'll stick with you for your whole durn life."

Clay was yanked out of his reverie by the jingle of Hewitt's spurs as he stepped back onto the porch. Clay stood and looked up at the big man.

"Son, this ain't nothing but evil. Any man that'd do what's been done here deserves what's coming to him. I'll get a posse together and be after those gents in the morning. First, though, we'll give your family a proper burial. Reckon they deserve that. Then you need to come over and live with us. We've got the room, and I know Sarah will be glad to see you."

"Mr. Hewitt, you can forget the posse. Those killers are long gone."

"But, Clay, they need to pay."

"Yes, sir. They'll pay. I'll get 'em no matter how long it takes. Will you walk with me?" Clay pointed to his hat on the hill and started toward it. Hewitt came down from the porch and joined him. "I've been thinking about what needs to be done. Pa had planned to join up with your drive to Kansas. We have about five hundred head that are ready for market. I know you've always liked our ranch, what with it sitting on so much water. Pa told Ma and me that you'd made him a fair offer. But they both loved this place. They'd never have sold it. If you still want it, I have an idea that might work for both of us."

Hewitt look stunned. "Clay, I won't dispute that I've always wanted this piece of land. But I'm not comfortable buying this from you now—not with what's just happened."

"Mr. Hewitt, I figure to make you a deal on the ranch. Not the cattle we were planning on selling. I'm thinking the five hundred head can be worked in with your cattle and sold in Kansas. I'll pay you a fee out of the sales price. I trust you. I know you'll be fair. Then you can just deposit the money in the bank in my name."

"Clay, what are you planning on doing?"

Clay's face was stern and set as he turned to Hewitt. "Like I said, I'm going after those killers. Those are men who don't deserve to be breathing the same air regular folks breathe. So, I reckon I'll do something about that."

Hewitt's eyes tightened, and his mouth drew into a straight line. "Son, you're not a killer. Why, you just turned seventeen in January. How can you even think about going after those men? They're hardened killers. You've filled out in these last two years, and you'll be a big man, but right now, you're only one boy."

"Mr. Hewitt, I've been doing a man's work since I was fifteen. Pa and Slim taught me how to shoot. I'm pretty good with a gun, whether a rifle or a handgun. I can use a bow and follow a trail as good as any Comanche. I figure I'll find those killers and read to 'em from the good book. They can't do what they've done and ride away scot-free."

"You're serious, aren't you?" Hewitt asked.

They had reached Clay's hat. He picked it up, dusted it off, and set it on the back of his head, his black hair hanging down over his forehead. "Never been more serious about anything in my life. Ma loved this country. Why, she planted those peach trees right after we moved here. I've loved this place, Mr. Hewitt. But I can't stay here. I just can't. Now, I know you like it. I reckon I've an idea that'll work for both of us."

"Talk to me about it tomorrow, when you come over to the ranch. I'm not happy about you chasing those killers, but I'll discuss the ranch."

The two men shook hands and started back to the graves. Luke had finished the digging. He and Bo were standing by the two bodies, waiting for Clay's return. Toby had brought their horses back and had gotten himself under control.

"I'll get Ma." Clay walked to the house and went into the bedroom. He wrapped the sheet tight around her and gently lifted her into his arms.

She's so tiny and light. Clay's face looked as if it had turned to stone. No tears flowed down his cheeks. He carried her to the grave and gently laid her in the hole. Bo and Luke picked up

Clay's pa and laid him in the grave next to his wife and put Slim in his final resting place, next to Clay's pa.

Clay slipped off his hat. "Mr. Hewitt, can you say a few words?"

Hewitt nodded, as he and the cowhands pulled their hats off. "Lord, these fine folks have come to a troubling end. This is rough country. Folks die in some mighty harsh ways. But these good folks were sent to you by evil men. We ask you to welcome them and let 'em know we'll be seeing 'em. We'd also like to ask that you watch over this boy as he heads out in search of these killers and keep him safe. Ashes to ashes and dust to dust."

Clay put his hat back on, and the other men followed suit. Bo had the shovel. He looked at Clay, and Clay nodded. "Start with Ma." Bo stepped over to her grave and started shoveling dirt into the hole. The rattle of the West Texas dirt striking his ma's body tore at Clay. With each shovelful, it felt like he was being stabbed. He wanted to walk away. But he stayed, forcing himself to hear and commit to memory every painful moment. He stood stone-still as the other two graves were filled.

It didn't take long. The burying was done, and the other men were standing around awkwardly waiting for Clay. He looked up and realized it was finished. "Thank you," he said. He brushed his hair back with one hand and put his hat back on, pulling it level on his head. "Mr. Hewitt, Bo, Luke, Toby, I appreciate all your help. Mr. Hewitt, it's getting late. You folks might as well head back home."

Hewitt said, "Clay, why don't you come on over to the house tonight, and stay as long as you want."

"No, thanks. I'll spend the night here. I'll be over tomorrow, and we can close the deal on the ranch and cattle."

Hewitt shook his head and waited for a moment. Finally, he said, "Come on, boys, let's get home." He turned his horse out of the yard with Toby alongside, Bo and Luke following.

It was twilight in the hill country. The sun had set over the western hills. Shadows were slipping across the yard as darkness overcame daylight. Clay walked over to Blue and rubbed his neck, scratching him between the ears. The western light cast an eerie pall over Clay's face. A face too grim to be so young. "We got a long trail ahead of us, Blue, boy. But we'll see those devils dead before we quit. Every last one of them."

2

Clay stepped into his ma and pa's bedroom. He grasped the bloody mattress and pillow, and pulled them into the yard. He did the same with the bedding from the other rooms. He checked for a breeze. There was none. Burning embers wouldn't be a problem. He pulled a match from his pocket and lit it on the butt of his .36 Remington. The match flared in the growing darkness and settled to a miniature blaze, the smell of sulfur drifting into the air. He tossed it onto the bedding.

The mattresses burned quickly, giving off a bright light in the early evening darkness. Clay stood silently and watched. The future he had dreamed about drifted up to the heavens with the tendrils of smoke. The fire cast a stark light across his face and body. No longer did he look seventeen. The weight of duty now rested on his shoulders.

His father had taught him to be a kind man and help those who were less fortunate. Clay had always been slow to anger, his temper roused seldom. But when it reached its zenith, he became deadly. Not the hot-tempered anger that stepped in swinging at one and all, but the cold fury that wouldn't stop until he was either knocked out or pulled off his unfortunate opponent. He had never killed a man. He had never even contemplated taking the life of a fellow human being. But now, with Ma and Pa and Slim in the ground, Clay was cold with anger. He knew what he had to do. He also knew he was young and inexperienced. He would have to be careful.

He turned back to the house and entered the kitchen. The burning bedding cast shadows across the sitting room. Clay stopped for a moment. He could feel the spirit of his ma in the room with him. He looked around the room. He could hear her playing the violin, the sweet notes drifting across his mind.

He sighed, the spell broken, and walked to the fireplace. Kneeling, he picked up kindling, put in some sticks, and then a couple of logs. He struck a match and slipped it under the kindling. Slowly, the flames took hold and licked up through the kindling to the sticks. Clay walked over to the kerosene lamp on the counter and lit it, adjusting the flame for maximum light. He started picking up books and putting them back in the bookcase. *Both Ma and Pa set great store by books. I guess I got that from them.* He loved to read. *They'd want me to take a few of these with me. Grandma and Grandpa can have the rest.*

After straightening the books, Clay picked up the lamp and headed for the barn. The mattresses had burned down to embers. He hung the lamp on a nail once he reached the barn. He lifted the pitchfork from its place on the wall, walked to the haystack, and started pitching hay. By the time he had cleared a path to the back wall, sweat glistened on his face and neck. He moved the lamp to a hook on the back wall of the barn, careful to keep it away from the hay. With the lamp hanging over the area he had just cleared, he knelt down and started sweeping away the dirt. It only took a moment to uncover the two six-inch-wide planks in the ground. He lifted them up and pulled the small safe from the ground. It wasn't really a safe, just a rectangular metal box about one by two feet, with a hasp on the front. Pa had called it their safe. There was no lock.

Clay opened the box. This was probably what the killers were after. His pa never liked banks. He kept some money in the bank in Uvalde, but most he kept buried in the ground in this box. Clay slowly started taking the items out. Lying across the top was a piece of paper, twice folded. He read it through. It was the contract Grandpa Barlow had given Pa when he awarded him the land grant. Clay folded it and put it in his vest pocket.

Pa had kept his old LeMat revolver in the box, loaded and primed. He hefted the heavy revolver. Its unique design included nine .42 caliber chambers and a single shotgun barrel beneath the cylinder. *Pa always liked the old LeMat. He figured if it was good enough for Jeb Stuart, it was good enough for him. Guess I'll hang on to it.*

The box contained gold bars and silver coins that his pa had saved throughout his life. *Pa had said there was close to three thousand dollars there. He and Ma were almighty good savers.* Clay walked over to his pa's saddlebags hanging across a rail in the barn. The leather smelled familiar. His hand rubbed across the burnished leather. *I'll get 'em, Pa. I swear I will.* After carrying the saddlebags back to the box, he slipped the gold, silver, and the old LeMat into the bags. He placed the empty box back in the hole and put the boards back. The saddlebags were heavy now. He set them against the wall, moved the lamp, and raked the hay back in place.

His young body was tired. He made a bed in the hay, unwilling to sleep in the house, and stretched out his long legs. *I made a promise to Ma and Pa. How am I going to accomplish it? How can I find those killers? Their tracks headed south. After stopping at the Hewitt's, I'll get some supplies in Uvalde and start after 'em. I'll catch—.*

Sleep overtook him. He dreamed of his ma and pa in the sitting room, smiling, laughing.

Clay awakened to Blue neighing in the corral. He looked at the sunlight streaming in through the barn doorway. Clay had slept way too long. He needed to get moving. He put some oats in the trough for Blue and tossed in some hay. "You'd better eat up, boy. We've got some riding to do."

The surrounding trees were filled with sound as he walked out into the yard. The mockingbird attacked the morning air with songs that he copied from other birds. A bright male cardinal trilled in the big oak. Today was like every day, except Ma and Pa were gone. "Why did they do it?" Clay asked, speaking to the silence. "If they were just trying to rob us, why would they be so brutal?" His young mind barely comprehended what had happened to his life. The cardinal looked at him with its head slightly cocked, but gave no answer. Brilliant red, it lifted on scarlet wings and sailed back to the orchard. A hummingbird zipped by on the way to Ma's flower garden.

The yard had been chewed up with horse tracks. Yesterday, he had seen the large blood spot in the yard. Someone else had been shot and hit hard. *Hopefully he's dead.* Several tracks had been clear. One of the horses' hooves were set deeper in the yard. It had been carrying a lot of weight, a big man. He turned abruptly and marched into the house. He didn't need much, his slicker, sugan, and groundsheet would make up his bedroll. They hadn't found the powder and lead, but they had taken all of the weapons. Pa's Colt and Winchester, Slim's rifle and sidearm, and Ma's pocket pistol that she had killed the Comanche with. Both shotguns were also missing. Clay had his two Remington Navy revolvers and his Winchester. He'd have to get more ammunition for the Winchester in Uvalde.

Books. He wanted to take some books with him, but books were heavy. Blue could only carry so much. Pa had his law books, his favorite *Blackstone's Commentaries,* and Ma her readers and math books that she had taught him and Running Wolf from. There were also books that Ma insisted on having. He, like her, loved reading *Robinson Crusoe* and *Gulliver's Travels*. He chose those three books, placing them in the chair next to the door. Clay walked into his room and looked around. This was home no longer. He had grown to a man here. His dream of adventure and travel, always returning home, had ended. The sweet smell of peach blossoms wafted into the study. Now resolute, he picked up the books from the chair and walked into the yard. Time to leave.

After saddling Blue, Clay tied on the bedroll and bulging saddlebags. He'd need to get the gold and silver in the bank quickly. He was sure there was no danger from the killers. They were probably miles away by now, but this country had more than its share of bandits and road agents. After one last look at the homeplace, he turned Blue south, toward the Hewitts' spread. He could rest for the night at the Hewitts', then go into Uvalde tomorrow. He'd draw up the contract with Mr. Hewitt, and deposit the money in the bank tomorrow. He'd devote the rest of his days to finding the killers, no matter how long it took. Clay swung into the saddle and looked across the valley. He could see the maples and cypress along the Frio. He hated to leave this country. It was his kind of land, sharp angles softened by oaks and mesquite, rivers clear as glass and cool as a fall morning.

He sat motionless for a moment longer, then swung Blue up the ridge toward the Hewitt ranch. He was getting a late start, but he'd be there a little after lunch. There'd be plenty of time to explain the idea he'd had to Mr. Hewitt.

～

IT WAS a little past noon when Clay paused on the ridgeline above the Hewitt ranch. Cattle were grazing along the Dry Frio west of the ranch house. Smoke from the chimney was lazily reaching for the puffy, white clouds. Someone worked near the corral. He'd seen this scene most of his young life. The Hewitts were good friends, and the families had visited one another often.

"Come on, Blue. Let's see if Sarah Jane has any vittles for a hungry cowboy."

Blue stepped out toward the ranch house as if he had understood. When they were only halfway down the ridge, he could hear Tyler Hewitt yelling. "Pa, I see Clay acomin'! He's comin' down the north ridge right now. Sarah Jane, did you hear me?"

A young woman stepped out onto the front porch and shaded her eyes with her right hand. "Tyler Hewitt, stop your yelling. I see him."

Clay smiled. He and Sarah had mostly grown up together. She wasn't quite a year younger than him. When Mrs. Hewitt had died of pneumonia, she had taken over the household for her father and had mothered Tyler and Toby. She was a strong-minded girl who never had a problem stating what was on her mind, and here lately, he'd felt that she had him on her mind way too much. He figured she had set her cap for him, and that made a man mighty uncomfortable.

Tyler met him as he pulled up at the corral.

That boy's growing. It's hard to accept he's only twelve.

"Howdy, Tyler," Clay said. "How're you doing?"

Tyler looked up at Clay with clear, serious eyes. "I'm fine, Clay. I'm sure sorry about your folks and Slim. If you want, I'll go with you to catch those killers."

Clay stepped down from Blue and put his hand on Tyler's shoulder. "Thanks, Tyler. That's mighty big of you. But you best stay here to help your Pa with the ranch."

"Clay?"

Clay turned to see Sarah standing close. Tears were brimming in her eyes. "Clay, I'm so sorry about your folks. That is the most horrible thing I've ever heard of." She reached out and rested her hand on his arm. "Is there anything that I can do?"

He looked into her big blue eyes, set wide in a strong face, framed by her long brown hair. "Reckon not, Sarah. But thank you."

The moment passed. "Well, you must be hungry. Come in the house. I left some food from dinner for you. Tyler, put Blue up." She turned to start back to the house.

"I'll put him up," Clay said. "He's had a hard morning, with all these hills. He needs a good rubdown."

"Let me do it, Clay. Blue likes me. He won't mind," Tyler said.

"All right, Tyler, thanks. Make sure he gets some water." Clay slid the Winchester out of the scabbard and untied the saddlebags, tossing them across his left shoulder. He joined Sarah, and they walked to the house.

Hewitt had come onto the porch. "Afternoon, Clay. How're you doing, Son?"

"I'm doing okay. If it's all right with you, could we get our business done? I don't mean to be abrupt, sir, but I'd like to get it done and out of the way."

Hewitt stepped aside and motioned Clay inside. "Sure, I understand. Come on into the office."

Sarah glanced at Clay in surprise. It was obvious she had no idea what they were talking about.

"Mr. Hewitt, if it's all right with you, I'd kinda like Sarah to sit in on this. The boys are also welcome. I'd be a mite more comfortable if everyone knew what was going on."

"Sure, Clay. Toby's out with Bo working cattle, but Tyler can come in when he's finished with Blue. Shall we?" he asked as he pointed toward his office.

Sarah walked in and sat in the second chair facing her father's desk. Clay took the first chair and waited until Hewitt sat down.

"Mr. Hewitt, I have an idea that may work for both of us," Clay said as he sat. "You want the grazing and the water on the Frio, and I need to be relieved of the responsibility of the ranch, for now."

Hewitt looked at Clay, a puzzled look on his face. "I thought you were talking about selling the ranch."

"No, sir. Pa was teaching me about business and talked about this idea in passing. He was talking as if he and Ma might go back East for a few years, and he knew how much you liked our ranch. Anyway, I'm going to be gone, I just don't know how long. I don't know if I'll even come back after I settle up with those killers. Right now, as much as I like the place, I can't stand to be there."

Sarah was looking at Clay, her eyes large, astonishment across her face. Clay looked at her and then looked back to Hewitt. The hurt in her eyes was obvious.

"Mr. Hewitt, what about me just turning the place over to you? You have all the grazing and water rights for as long as I'm gone. If—"

"Clay, are you sure you don't want to sell the land? You would be done with it, nothing to worry about. I'll pay you a good sum for it."

"No, sir. I'm not interested in selling right now," Clay said, his mind centered, for a moment, on the paper he'd found in the safe. "Pa taught me not to make a major decision when emotions are high."

Sarah was still focused on Clay. "Are you really leaving?"

"I can't stay, Sarah. There's a bunch of killers running loose. I've got to find them."

"Clay," Hewitt asked, "what kind of terms did you have in mind?"

"Mr. Hewitt, I'll give you a ten-year guarantee. After that, we can talk about renewing. I won't take it back before then. You can figure what you should pay me for it. I trust you. You can make it monthly or once a year, I really don't care. Just deposit it in the Uvalde bank."

Hewitt leaned back in his chair. "You're awfully trusting, Clay. I could pay you nothing, based on your request."

"Yes, sir, you could. I just want the land looked after. I'd like you to take our cattle, those that are ready for market, on the drive. You figure what's fair to charge me and deposit the rest after the sale. Pa, Slim, and I had about finished the gather. The cattle are holding along the Frio, south of the place."

"Son, you've got a deal, except for one thing. I don't want a ten-year contract. We'll just make it until you return and decide what you want to do. Does that sound fair to you?"

"Yes, sir, that's more than fair."

"Good. I'll draw up the contract. We'll sign it, and I'll have Luke witness it. I'll also make you a copy."

Hewitt came to his feet and extended his hand. "I hate to see you leaving, Clay. You've bitten off more than most grown men would want to chew. You sure I can't talk you into staying?"

"No, sir. If you don't mind, I'd like to spend the night and leave for Uvalde in the morning. I also need a couple of your horses, if you have any for sale. The killers took the horses around the house, and I don't have time to roundup any others."

"Sure, we've got some good stock in the corral. I'll get Bo to pick out a couple of good ones. We'll make them part of the deal."

Clay rolled and unrolled his hat brim. Then he ran his right hand through his black hair. "I've one more request, Mr. Hewitt. I hate to ask this, but I just don't have time to do it. You know my grandparents live in D'Hanis. They need to know, but I've got to get after those killers. I'd be obliged if you'd send a hand over and tell them what happened. Also, tell them to come over, get the books, and whatever they want out of the house. What they don't want, you're welcome to."

"I'll be glad to, Clay. Though it would be better coming from you."

"Yep, reckon it would."

"Papa, I know Clay must be starving. I'll take him into the kitchen and get him something to eat."

Without waiting, Sarah turned and strode into the kitchen.

Hewitt watched his daughter, then shook his head. "She's upset, Son. Go easy on her."

Clay nodded, and followed Sarah into the kitchen.

She looked up as he stopped at the door. "Why, Clay? I thought you—I thought we—it's just not right. You don't have to leave. The sheriff can chase the killers. You're just seventeen."

Clay lay his hat on the table as Sarah continued to put food on the table. "Sarah, I'm really sorry. But it's my folks who have been killed, not the sheriff's. And I'm getting almighty tired of people telling me I'm 'just seventeen.'"

"Sit down and eat," Sarah said. "Your ma and pa talked about you going back East to school, what about that?"

"It'll have to wait." He picked up the knife and fork and cut a piece off the steak, following it with a bite of cold biscuit.

"You were looking forward to going. Don't you still want to be a lawyer like your Grandpa Barlow?"

Clay looked up from the steak, the exasperation showing. "Sarah, do you understand my folks are dead? They were brutally murdered by scum that probably never worked a day in their life. That type of trash has to be stopped!"

Tears were flowing down Sarah's cheeks. "Must you be the one to stop them? What's going to happen to you? What about us?"

"I'm sorry, Sarah. There is no us. I'm going to see those men in their graves. I know I'm young, but I'm the only son my parents had, and it's up to me to see that justice is served, no matter how long it takes."

Sarah ran from the room. Clay could hear her footsteps disappear into her room. Gloom settled over him. *I'm only one man. Can I really do this? All I know is they left our ranch headed south. I have no idea where they're headed. Am I too young?*

3
_____

C lay stepped into the saddle. Dawn was just slipping over the cedar ridge. He was giving Blue a break and riding the sorrel. Blue and the buckskin were in trail. Hewitt, Bo, and Luke were out to see him off.

"Sorry, Clay. I guess Sarah's still upset. She'll get over it."

"Mr. Hewitt, Sarah needs to forget me. I don't know how long I'll be. This could take years, and I might not even make it back. She needs to get on with her life."

"Son, that'll be hard for her. She had big plans for you two."

Clay patted his vest pocket, where the new contract lay. It had been more than fair. "Thanks for everything, Mr. Hewitt.

"Bo, Luke, thanks for all you've done. You're good friends."

"Take care of yourself, boy," Luke said as he shook Clay's hand.

"Good huntin'," Bo said, and patted the sorrel on the rump.

Clay looked around at the ranch house and yard where he and Sarah had played since they were children. He leaned over and shook Hewitt's hand. "Thank you. Tell Sarah I'm sorry. _Adios._" He wheeled the sorrel to the south, and with Blue and the buckskin in tow, trotted out of the yard.

CLAY RODE out of the hills, north of Uvalde, around noon. He pulled up the horses for a moment, watching the small town. The county seat was bustling with activity. There was a caravan of freight wagons bound for San Felipe del Rio. He watched the town for a few minutes, then trotted forward. He rode through town to the south end, pulled up at the stables, dismounted, and tied his horses. He pulled off his hat and beat the dust from his chaps.

"Howdy, Clay. Whatcha doin' with Hewitt's horses."

Clay looked over the grizzled little man. His skin looked like it had been fried in the sun and tanned by the wind. He was so wrinkled it was hard to tell his age. But he still had a spring in his step a young man might envy.

"Hi, Mr. Johnson. Mr. Hewitt sold me a couple of horses. I've got the bill of sale if you need to see it."

"No, Son, don't need to see nothin'. But why in blue blazes are you buyin' Hewitt stock? Your pa's got plenty to choose from."

Clay walked the three horses to the water trough. "Pa's dead. Ma and Slim too. Killers hit our place five days ago. I was out working cattle and didn't find them till day before yesterday."

The old man was stunned into silence for a moment. Then, "I'm danged sorry, Son. Your folks were fine people. So was Slim. You have any idea who done it?"

"No, sir, but I aim to find out. There was six of them. One of them was hit pretty hard, bled a lot in the yard. There's also a mighty big man with them. They headed south when they left the ranch."

"You best tell the sheriff. He'll see 'bout getting a posse together and git after that scum. You say they killed your ma too?"

"Yep, killed Ma. But I'll tell you, Mr. Johnson, I don't need a posse. I just need to catch 'em."

"Boy, what'er you goin' to do when you catch 'em?"

Clay turned to Johnson. "Why, Mr. Johnson, I'm gonna kill 'em, every one. Now, would you look after my horses? I've got some business to take care of. I'll be leavin' town shortly."

The tall young man pulled his saddlebags from the sorrel and tossed them over his left shoulder, leaving his gun hand free. Then he turned and headed up the street toward the bank.

Clay stepped into the bank and paused to let his eyes adjust to the light. The building had few windows, mostly on the front. Only moderate light filtered inside.

The banker stepped out of his office and saw Clay. "Clay? Uh . . . how are you doing today? How's your folks?"

"My folks are dead."

Besides the gasps of the two ladies at the teller's window, a pin dropping would have been heard by all.

The banker took his handkerchief from his pocket and, with a trembling hand, wiped his forehead. "How did it happen, Clay?"

"Mr. Houston, I've got some business to transact. Can we go into your office?" Clay could feel all eyes on him as he followed Houston into his office and closed the door.

"Have a seat, Clay," Houston offered as he moved to sit behind his desk. "Now tell me, what in the world happened?"

Clay stated, again, the gruesome details. When he had finished, Houston took off his spectacles and began to clean them on his shirt front. "Really sorry, Clay. Really sorry. Your folks were good people."

"Yes, sir, thank you. But I've got some business to take care of. Pa has an account in the bank?"

"Yes, Clay, he does. He doesn't keep much in it, but he does have an account."

"Then I'd like to get it changed into my name and make a deposit."

The banker looked at him for a moment. "Yes, that will be no problem. We'll need to fill out some papers, but that can be done right now." He reached into his desk drawer, pulled out a form, and started filling it out. "How much do you want to deposit?"

Clay started taking the gold and silver out of his saddlebags and stacking it on the desk. "The way I count it, Mr. Houston, there should be three thousand dollars."

"My goodness, Clay, where did you get that kind of money?" Houston asked, patting the perspiration off his upper lip with his handkerchief.

"Ma and Pa were good savers."

"Indeed. They must have been." Houston moved his scales to a more advantageous position and began weighing the gold and silver.

"Yes, sir. I'd like to get three hundred back."

Houston looked up from the scales. "Clay, what do you need with three hundred dollars?"

Clay locked Houston in an icy gaze. "I don't ask what you're going to do with your money. I don't expect you to be askin' me."

Houston cleared his throat. "Yes, well—I see—yes, I see. Certainly, you're right." He quickly looked down and focused his attention on the scales.

"You'll be givin' me a receipt for that money?"

"Yes, surely I will." Houston regained his composure. "Of course I will. That's just the proper way of doing business. Would you like to come back to pick it up?"

"No, sir, I'll just wait right here until you have it, and my three hundred dollars."

"Yes, well, uh, excuse me. I'll only be a few minutes."

Houston returned, counted out Clay's money, and gave him his receipt. "I'll be able to get the money I've left here from anywhere in the country, won't I?"

"Yes, Clay. Just have the other bank notify us and we'll wire the money right away."

Clay stood, towering over the banker. He had never realized until now how small the man was. "Thank you." He shook the limp, sweaty hand the banker extended and walked out, glad to be leaving.

He waited for a moment and turned right for the sheriff's office. He noticed people whispering and looking at him as he walked north up the street. *Sure didn't take long for bad news to get around town.* He could see through the sheriff's office window. The sheriff was behind his desk, going over wanted posters. Clay opened the door and walked in. "Hello, Sheriff Haskins."

The sheriff stood as Clay entered the small office that fronted the jail. "Come in, Clay. Have a seat. I was just going over some wanted posters."

"I guess you've heard."

"Bad news travels fast in a small town, Clay. Tell me everything from the beginning."

Clay started the story again, but this time, he shared every detail he could remember with the sheriff.

After he had finished, Sheriff Haskins sat silently at his desk, leaning forward. His elbows rested on the desk, and his big, sunburned hands were steepled in front of him. His brow was wrinkled, and he was far away in thought.

A few more seconds passed. The sheriff took a deep breath, blew it out through his hands, and leaned back in his chair. "Clay, bad things come to good people. Not much sense in trying to get a posse after 'em. They're long gone by now. But I'm pretty danged sure I know who did this. It's a long story. You want some coffee?"

"No, thank you."

The sheriff walked over to the coffee pot sitting on the potbellied stove. He picked up a towel and grabbed the coffee pot by the handle. "I hate burning this danged stove. The office gets hotter than the hinges of Hades, but I've got to have my coffee." He poured himself a cup.

"Clay, you've grown mighty big. You look a lot like your father. How tall are you now?"

"Just under six feet, Sheriff Haskins. Pa said I'll probably make it a couple more inches."

"Well, Son, you're big now, but when you finish filling out, I figure whoever ties you on is gonna have to bring a lunch." The sheriff took a sip of his coffee, grimaced, and set the mug down. "Clay, I've got a story for you. You were born in '56, right?"

"Yes, sir."

"Your pa's about four years younger than me. In 1854, I was sheriff of Comal County. Office was located in New Braunfels. I was looking for a deputy, and your pa was recommended by Senator John O. Meusebach. I met with your pa, and we hit it right off. I hired him as a deputy, and he never looked back. Your Grandpa Barlow was an attorney in Austin. He'd been in Texas nigh on to twenty years, at that time.

"Anyway, your pa had to pick up a prisoner in D'Hanis later in the year. That's when he met your ma. She was a real looker, and just as sweet a little French girl as you could ever find. But let me tell you, her pa was none too thrilled about a deputy sheriff sparking her. I think he felt a little better when he found out who your pa's pa was."

Sheriff Haskins stopped for a moment and watched a wagon roll north toward the freight caravan. He took a long sip of his coffee and sighed.

"In '57, when you were a year old, I had to go to San Antonio. I'd no sooner left, when your pa got word the Pinder Gang was headed to New Braunfels to rob the city bank. He deputized some of the citizens. Let me tell you, those old German military men were some tough cookies. The Pinder Gang didn't know what they were in for."

Clay moved to the edge of his seat. He'd never heard this story. Pa didn't talk much about his days as sheriff or in the war.

Sheriff Haskins continued. "So your pa stations his deputies around the bank, and he puts himself inside as a teller. He carried a couple of 1848 Colt Baby Dragoons. They were only five shot, .31 caliber weapons. But in your pa's hands those Baby Dragoons were deadly. He also had a sawed-off shotgun leaning next to him behind the counter.

"Well . . ." The sheriff paused and took a long sip of his coffee. "The Pinders rode in big as you please. There were five of them. Gideon's the oldest. He's a big son of a gun. He must have weighed two fifty."

Clay had not been able to figure the point of the sheriff's story until he mentioned Gideon's size. Immediately, he thought back to the heavy weight that horse had been carrying at the ranch.

"They left Harly and Quint with the horses. Gideon, Emmett, and Micah went into the bank. Only Gideon made it out, and he had a bullet in his chest. Your pa killed Emmett and Micah. When those boys pulled their guns they signed their death warrants. Hear tell, it sounded like a young war in the bank. Your pa drew those two Baby Dragoons and put two shots right in the hearts of Emmett and Micah. He got one shot into Gideon as he was backing out the door. Gideon was lucky he lived.

"That was all the shooting. The boys outside tried to get onto their horses, but those Germans had 'em surrounded and just dared 'em to go for their guns.

"What beat all was that Bill, your pa, came out of it without a scratch. I think he scared those Pinder boys so bad they couldn't shoot straight."

Clay stared silently out the window for a moment. He turned his head and looked directly at the sheriff. "Pa never told me any of that."

"Your pa weren't no braggart. And, Son, you've got to know, he was much of a man.

"Anyway, at the trial, Gideon Pinder swore he'd get your pa. They were all sentenced to fifteen years. That means they would have gotten out the end of last year."

Clay got up and walked to the window. He stared at nothing

for a moment, then turned back to the sheriff. "You think it was them, Sheriff? There were tracks of six men, not three."

"Son, I don't know it for a fact, but were I a bettin' man, I'd sure bet on it. The word is that they've picked up some other lowlife to ride with 'em. There's Birch Hays. He's slick, some say mighty handsome, and smooth with the ladies. But he's a fast gun. A real killer. I know of three men he's killed in Texas. There's also Milo Reese. He's supposed to be a dead-eye with the rifle. He was a sniper in the war and got to where he liked killing. But, like they all do, he made a mistake. He killed a councilman in Fort Worth. There were witnesses.

"Now, in my opinion, the worst of the new men is Zeke Martin. People call him Mad Dog. The name fits. For some reason this sick coyote likes to burn people. He burned a whole family down in Goliad. There's a dead-or-alive poster out on him, with a reward of two hundred and fifty dollars."

Clay returned to the chair and sat down. *I've sure got my hands full. But Pa taught me how to shoot and how to fight. I reckon I can be just as good at killin' as they are.*

Clay realized the sheriff was looking at him. "Son, you still want to go after these killers?"

"Yes, sir. I'd be obliged if you have any pictures or likenesses of 'em. I'd like to know who I'm looking for."

"Just so happens I do. That's what I was doing when you came in. Here are some old posters of Gideon, Quint, and Harly. They're pretty good likenesses—course, they're fifteen years old. Up until now, they weren't wanted for anything new. These other three are current and show the posted rewards."

Clay picked up the posters. "You mind if I take these, Sheriff?"

Haskins took another sip of his coffee. It was cold. He turned and spit it out on the floor. "I hate cold coffee. Go right ahead, Son."

Clay stood up. "Much obliged, Sheriff. I've got to pick up

some supplies. Has anyone mentioned seeing the Pinders around here?"

"There was a fella came through from San Felipe a couple of days ago. He mentioned dust from riders coming out of the hills heading west. Now that could've been Comanches, Apaches, the Pinder Gang, or just some riders. That's all I've heard. Not much to go on."

"That's more than I had. I'll head for San Felipe del Rio."

The two men shook hands, and the sheriff walked outside with Clay. The southeast wind lifted the dust in the street, spreading the grit over the town. Clay pulled his hat tight on his head. "Thanks, Sheriff."

"If you're leaving today, you might check with the freighters. They'd probably welcome an extra gun. There's safety in numbers, what with all the Apaches west of here."

"Appreciate your help." Clay stepped off the boardwalk and walked across the dusty street to the general store. When he opened the door, he could see Mrs. Graham behind the counter. She was putting cans on the back shelf. She glanced over her shoulder to see who it was. When she recognized him, she immediately yelled to the back. "Mr. Graham, Clayton Barlow is here." She came out from behind the counter, then ran to Clay and gave him a big hug, the top of her head coming just under his chin. "Clayton, I am so sorry to hear about your folks. They were such good friends and good people."

She held him by the arms and looked up into his face. "It's good to see you. You've grown so big. You're not the little boy I used to slip candy to when your father wasn't looking."

Clay grinned. "I still like candy, Mrs. Graham."

She let out a tinkling laugh. "I bet you do, I just bet you do. How long are you going to be here? Of course, you can stay with us while you're here."

Mr. Graham had walked in from the back while his wife was

talking. "Sorry about your folks, Clay. They were mighty good friends."

"Thanks, Mr. Graham. I've got a list of supplies here that I'd like to get filled as soon as you can. Mrs. Graham, I'll not be staying. I'll be headin' out as soon as I've got the supplies. In fact, while you're filling the list, I'll go down to the stable and bring up my horses."

Mr. Graham took the list and looked it over. "You've got quite a list here, Son. You planning on doing a lot of traveling?"

"Yes, sir, I am."

The Grahams paused for a moment.

Finally, Mrs. Graham said, "Clayton, are you going after those killers?"

"Yes, ma'am."

The Grahams looked at each other for a moment, then Mr. Graham turned and said, "Well, we best be getting your supplies. We wouldn't want you to go hungry out there. Mrs. Graham, come on and give me a hand."

Mrs. Graham patted Clay on the arm and scurried about the store, picking out supplies.

Clay walked out of the store and turned down the street to the stables. He'd miss folks like the Grahams. Pa had even helped Mr. Graham get his store going in Uvalde. They had been close friends.

Clay could see Gabby saddling Blue. He had the gear tied on and ready when Clay got there. "Mr. Johnson, I need an extra saddle and a couple of cloth panniers to hang across the saddle. You have something like that?"

"I've got that, boy, but I got a pack saddle back there that would carry a lot more load."

"No, sir. I'll have more weight than I can carry in my saddlebags, but not so much I need a pack saddle. In fact, the panniers don't need to be real big."

Gabby came out with an old saddle. "This is old, but it's in good shape. I've also got a nice clean blanket for it. These are well-made panniers that should ride well and not rub at all."

Clay looked them over. They would work for what he needed. He tossed the blanket across the buckskin's back, smoothed it out, and saddled the horse. He and Gabby fastened the panniers across the saddle. Clay checked for rubbing, but the panniers were short enough to rest mostly on the side of the saddle and the stirrup leather. "This seems fine, Mr. Johnson. What do I owe you?"

Gabby rubbed the stubble on his chin with his thumb as he mentally calculated the price. "The saddle's old but good, I'd say twenty-five, two bucks for the blanket, five dollars apiece for the panniers. You planning on hobbling or picketing these animals?"

"I reckon picket."

"You don't have enough rope for the three. I'll toss in some good hemp for five dollars. Clay, I'll tell you what I'll do. It comes to forty-two dollars, but I'll let you have the whole shootin' match for forty bucks. How's that sound to ya?"

"Mr. Johnson, that sounds more than fair." He pulled out the wad of three hundred dollars and peeled off forty before slipping the remainder of the money back into his pocket.

Gabby took the money and slid his old, beat-up hat to the back of his head. "Clay, I'm gonna give you a piece of advice. I know fer sure, most advice is worth exactly what you pay for it. But, Son, you don't want to be flashing that kind of money around. There's plenty of folks who'd shoot you or knock you in the head for way less than what you've got there. Split it up. Put some in each boot. Slip a little in yore saddlebags. That way it ain't in one pile. Understand what I'm saying?"

Clay immediately recognized the sense in what Gabby had told him. "Yes, sir, I do. I guess I've got a lot to learn. Thanks."

"Nary important to mention it, boy. I'm just glad to help. You'll learn. Your size'll help you. But always be on the lookout. Just because you're amongst a bunch of white men, don't mean you're safe. But I guess you already figgered that one out for yourself. Good luck to you."

Clay mounted Blue and nodded to Gabby. "Be seeing you."

He led the sorrel and the buckskin toward the general store. Puffs of dust from the horses' hooves disappeared quickly in the afternoon breeze. He pulled up in front of the general store, tied the horses, and went in.

The Grahams had divided his supplies up into two potato sacks and set them on the counter. "Clayton," Mrs. Graham said, "here's your list. All your supplies are in these two bags. I also put you some lunch in there. Part of me wishes you weren't going after those men. The other part wants you to catch them and kill them for what they've done. Please, be safe."

"Yes, ma'am, thank you. I plan on it. By the way, do you have any of that hard lemon candy? I've had my mouth set for some."

Her musical laugh filled the store. She filled a small bag with lemon candy and handed it to Clay, squeezing his big hands in hers. "You always did have a sweet tooth."

Mr. Graham came from the back carrying a shotgun and a box of shells. "Son, you know your father helped us get this store started. We owe him more than you can ever know. I have long wondered how we could repay him. Now I know. We can contribute, in a small way, in keeping you safe. This is for you."

"Mr. Graham, I can't take that." Clay eyed the single-barrel shotgun.

"You can and you will. This helps us pay our debt to your folks."

"I've never seen anything like it."

"Clay, this is a Roper 12 gauge repeating shotgun. You lift this cover to load and fire. To load it—" Mr. Graham took four shells from the box, "—you press the shells down into the revolving cylinder. It holds four. To fire, just pull the hammer back. You'll find it a little stiff, but just pull hard and let her rip. I planned on using it for protection around here, so I had the gunsmith shorten the barrel. It won't be good for bird hunting, but it'll danged sure stop anything up close. It fits perfectly in this scabbard."

"Mr. Graham, I don't know what to say."

"Say nothing. Just pay me the fifteen dollars for the supplies, and you can be on your way."

Clay paid for the supplies. Mrs. Graham began to tear up. He picked up the bags, took them outside, and loaded them into the panniers. He walked back into the store. Mrs. Graham hugged him, and Mr. Graham shook his hand. No other words were said. He picked up the scabbard with the Roper, nodded, and went through the door. He tied the scabbard on the buckskin's saddle, walked around the horses checking the gear, and swung up onto Blue.

Mr. and Mrs. Graham stood quietly on the boardwalk. He tipped his hat to them and nudged Blue. Blue started walking north toward the freight outfit. Sheriff Haskins leaned against a post in front of his office. They nodded to each other as Clay passed. *Will I ever be here again?* Clay lifted his eyes to the freighters and clucked Blue into a trot.

4

Clay stopped at the lead wagon. A solidly built man was checking a water barrel. "Howdy," Clay said, "where can I find the boss?"

The man nodded at two men riding toward the wagons. They had come into view after topping a low rise to the west. Clay rode out to meet them. One of the men was older, gray hair showing out from under the hat that had once been white. The man was big, but now going to fat. The other man was wide-shouldered, slim in the waist, with long, wavy brown hair. He was sporting a well-trimmed mustache and goatee.

They pulled up as they reached Clay. "Howdy, young feller," the older man said, "vhat is it ve can do for you?"

"My name's Clay Barlow. I was wonderin' if I could ride west with you? I'm headed for San Felipe del Rio."

The other man appraised Clay. "You any kin to Bill Barlow? Used to be deputy sheriff in New Braunfels?"

"Yes, sir, that was my pa."

"Was?"

"My ma and pa were murdered a few days ago."

The older man shook his head. "It is a shame to have such a

thing happen to one's family. I am very sorry. My name is Helmutt Tropf. These are my vagons. We have irrigation supplies to drop off in San Felipe, and then ve'll be going on to El Paso. You are most welcome to join us. We can always use another gun."

The long-haired man said, "Name's John Coleman. My friends call me Jake. Met your pa shortly after he caught the Pinder Gang. He was a man to reckon with. You say your ma was killed too?"

"Yes, sir, my ma, pa, and Slim, our friend. They shot, hanged, and burned Pa."

Coleman spit a slug of tobacco juice and hit a prickly pear dead center. "Whoever did that needs killing, and soon, before they do it again. Any idea who might have done it?"

"I was talking to the sheriff. He figures it's the Pinder Gang."

Tropf nodded to Clay and Coleman. "I've got to get these wagons rolling. Ya, you're velcome to tie your horses behind the first wagon. I'll talk to you later." He trotted his horse toward the lead wagon.

"Let's move off the road," Coleman said.

Clay walked Blue and the other two horses over to where Coleman sat.

"Where you headed?" Coleman said.

"Mr. Coleman, I'm after the men who killed my folks."

"Call me Jake. You know how to use those Remingtons?"

"I do."

"Ever shot a man?"

Clay could feel his face getting hot. "No, but I'll be up to it when the time comes."

Coleman studied the boy for a few moments. "You just might. Tie up those two horses and ride with me."

Clay joined Jake Coleman after tying the sorrel and buckskin behind the first wagon. The wagons had started moving as he and Coleman topped out over the first hill. They rode along in silence, watching the countryside. Though it was dry, the rolling hills were lit with color. The light green of the mesquite trees was accented by purple thistle and yellow acacia tree blooms. This was rough country, but still provided colors that were easy on the eyes. The thick, tan bunches of buffalo grass spread as far as they could see.

Clay glanced over at Jake. He was examining the hills, keeping a close lookout for anything out of the ordinary. "You going all the way to El Paso?"

"Reckon," Jake said. He shot a stream of tobacco juice at a jackrabbit in the shade of a prickly pear patch. The tobacco hit him on the left shoulder. The surprised rabbit leaped from under the prickly pear and dashed a few yards, stopped, and looked back.

Clay laughed. "You as good with a gun as you are with that tobacco juice?"

Jake leaned back in his saddle to stretch his back. His mustache moved in what could have been taken for a smile. "Maybe."

Several miles were covered without a word being spoken. The sun was casting shadows from the mesquite and prickly pear. Jake pulled up at the crest of a low ridge. The west side of the ridge sloped down to the Nueces River. "You familiar with Injuns?"

"Yes, sir," Clay said. "We had a tribe of Tonkawa who wintered near our ranch for years. I had a friend about my age. We spent a lot of time together. Ma schooled him some, along with me."

"Is it true the Tonkawa eat their enemies?"

"I never saw it. They took me in like their own and helped us fight off Comanches. Pa always said they were good people. Those Tonkawa taught me a lot."

"Son, my friends call me Jake. Not sir. I'd be beholden if'n you'd stop with the sirs."

"Sorry, just the way I was raised."

"I'm sure your ma was a fine lady and taught you right. For young folks, that's good to learn. But you being in a man's world, you best leave it behind. Some folks'll take it as a sure sign of weakness. They're like wolves, they smell weakness and they go for your throat."

Jake headed down to the Nueces. Clay followed by his side. "We'll ford and camp on t'other side," Jake said. "By the time the wagons get here, it'll be gettin' close to dark. We'll circle up and keep the animals inside the circle. Don't want to tempt anyone."

They crossed the ford and examined the west side of the river. "Looks good," Jake said. "Let's head back."

THE WAGONS HAD CIRCLED up and campfires were burning. They had managed to get the stock unhitched and watered before dark, and now everyone was enclosed in the circle of wagons.

"Clay," Jake said, "this is our wrangler, Arlo Paxton. Arlo, Clay Barlow, out of the hill country."

"Howdy, boy. You goin' to be ridin' along with us?"

"Yes, sir, I'm headed for San Felipe del Rio."

"Good, we can always use another gun. Why don't you toss your extra gear in a wagon and run your horses with the remuda. Two more won't make a heap of difference."

"Ya, dat's a goot idea, Clay," Helmut Tropf said. "Put your things in the third wagon. There be extra space in that one."

"Why, thank you both. That'll make it some easier."

Clay picked up his extra saddle and panniers and headed for the third wagon. He was just pulling the Roper out of its scabbard when a bearded, burly man walked around from the opposite side and placed his hands on his hips.

"Whatcha doin' at my wagon, boy?"

Clay nodded. "Howdy. Mr. Tropf said it was okay for me to put my gear in this wagon." He picked up the saddle and dropped it into the back of the wagon.

"Well, I sure as blazes didn't. Now git that saddle out of there, and git it out right now."

"Mister, I'm not looking for trouble here. Mr. Tropf owns this wagon, and I reckon what he says goes." Clay picked up one of the panniers and dropped it into the wagon.

The big man's face clouded over, and his little, beady eyes almost disappeared under thick eyebrows. He stepped forward, his hands clenched.

"Nestler! Leave the boy alone," Tropf yelled from the fire. "I told him to put his tack in your vagon. If you have a problem with that, you can take it up with me."

Nestler glared at Clay. "We ain't done, boy."

Clay said nothing as he picked up the remaining pannier with his left hand and dropped it into the wagon, his shotgun loosely gripped in his right hand.

"Yes, sir, Mr. Tropf," Nestler said. "I just didn't know he had permission, what with the weight and all. Just wanted to save your stock."

Tropf nodded and turned back to the fire.

Nestler strode toward the second fire, his fists still clenched.

Clay walked over to where Jake and Arlo were standing, away from the fire. Darkness had settled on the countryside. A couple of coyotes on the north ridge, above the camp, were serenading the moon. Night animals were shuffling in the brush outside the wagons.

"You got a problem there, boy," Jake said. "His name is Cain Nestler. Don't know much about him, except I don't like him."

"Yep," Arlo said. "I reckon he's mean clear through. Always pickin' on the other men. 'Specially those he thinks he can buffalo. He's hard on the stock too. Never liked a man what didn't treat his stock right."

"Mr. Coleman, I'm not looking for a fight. But I won't run from one either."

"You'll have it to do, Clay, I promise you," Jake said. "Now, what kind of shotgun you got there?"

"This is a Roper. It shoots four shells just as fast as you can pull the hammer back."

"You don't say," Arlo chimed in. "Never in my life seen a shotgun like that. What with that one, short barrel, I took it for a single shot, muzzle loader at that."

"Let me show you how it works. You open up this gate on the top, and you can put the shells right in here. It'll take four. Then, when you're ready to shoot, just pull back the hammer."

Both Jake and Arlo had leaned over, examining the Roper. "What'll they think of next?" Arlo said. "Just imagine, four shots without reloading, coming out of a single-barrel shotgun. That'll sure be a surprise for whoever's on the receiving end."

The three moved over to the fire and got some beans and venison, then moved back. Jake and Arlo leaned against a wagon wheel, and Clay sat cross-legged on the ground. Clay ate quickly, then got up and spooned out another plate of beans. "Mighty good," he said.

The others looked up and laughed. "Don't let Cookie hear that, it'll go to his head." Guffaws followed the man's comment.

"You shut up, Wilson, or you'll be sucking on rocks and eating loco weed." Cookie grinned at Clay. "Eat up, boy. It's good for you."

Clay grinned back at the cook, nodded, and walked back to Jake and Arlo.

"You feel like taking the first watch tonight?" Jake asked Clay.

"Yes, si—Jake, sure do."

"Good, there's a knoll about twenty yards north. Make a good stand. If someone comes slipping into camp, they mean no good. You do what you have to do. Wake me in three hours. Arlo, you up to the last watch?"

"Yep."

Clay finished his supper and sanded out his plate. "Reckon I'll get on up there."

He rolled out his bedroll next to a wagon, pulled his moccasins from the saddlebags, and slipped them on. They felt good on his feet. Running Wolf's ma had taught him how to make them, and he always carried two pair with him. His feet had grown thickly calloused through the years. Unlike most cowmen, he was as handy on his feet as in the saddle. He and Running Wolf had run all over the hill country around the ranch. He could run for hours without slowing down. He missed those days, Running Wolf, Ma, Pa, Slim. Now they were gone, Running Wolf probably up near Fort Griffin. He'd like to see him.

Clay slipped out to the knoll and found a place screening his back with a huge bunch of prickly pear. He cleared the ground of spines and sharp rocks and sat down. The stars were sprinkled across the heavens like fireflies that frequented the Frio during the summertime. The waning moon was just peeking up in the east. Yellow, it was, like the butter that came out of Ma's churn. The howling of the coyotes had disappeared into the night. They must be hunting. The only sound came from the cicadas singing their rough tune and the nighthawk's rattle.

Time passed quickly. Two deer moved silently between the knoll and the wagons. Alert to danger, they walked slowly to the Nueces for water. Clay took one last look at the stars. It was time. He moved silently back into camp, moved up to Jake, and touched him on the leg.

"You move awfully quiet, Clay," Jake said. "Anything?"

"Just a couple of deer moving to the river. You awake?"

"Yeah. I'll see you in the morning."

Clay moved over to his bedroll, slipped his moccasins off, and lay down. *Don't know what lies ahead, but I plan on burying some men before I die.* He lay there for a moment more before sleep came.

5

Two uneventful days had passed since their camp on the Frio River. The sun was overhead when Fort Clark came into sight. Clay, astride the buckskin, riding next to Jake, was anxious to get into Brackett and the fort. This would be his first opportunity to confirm he was on the killers' trail.

"Let's ride on into town, Clay," Jake said. "The Pinders could be here. They've got no idea anyone is following them, so don't go off half-cocked if you see 'em. We'll try to check in with the fort commander and see if those soldier boys know anything—at least let them know what's happened. We don't want them coming down on the wrong side if shootin' breaks out. You keep that shotgun handy."

The two rode up to the fort. "Howdy," Jake said to the private on guard. "We got freight wagons coming on behind us. Should be here in a couple of hours. You happened to seen or heard of six riders coming through these parts?"

The private thought for a moment. "Yes, siree, they was six come through here 'bout four days ago. Rough-looking characters. One was shot bad. Said they run into some Apaches. They took him to the infirmary." He pointed to a sturdy rock building. "Reckon he's still there. Can't believe he ain't dead, but he ain't."

Clay spurred the buckskin. The surprised horse leaped into a gallop toward the infirmary. Jake was right behind. Clay swung down off the horse and jumped onto the infirmary porch just as an army captain in a white coat stepped out the door.

Startled at seeing this big young man standing in front of him with a shotgun in his hand, he took a step back. Jake jumped up on the porch right behind Clay. "What's going on here?" the surprised captain said.

Clay started to push past him when Jake grabbed his arm. "Clay, simmer down. Just hold on. We'll git this figgered out."

Clay turned on Jake with a fierce glare. "He's in there, I know it."

Jake held on. "Think, boy. Just cool down and think." He looked around and could see several soldiers had stopped what they were doing and were watching. A couple had started for the infirmary. "We don't want to make a ruckus here, Clay. Slow down."

Clay looked around. He felt reason beginning to return. He took a deep breath, and turned back to the captain. "Captain, you've got a civilian in there who's been shot up some?"

"I might," the captain said, "but I asked you what's going on here, and I mean to find out before you go a step farther." The captain turned to the advancing soldiers and waved them off.

"Captain, that man is a member of a gang, the Pinder Gang. They killed my ma, pa, and a friend. They shot, hanged, and burned my pa and raped my ma. I reckon I have a right to see if the man you have is one of them."

"How do you know it was this man?"

"The sheriff had posters on all those killers. I can identify them with the posters."

"Captain, what's going on here?"

Clay and Jake turned. The hard voice issued from an army colonel flanked by two armed soldiers.

The captain quickly explained what he knew.

"My name is Colonel Ranald Mackenzie. I am in command of this fort. What are your names?"

Clay and Jake introduced themselves.

"Mr. Barlow, no man races into my fort armed. You will put your weapons on your horse. That goes for you too, Mr. Coleman. Then we will go inside and see if this is one of the men you are after."

Clay slid the Roper into the scabbard, then unfastened his six-guns and looped them over the saddle horn. Jake followed suit. The two men stepped back onto the porch as Colonel Mackenzie opened the door of the infirmary. They followed the colonel and captain inside. The infirmary had eight beds, four on each wall. Half the beds were occupied. The captain headed for the one at the far end of the room.

The man, apprehensive, watched their approach. Clay immediately recognized him as Birch Hayes, from the wanted poster. "That's one of them, Colonel. He's Birch Hayes, wanted for murder in San Antonio."

"That's a blamed lie," Hayes said. "I don't know who you are, boy, but you've got a loose mouth. If I wasn't laid up here, I'd teach you to have some manners for your elders."

Clay shuffled through the wanted posters, found the one he was looking for, and handed it to the colonel. "No lies, Hayes. You're going to swing, and I'm going to watch."

The colonel looked at the poster, then at Hayes. "You're right, boy. This looks like your man."

Hayes swung his head between Clay and the colonel. "Now see here, Colonel, there ain't no proof. Anyway, I ain't fit to travel. I'm lucky to still be alive, what with those Apaches attackin' us and all."

It was all Clay could do to hold back from choking the man to death. "You weren't attacked by Apaches, you lying piece of dirt. You were shot by Slim when you rode into our ranch."

Hayes looked nervously to the colonel. "Now, Colonel, I don't know what this here boy is talking about. It was Apaches that done this, almost done me in too. We ain't been around any ranch."

"Colonel," Clay said, "if you'll let me get my bowie knife and give me just a couple of minutes, I'll have this liar singing like a mockingbird. He's lying, and it won't take much to get the truth."

"There'll be none of that," Colonel Mackenzie said. "I'll hold this man until he's able to travel, then he'll be escorted to San Antonio and turned over to the sheriff."

"Doctor, when your patient is ready to travel, let me know."

"Yes, sir," the captain said.

"Gentlemen." Mackenzie motioned toward the door.

Clay's vision was riveted on the killer. Jake took him by the arm. "Boy, we've got to go. Now."

Clay turned for the door, then back to Hayes. "We're not done, Mister. Not by a long shot." Then he turned and followed them out of the infirmary.

"Mr. Barlow, I understand your desire for justice," the colonel said, "but I want no violence on this post. Do you understand?"

"Colonel, that man was one of those that killed my folks. I reckon I know what kind of justice he needs." Clay swung the gunbelt around his waist, fastened it, swung up onto his horse, and, without looking back, rode out of the fort.

Jake followed him. "So what's your plan?"

"I'll just wait and watch. I'm bettin' he's mighty nervous right now. As soon as he's feelin' up to it, I think he'll try to escape. When he does, I'll be waiting for him."

"You plan on killing him?"

"That depends on him. I want him dead. If it's a rope, I'm good with that, but if he forces me, I'll kill him myself. Right now, I just want to question him and find out where Gideon Pinder's going. I'm sure Pinder will have his gang with him. Then I'll be able to even the score."

"That's a mighty big bite, boy, even for Bill Barlow's son. You could be gettin' in way over your head."

"Jake, I realize that, but I don't know what else to do. Those men killed my folks, and you know they'll kill again. Their type has no remorse. They've got to be stopped. I just don't see anyone else signing up for the job."

Jake took his hat off and brushed his long hair back with his fingers. "Look, the wagon train's in Brackett. Mr. Tropf will be unloading some of his supplies at the general store. He'll spend the night here. We'll be heading on for San Felipe del Rio in the morning. You're welcome to continue on with us."

"Thanks, Jake, but I think I'll hang around here and see what happens with the army's prisoner. I don't imagine he wants to go back to San Antonio. If he tries to escape . . . No telling what kind of conversation we could come up with."

"Reckon I'd do the same thing, were I you. But he ain't goin' to be doin' any traveling for at least a couple of days. Come on with me. We'll go into Brackett and get us some vittles that weren't burnt over a campfire. Maybe I can round up something to wet my whistle."

Clay agreed, and the two men rode the short distance into Brackett.

Jake stopped in front of the Cattleman's Saloon. "The food's mighty good. The liquor ain't bad either. You a drinkin' man, Clay?" Jake said as he stepped down from his horse and looped the reins over the hitching rail.

"Nope, Pa didn't drink. Reckon he set me a good example. Although, I always did like a good sarsaparilla." Clay followed Jake and looped his horse's reins over the hitching rail.

The two walked into the saloon. Several of the bullwhackers were already inside. A couple of them nodded and went back to drinking. Jake walked over to a table and sat down, then motioned to the barkeep.

"Hildi," the barkeep called to the back.

A tall woman of indeterminate age came out of the back and looked toward the bartender. He nodded toward Jake and Clay. She marched over to their table, gave Jake a look, and said, "If you're looking to eat, we got some fine steak, and we'll toss in some beans to go along with it. I've whipped up a tasty peach cobbler, if you've a need to cater to your sweet tooth."

Clay smiled. "Ma'am, all that sounds mighty good. Could I have a sarsaparilla to go along with it?"

Jake grinned. "Hi, Hildi, been a while."

"Quite a while, Jake. Understand you're scoutin' for this freight outfit."

"Yep, keeps me eatin'."

"Jake, you hear next year they may be startin' the Rangers up again?"

"I heard that, Hildi. If we can get Coke elected and get that carpet-bagging Davis out of office, it just may happen."

"You gonna sign back up, if'n you get a chance?"

"If they'll take me, I imagine so. But here now, where's my manners? Hildi, this sarsaparilla-sippin' feller next to me is Clay Barlow. Reckon you remember his pa, deputy in New Braunfels back in the fifties."

"Why, I sure do, had my cap set for him, but he never knew I was around. That little French girl from D'Hanis had his attention." Hildi stuck her hand out. "Nice to meet you, Clay. You look just like your pa, only bigger. How are your folks?"

Her hand disappeared in Clay's when he shook it. "Nice to meet you, ma'am. My folks are dead. Murdered just over a week ago."

Hildi stood silent for a moment, shocked by the news. "I'm mighty sorry. You'll be looking for those who done it, I imagine."

Clay nodded. "Yes, ma'am, I'll sure be doing that."

"Hildi," Jake said, "this here's a growing boy. Reckon we could get him some food? I'll have the same, but with a beer. We'll talk later."

Hildi nodded, her smile returning. "I bet we can do that mighty quick." She turned and started for the kitchen.

"You better hurry up there, girl." Cain Nestler was sitting with the bullwhackers and had already tossed back a few drinks. "That boy looks like he's in mighty serious need of his sarsaparilla." The other two men at his table roared along with him.

Clay looked over at the big bullwhacker. It was obvious the man was on the prod. Even at his young age, Clay knew what a bully looked like. *I'm tired. I really don't want to get into a fight with Nestler. It won't accomplish anything.*

"Ignore him," Jake said. "He's trying to needle you into a fight. In his mind, he knows he can beat you. You're going to have to fight him, but it doesn't have to be now."

"You're right, Jake. I've more important things to do than fight a loudmouth."

"What's a matter, boy?" Nestler said. "You miss your mommy?"

Clay was on his feet instantly.

Nestler was grinning, as if he relished the opportunity to whip the kid. But Nestler's type liked to talk, build up to a fight, belittle his opponent. He leaned back in his chair just as Clay walked up to him. Clay kicked the chair's back leg, sending the big man sprawling. Nestler scrambled to his feet and met the barrel and charging handle of Clay's Navy Remington with the side of his head. He crumpled to his hands and knees, and Clay hit him again across his left ear and head. His ear and scalp split, sending blood across the floor, but Nestler didn't care. His nose smashed into the cedar planks of the floor, as he collapsed, unconscious.

Clay thumbed the hammer back on the Remington and

swung the muzzle to cover the other bullwhackers who were with Nestler. "I aim to have my sarsaparilla in peace. I want no trouble. You might ought to have your friend looked at by the doctor before he bleeds to death." His hands were steady, and his voice was calm, but inside, he was shaking like a cottonwood leaf in a windstorm. He'd had fights as a youth, and a couple of times he had felt anger build, but never had it reached today's point. When Nestler spoke of his ma, all he could think about was killing the man. He wasn't interested in fighting him. He just wanted him dead. Looking down on him now, he felt a twinge of regret. The man lay bleeding on the floor, blood pouring from his head wounds. Rage had taken over his mind. Adrenaline had coursed through his body, and this was the result. He felt small regret for Nestler, but more for his loss of control.

The two bullwhackers got up and went over to Nestler, stepping carefully to keep their boots out of the blood. One turned to Clay and said, "Boy, you might of killed him. He'll be almighty mad when he comes to—if he does. You best watch out."

Clay turned back to his table, holstered the Remington, and sat down. "Tell him to look me up anytime. When he does, he better be healed. There's too many of his kind in this country. One less won't make much difference. One more thing, Mister. I may be young, but I'm no boy. Remember that."

The two men dragged Nestler out of the saloon, a trail of blood marking his passage.

Hildi came from the back carrying their drinks. The bartender had watched the altercation, silently cleaning a beer mug. When she came through the door, he said, "Hildi, after you get them their drinks, clean up the floor."

She set the drinks in front of the them and reappraised Clay. "I'd say you're a chip off the old block. Your pa could be sudden, just like that. I'll bring your food in just a minute." Smiling at Clay, Hildi said, "Gotta clean up this mess you made first."

The two men picked up their drinks, saluted each other, and

let the liquid flow down their throats. The sweet, cool bite of the sarsaparilla was soothing to Clay. He took another sip and set the bottle back on the table.

Jake wiped his mouth with the back of his hand. "You can be a mighty sudden feller."

"He spoke ill of my ma. I'll not abide any man doing that."

"Understand, rightfully so. But, I've gotta tell ya, that six-gun came out of your holster unholy quick. I thought Nestler was dead. I reckon his two partners did too."

"Pa and Slim taught me. They worked with me when I felt I was too tired to draw another time, but I did. Pa always said this is tough country and I needed to be ready."

Jake chuckled. "I'd say you were ready. A word of caution: Keep your head. I saw your eyes. You were totally focused on Nestler. If there woulda been other men gunning for you, you'd be dead. 'Course I might've taken care of one or two, but the point is, always be aware of your surroundings. That'll keep you alive, the other won't."

Clay took another sip of his sarsaparilla and nodded. "Thanks, Jake. I know I've got a lot to learn. I just hope I learn enough before I catch up to the Pinder Gang."

Hildi had walked up with their food as they were talking. She set the plates out in front of them. "Did I hear you say Pinder Gang?"

"Sure did," Clay said.

"You know, they were through here a few days ago. Are they the ones who killed your family?"

"Yes, ma'am. They surely are."

"I never did like Gideon Pinder," Hildi said. "I don't think he has a kind bone in his body. Saw him shoot a boy's dog when the dog didn't move fast enough to get out of his way. He's bad clean through, and him always quoting scriptures. But, Clay, I did hear them say they were going to hole up north of San Felipe. That's all I heard, other than the fact that Birch Hayes is in the infirmary, with a bullet hole in his chest. They said he got it from Apaches. But now I reckon I know where he got it from."

"Ma'am," Clay said, "you don't know how much I appreciate you telling me this. I was concerned they were headed for El Paso. San Felipe is a lot closer."

"Glad to help," Hildi said before she headed back to the kitchen.

Jake cut into his steak and took a big bite. After moving it to the side of his mouth, he said, "What are you going to do now?"

"If they're going to ground in San Felipe, I reckon they'll be there for a while. I still want to talk to Hayes and get the truth out of him. What with the time I spent with the Tonkawa, I should be pretty persuasive."

"You be careful. Birch is fast with a gun and knife. Smart too. Even with a bullet through him, he's a handful. But, Clay, your trouble's not near over when you finish with him. I wish you were coming with us. A lone man on the trail between here and San Felipe del Rio is a sitting duck for the Apaches. I'm serious, now. There's word they're out, and you don't see Apaches until they're on you. Keep that shotgun handy."

"Thanks, Jake. I'll keep my eyes peeled. Now let's finish this steak."

6

Clay watched the shadowy figure of Hayes approach. The moon was up. It provided very little light, but enough to recognize Hayes. Clay had been hiding in the thick mesquites behind and to the west of the infirmary for the past five nights. Tonight was to be the last night, and he would have to give up and head over to San Felipe. But now he waited, watching as Hayes drew closer.

"This shotgun makes a mighty big hole at this range. Gently unfasten that gunbelt, hang it over the saddle horn, and step away from your horse."

Hayes froze. Clay didn't want to kill him—he wanted to question him. He'd never killed a man, but if he went for his gun he would. Clay waited for a few more moments. Then Hayes's body relaxed, and he slowly unfastened the gunbelt and dropped it to the ground.

"I told you to hang it on the saddle. Pick it up and do what I say."

Clay was close enough to see Hayes's right hand go to his belt as he bent over to pick up the gunbelt with his left. "Hayes, you pull that gun and you're dead. At this range, this buckshot will make a mighty nasty hole. Now, git that right hand up, empty."

"How'd you know I'd be here?"

"Walk over to me, slowly."

"They'll hang me, if you take me back."

Hayes walked to Clay with his hands up. Clay shoved the shotgun barrel against the man's throat, then reached under Hayes's belt and pulled out a double-barrel derringer. He stuffed it behind his belt, and with the shotgun still tight against Hayes's throat, he pulled out the piggin' string. "Lay down, face-first," Clay said. He remembered how Pa talked about tying a man up when he was alone.

"There's goat heads, grass burrs, and mesquite thorns, not to mention cactus. Why, I just ain't—"

"Fine, I'll just knock you in the head."

Hayes laid down, carefully, face-first.

"Now spread your feet and stick your hands in front of you as far as you can."

Clay walked around in front of Hayes. He wasn't afraid of Hayes overpowering him. Hayes was still a sick man, but he could have another hideout gun or knife. He laid the shotgun down and quickly tied both of Hayes's hands together.

"That's too tight."

"Get up."

Clay picked up the other gun and pulled the gunbelt off the other man's horse. He moved back to Blue, who had been standing quietly a few feet from the two men, and slipped the three guns and holster into his saddlebags. While keeping his eyes on the shadowy figure of Hayes, he mounted Blue.

"Mount up."

Clay picked up the reins of Hayes's horse and handed them to him.

"Ride slow and quiet into that little dry creek. It'll take us away from the fort and Brackett. Take it nice and easy. My trigger finger is gettin' tired."

The two men rode into the dry creek bed and headed southwest. After a mile, Clay motioned Hayes out of the branch and pointed west. The two men turned west, and Clay prodded Hayes to pick up the pace. The two horses picked up a lope for the next two miles. Clay slowed them down to a fast walk, and they continued their journey west.

"Where you takin' me?"

"Why'd you kill my ma and pa?"

"I don't know what you're talking about. This bullet came from an Apache. I've never been near your ma."

"Mister, I know who you are. I know who you were riding with. I can take you back to the army and you'll end up getting hanged. Speakin' of the army, how'd you get away? You sure didn't tie out your own horse, for yourself, with all your gear."

"I had help."

"I reckon. Go on."

"An orderly. He got my gear and horse and tied them out behind the hospital. I paid him."

"Guess he'll be in some trouble."

"Reckon not. After we got outside the hospital, he kind of stumbled and fell on my knife."

Keep an eye on this guy. He's as dangerous as a rattler.

They hit Maverick Creek and turned southwest, riding until they found a thick grove of oak along the creek.

"Git down."

Clay had found the perfect limb he was looking for. "Come over here."

Hayes walked over. Clay could tell the ride had exhausted the man. He was still not in good shape. Clay took the end of the rope, pulling Hayes's hands up, and tied him to an oak limb that paralleled the ground. The limb was high enough where Hayes's arms were stretched above him.

Clay rode back to the horse, picked up the reins, and took both horses to the creek. There, they drank their fill. Then he rode back and ground-reined them both on some good grass. Hayes had turned and was watching him.

"What are you going to do with me?"

"Up to you."

"I need to sit down. I'm tired."

"Why'd you kill my ma?"

"I told you, I didn't—"

The sound of the slap was like a pistol shot. It caught Hayes fully on his left cheek and sent him spinning on the rope.

"Why'd you kill my ma?"

Hayes had regained his footing. Light was beginning to break in the east and slip through the maze of trees.

"I'm telling you, I—"

This time the slap caught him on the right cheek and knocked him spinning like a top in the opposite direction, flopping on the tree limb.

"I've been shot. I could die. You can't do this."

"Mister, I've got a lot more time than you. Did I tell you that I was raised by the Tonkawa? I spent nearly as much time with them as I did with my folks. They have truly fascinating ways to help people speak the truth. I'm bettin' you'd like me to show you." Clay pulled out his bowie knife, the blade glinting in the early morning daylight. He knelt down and pulled off the boot from Hayes's right foot. When he did, the slim dagger on the inside of the boot came into view.

"You've been holding out on me. Here I thought I had all of your weapons." He quickly checked the other boot. Nothing.

Clay checked the edge of the dagger. "Why, I believe your knife is sharper than mine." With that, he slid his bowie knife back into the scabbard.

"Now where was I? Oh yeah." Clay reached down and pulled the man's sock off.

Most folks Hayes had met would think he was a brave man. He was fast with a gun and knife, and wouldn't hesitate to use them. Now, though, he was sweating. The cool morning breeze was little comfort to him. His eyes, wide with fear, tracked the knife with the intensity of the damned.

"Ever seen a man's foot split? You can make a man's toes as long as you want. Why, I could slice between, say your big toe and the next one, all the way to your ankle. It'd make it mighty difficult to walk."

"Why do you want to do that? I've been shot. I'm a sick man!"

"Mister, I'm through funnin' with you. You either start talking right now, or I start slicing." Clay reached down and grabbed the man's foot. Hayes tried to kick him with the other foot, but was too weak to lift his foot high enough.

Clay made a slight nick between his toes.

"All right, all right," Hayes sobbed. "I'll tell you, just please don't cut me. Don't cut me."

Clay dropped the man's foot, threw the dagger into the dirt, and stepped back. He was sick to his stomach with what he'd done. That seventeen-year-old boy who loved his ma and pa would never have done this to a man. But he was afraid, deep down, that if the man had not broken, he might have cut him until he did.

"Tell me quick, Mister. It'd better be true. If I catch you lying, I'll start again and won't stop."

"It was Gideon. He'd been going on how he was going to get your pa for killing Emmett and Micah. All he could do was quote scriptures and curse. So that was going to be our first job after getting together.

"Gideon said we'd kill two birds with one stone, cause your pa had money. Can you please cut me down? I swear my arms are about to pull out of their sockets, and this bullet hole, I think it may be bleeding again."

Clay turned Hayes around till his back was to him and sliced the rope, letting the man fall in a heap at his feet.

"Keep talking."

"Quint suggested to Gideon that he put Milo on the ridge overlooking the front of the house. That way if anybody went for a gun, Milo could drop them. Milo's a dead shot with that Sharps.

"So we come riding up, your pa walks out on the porch, recognizes Gideon, and goes for his gun. He didn't stand a chance. Milo was already zeroed in, and it just took a squeeze of the trigger. That hunk of lead caught him right in the side of his head, though Milo was off a little. It hit just a tad low, but tore a mighty hole in him. Knocked him across the porch. What was amazing, he was still alive."

Clay's hands shook. He could feel the rage building. Never had he killed a man, but this man was treading close.

"Go on."

"Well, right after Milo shot, this tall drink of water—"

"Slim."

"Slim steps out of the barn, and before Milo can shoot, he puts one in me. Then we all opened up and shot him to dishrags.

"While that was happening, your ma comes running to your pa. Gideon, he's off his horse faster'n a jackrabbit and grabs her. Funny to see a man that big move so fast. She got a shot off from her little pistol, but didn't hit anyone. Gideon, he just wrenched that gun from her hand."

"Gideon's never been good with women. He's mean."

Clay didn't know if he could listen to this. It was all he could do to keep from beating Hayes to an unrecognizable piece of meat. He held himself in. *I've got to hear this so I'll know. Just let me be strong.*

"Gideon, he drags her into the house. We heard her screaming. By now, I can barely keep the saddle. I was bleeding pretty bad. I sure figured I was a goner.

"Quint yells and leaps out of the saddle. Your pa had

managed to get his gun out, but couldn't quite lift it. I could see his eyes. He wanted to kill us all. Quint kicked the gun out of his hand and kicked him in the head. Then he ran back to his horse and got his rope. He tossed a loop around your pa's neck and dragged him over to that big oak tree and strung him up. There weren't much life left in him and he died quick.

"Say, could I get a drink of water? I'm mighty dry from all this talking. I surely am."

"You keep talking," Clay said, "and I might not leave you out here for the buzzards."

Hayes looked up. Hate seeped from every pore.

"I said, keep talking."

"You're hard, boy. If you live long enough, you'll be a mean *hombre.*

"The screams from the house stopped. A few minutes later, Gideon comes out, looking pleased as punch and spouting scriptures. He sees your pa in the tree and smiles like it's Christmas time. Then he turns to us and says to git into the house and find the money. I'm just hanging onto my horse, but the other boys, including Milo, who's just come riding up, jump off their horses and start searching the house.

"We found nothing. Boy, can you help me lean against this here tree? It ain't far, and I'm mighty tired."

Clay grabbed Hayes's hands and dragged him over to the tree and dropped him. He kept an eye on him as Hayes painfully pushed himself into a sitting position against the tree. Then Hayes looked down at the blood on his bare foot and wiggled his toes. "You're mean, boy, mighty mean.

"We couldn't find anything in the house or barn. By now, everybody's mad and Mad Dog is almost foaming at the mouth. 'There ain't no money here, Gideon,' Mad Dog yells. 'There ain't a cent.' He turns to your pa hangin in the tree. 'We oughta burn ya, that's what we oughta do.' He turns back to Gideon and Gideon nodded. Mad Dog raced back into the house and got a lamp full of kerosene and doused your pa with it. He pulled out a store-bought match and struck it, stuck it up to your pa's leg, and cackled like a hen when your pa started burning. That's about it, boy. I told you true. The least you could do is get me some water."

Clay walked to Blue and untied the canteen. He turned back to Hayes. As he neared him, something didn't look right. What was wrong, what had he missed? His hands. They were above his head.

Hayes struck like a viper. He whipped the knife out of the holster hanging between his shoulder blades and threw it with all of his remaining strength. The blade buried to the hilt in Clay's neck, the point sticking out below and behind his right ear.

Clay's hands flew up to the knife, but he couldn't pull it out. It was tight and he was bleeding—bleeding bad. He felt his legs going and he crumpled to his knees. He tried desperately to get out his gun, but his hands weren't working. Clay watched as Hayes stood up, his face covered with an evil smirk.

Hayes sauntered over to Clay, looked down at him for a moment, and kicked him as hard as he could in the chest. Clay sprawled back on the grass under the big oak trees. He looked up at the blue sky. The sun was up, and the woods were busy, birds singing, squirrels barking, and armadillos rooting. A beautiful Texas day. *But I'm dying. I'm sorry, Ma. I promised, but I'm dying.*

"How's it feel, kid? Tide's turned, hasn't it?" Hayes stripped the guns from Clay, then reached up to pull his knife out of Clay's neck. He pulled and tugged. The knife wouldn't budge. He put his heel against Clay's throat and pulled. No knife. "Boy, I'm gonna make a trade with you. All your gear for my knife. I'll just leave it there while you bleed to death. Ain't life great? I just knew it'd work out good for me. It always does." He searched Clay's pocket and found his twenty-five dollars. "Yes, sir, it always works out for me."

Hayes picked up the knife Clay had found and slipped it into his neck scabbard. "Boy, you're just too green. You should've searched me better. Good for me you didn't." He slipped his sock and his boot on, gathered up the reins, and pulled himself up into the saddle. "You had me going, boy. I've got to tell you, I knew you were going to split my foot from toe to ankle. But you didn't, and I win. I always win, boy. I always win."

Clay watched him cross the creek. He hated to lose Blue. Blue was a good horse and friend. They'd been together for a long time. But it didn't matter, he thought. Time for him was about to end. He could feel the blood coursing from his neck. He wondered how long it would take him to die. It was getting darker, but he knew it still wasn't noon yet. Why was it getting dark?

The last thing he remembered was the coyote sitting on his haunches, watching him, waiting.

~

"Boy, can you hear me? If you can hear me, don't try to talk, just blink."

Who was talking? Was he in heaven? No, if he was in heaven, they'd know his name. His eyelids were so heavy. He worked hard to open them. They wouldn't move.

"Son, open your eyes. I know you're in there. I know you can hear me. Open your eyes and blink."

Clay could feel himself getting mad. How does he know I can hear him? But I can. Wait, I can hear him! Clay gradually came back to consciousness. His first sight was the captain he had run into when he tried to get into the infirmary, the doctor. He was sitting next to him, in a chair.

"Good. I knew you could do it. You're way too determined to die from a little knife cut. You had us worried, but you're doing better. You lost quite a bit of blood, so you'll be weak for a while."

Clay tried to ask how long he'd been there, but all that came out was a croak.

"Listen to me. Don't try to talk. You're very lucky. The knife missed everything vital. It went all the way through your neck, and one side of the blade lodged in your jawbone. You'll be sore for a while, but you'll recover. Even your voice should return to normal. You're one lucky young man."

Clay could feel reality returning. He looked around. He was in a bed in the infirmary. There were two or three soldiers scattered in the other beds. The bed felt good. It felt so good he thought he'd close his eyes for a moment. Just a moment, then he'd talk to the doctor again.

He was alive.

7

I t was still daylight when he awoke. He looked around. Only two soldiers were in the other beds. He felt stronger. Gripping the sides of the bed, he pushed himself up against the wall. It felt good to sit up. His right hand went to his throat. He was bandaged from his chin to his chest. His neck hurt like the dickens. He tried to yawn, but his jaw was almighty stiff. The jawbone just below his ear felt like he'd been kicked by a mule, and he had a major earache.

Clay gradually remembered what had happened. Hayes had stashed another knife in a scabbard behind his neck. What an idiot. Jake had said to be careful. He needed to learn, to build experience. I guess this is building experience the hard way, he thought.

The door opened at the end of the infirmary and the captain walked in. He was carrying a pad and pencil, and was accompanied by Colonel Mackenzie.

"Looks like my patient is feeling better," the doctor said. "You shouldn't be talking, but you can write. You can read and write, can't you?"

Clay nodded.

"Mr. Barlow, I'm glad you are alive," Colonel Mackenzie said. "Hayes knifed and killed one of our orderlies and escaped. At least, he escaped until he got to his horse."

Clay's eyebrows went up.

"Oh, yes, our Indian scouts were able to tell us exactly what happened. You can correct me if I'm wrong. Although, I doubt that my account will be anything less than accurate.

"You captured Hayes and went west with him. When you reached Maverick Creek, you stopped and interrogated him. I would be grateful if, when you feel up to it, you would write down everything he told you. But having a kind heart, you cut him down from where he was tied. Tying him as you did was an excellent idea. However, cutting him down was your second mistake and led to your undoing. The first was not thoroughly searching him. He was able to stick a throwing knife into your throat, and with more luck than anyone deserves, the knife missed anything vital. Hayes made away with your horse and guns and left you to die. That was your second great piece of luck. He didn't outright kill you. Your third piece of luck arrived in the form of our patrol. Again, thanks to our Seminole scouts. Your fourth piece of luck was our having Captain Dixon with the patrol. He would not have normally been there. But he success-fully presented his case to me that he should be allowed on some of the patrols to provide him with more experience. Had he not been there, you would probably have died. So, young man, I take my hat off to you. With all these coincidences, I feel you were meant to stay on this Earth."

Clay couldn't help but agree. He should have died. Thanks to everyone who was involved, he thought, I am still here today, listening to Colonel Mackenzie tell me how lucky I am. He started to swing his feet out of bed and stand up.

Captain Dixon stopped him. "No, no, no. You cannot be up by yourself for several more days. You've lost too much blood, and you're extremely weak."

Clay settled back down and picked up the writing pad and pencil. **How long?** he wrote.

Captain Dixon picked up Clay's legs and swung them back on the bed. "At least a week, maybe more. You can stay here until you're well enough to leave."

"That's right, Clay," Colonel Mackenzie said. "You're welcome to stay here until you're fit enough to move out."

Clay wrote again. **What about my horses and gear?**

The colonel spoke up, "The gear and horse you had with you are gone, but if you're talking about the two you stabled, they're fine, and so is your gear. I sent someone to check on it with the hostler. You're paid up for quite a while."

He didn't happen to throw my books out of the saddlebags?

"What books?" the colonel asked.

I had three books, Clay wrote, **Robinson Crusoe, Gulliver's Travels, and Blackstone's Commentaries.**

The colonel tossed a surprised glance at the captain, and said, "Who taught you to read such books?"

Clay wrote, **Ma, mainly, but Pa read Blackstone's to me, when I was older.**

"*You liked it?*"

Yes, sir, I did. I like the law, Clay wrote.

"You can be proud of your parents," the colonel said. "They were truly bringing you up right. When this is over, I hope you're able to pursue your education." the colonel said.

Thank you. I am proud of my parents, he continued to write. **Two more things. What about Hayes and when can I start talking?**

"Hayes is in the wind, I'm afraid," the colonel said. "Our priority was getting you back to the infirmary as quickly as possible. We'll keep an eye out for him, but he is gone for now. However, he is now wanted for murder of a member of the military. That will be turned over to the federal marshal, and when caught, Hayes will be tried in a federal court and hanged by a federal hangman."

Doctor Dixon spoke up. "Clay, you've had some damage to your vocal chords. I can't tell you how long it will take to heal."

Clay felt panic rising in his chest. Would it be possible that he would never be able to speak? How could he go about his life without his voice? How could he communicate? How could he catch the killers? He scribbled quickly: **Will my voice return?**

The doctor looked down and then up at him and hesitated. "Clay, I can't say. There is a lot of swelling in your neck from the injury. To complicate matters, Hayes either struck you in the throat or braced his foot against your throat to pull the knife out. In doing so, he applied quite a bit of pressure to your larynx—sorry, your voice box."

I'm only seventeen. Clay could feel pressure building in his ears, and his breathing became rapid. He hadn't felt this kind of fear since the steer had him cornered in the draw. If he hadn't shot that steer, both he and Blue would be dead. *But this isn't something I can shoot or whip. This is out of my control.* He felt tightness behind his eyes, and his ears started ringing. *Wait. Hold on. Remember, Pa said that panic takes away your mind.* His heart was beating like a Tonkawa drum.

"With the swelling," the doctor continued, "we won't know anything for a while."

Clay scribbled, **How long is a while?**

The doctor shook his head. "We just don't know. It could take a week for your voice to return—or more."

I've got to get control of myself. Take a deep breath. Pa always said that when you were afraid, a few deep breaths would help calm you down. Clay started breathing deeply. He could feel the panic receding and control returning. The pressure in his head was decreasing.

"Clay, you have youth going for you. What is needed now is for you to rest. Don't try to use your voice until I give the okay.

"Colonel, if you are through, my patient needs his rest."

"Yes, yes, of course, Doctor." The colonel nodded to Clay and started to leave, then turned. "Mr. Barlow, I need that report as soon as you feel up to it."

Clay nodded to the colonel's back as he strode out the door. The ringing in his ears was subsiding.

"He's a good man. Strict, but good, and for some reason, he's taken an interest in you. He was a highly decorated general in the war."

Clay was feeling tired. The momentary panic had exhausted him. He could tell that he had little strength. His eyelids were getting heavy.

The doctor immediately noticed. "You're tired. Get some rest, and I'll see you tomorrow."

THE WEEK HAD PASSED SLOWLY. For two more days he had remained in bed. Then, with some protest from the doctor, he started walking in the infirmary. By the end of the week he was jogging around the parade ground, taking care not to interfere with the soldiers' activity. It was almost the middle of May, and the fort was buzzing with excitement. The men were preparing for what appeared to be a large patrol.

His voice had not returned. The swelling in his neck was slowly disappearing. The pad and pencil went with him everywhere. Each time he thought about his voice not returning, panic began to rise. But, with practice, he was able to send it back to that dark place it came from.

Today, Captain Dixon had cleared him to walk into Brackett. He needed to purchase some new weapons and wanted to check on his horses and gear at the stable. His strength was returning quickly. His throat still hurt, especially his jaw, when he ate, but it was getting better.

Clay stepped out across the footbridge that crossed the stream from the Las Moras Springs. At the sound of his steps on the wooden bridge, a fox squirrel ran out on the oak tree limb and started barking at him. It felt good to be out. The army had kept the money for him that he had stashed in his boots. It came to about a hundred dollars. He had another seventy-five squirreled away in his panniers. He'd need to get some more money sent over from the Uvalde bank. Buying another complete set of gear was costly.

The first place he came to was the Brackett General Store. He'd already made a list of the things he needed. The bell over the door tinkled when he stepped in.

"What can I do you for?" a brittle voice asked from the back of the store.

Clay walked to the counter in the rear of the store and slid his list across the top.

The wizened old man stepped around the end of the counter and came toward Clay. "How you doing, young feller?"

Clay nodded to him and pointed to the bandages around his throat. He saw the pity in the man's eyes, and felt a burning shame. *This is what it'll be like my whole life if I don't get my voice back.*

"Knowed a man back in '42 got attacked by a bear. Old boy killed the bear, but not before that there bear took a swipe at his throat. Lucky he lived. But he weren't never able to say another word. Terrible hard on him. Died just a few years later. I suppose it was just grief from not being able to talk."

Clay tapped hard on the list. The man looked down at the list and then up into Clay's hard eyes. He cleared his throat and got busy picking out the items on the list. I can live with this if I have to, Clay thought. It won't be easy, but I can do it.

When the old man came to the guns on the list, he stopped. Clay had written down a pair of .36 caliber Remington Navy revolvers. The old man turned to Clay, and, in an overly loud voice, said, "I've got the Navy Remingtons, but you might want to look at the Smith & Wesson Model 3. It's—"

Clay motioned the storekeeper over to him. While he walked over, Clay wrote, **I can't talk. My hearing is not affected.**

The old man looked up at him for a moment, then took a rag from his pocket, removed his spectacles from his face, and started cleaning them. He looked back up at Clay through rheumy old eyes, wisps of matted gray hair hanging out of place. "You'll have to forgive me, Son. Sometimes I talk too much, and often I'm just blamed inconsiderate. If my granddaughter was here, she wouldn't hesitate to set me straight.

"Can I show you the Smith & Wesson?"

Clay nodded yes. He wanted to see the gun. He'd heard about it, but had never seen one.

The old man pulled it from inside the case and laid it on top of the counter. Clay picked it up and felt the balance. Then he snapped it a couple of times. He didn't like snapping an empty gun, but he had to check the trigger pull. It was crisp and light. He liked it. He looked for the loading lever, realizing he did not know how to load this weapon.

"This here's a different kind of six-shooter." The old man set a box of .44 American cartridges on the counter. "This is what it shoots. It's a hefty .44 load. Mind if I have it for a moment?"

Clay handed over the Smith & Wesson.

"This here is how you load it." The man pushed back the latch in front of the hammer, and the cylinder rotated up as the barrel was pushed down. "Now, when you open it fast, like this, the ejector pops out all six cartridges. Or you can do it slow and the ejector comes up slowly, so you can select the empty cartridges you've already shot."

Clay looked it over. It would sure speed up reloading. He loved the Remington Navy, but it took time to reload the chambers, even if you were just switching cylinders. He liked the looks of this weapon. It felt a little heavier than the Remington, but not much. The revolver had a half-ring, facing forward, just beneath the trigger guard. It looked like they intended it to be a separate finger grip. He didn't like that. He pointed to the half-ring and shook his head.

"Don't like it either," the old man said. "We've got a fine gunsmith in town. You buy the gun and I'll foot the bill for having the ring removed. He'll smooth it out so you never knew it was there."

Clay jotted on the pad, **I need to shoot it.**

"Yessiree, I imagine so. We'll just step out the back of the store. I've got a couple of peach cans that you're welcome to try it on."

Clay took the revolver, opened it, and loaded five rounds, leaving the cylinder under the hammer empty. Pa had always said to never let the hammer ride on a charged cylinder. A single jolt and you could have a hole in your leg. He snapped it closed. The old man brought a gunbelt with two holsters and the ammunition outside with them.

"Try this gunbelt, Son. It fits the Smith & Wesson."

Clay buckled the gunbelt and slid the revolver into the holster. It went in smooth. He adjusted the belt and tied the leather string, hanging from the holster, around his leg. The old man had set up two peach cans. When the man was out of the way, Clay drew the revolver and fired. One dead peach can. He slid the revolver back into the holster.

This time he tried for speed. The muzzle cleared the leather and lifted in a straight line to the second can. As soon as it leveled, Clay fired, thumbed the hammer back, and fired again—three more times. The can danced across the ground, never coming to rest until the last shot. He slid the gun back into the holster. This gun was a real shooter.

"Woo-wee. You make that six-gun sing. Reckon I've never seen anyone that fast, except maybe Bill Barlow from up New Braunfels way. He was mighty fast. Good man too."

The old man's statement startled Clay. He turned, walked back into the store and jotted down a note. **How much?**

"Fifteen dollars for one. You can have two for twenty-five, and, if you'll leave them with me tonight, I'll get the gunsmith to smooth down that trigger guard."

Could I see another one? Clay wrote on his pad.

"Surely," the old man said and pulled a second Model 3 out of the gun case. He handed it over to Clay.

Clay tried it, and it felt as good or even better than the first one. **I'll take it, but I still need a knife and a rifle, and can you make the left holster a crossdraw?** he wrote.

"I sure can set up that gunbelt and holster for you," the old man said. He reached up to the gun rack and pulled down a Yellow Boy. "Here you go, Son. This 1866 Winchester Yellow Boy has a little age on it, but it shoots straight and fires every time you pull the trigger."

Clay worked the action. It was smooth and solid. He looked it over, noticed a few light dings in the wood, then wrote on his pad, **How much?**

"Well, seeing it's been used some, I'll let you have it for twenty dollars, and I'll toss in this Boker single blade knife for free."

Clay scribbled quickly on his writing pad, **Make it fifteen and I'll take it, plus two hundred fifty rounds for the six-guns and two hundred for the rifle.**

"You drive a hard bargain, Son, but you got yourself a deal," the old man said.

The bell on the door tinkled. Clay turned slightly to see who had just entered the store, and his breath caught when a vision came floating into the dusty old general store. He guessed she was about his age, maybe a year younger. Her black hair cascaded about her shoulders, setting off her soft, tanned skin. Her eyes were dark, maybe blue, but, in this light, they looked a deep violet. He'd never seen eyes that striking.

The girl's cheeks turned pinker under his gaze.

"Do you make a habit of staring at women, young man?"

Her voice was musical, with a happy lilt, slightly teasing.

"What's the matter, cat got your tongue?"

At that, he came out of his reverie. His cheeks turned red with embarrassment and shame. A frown settled on his face. Turning, he wrote on his pad, **I can't talk**, and handed it to her.

"I'm-I'm sorry," she stuttered. Her face was flaming with embarrassment. "I-I didn't know."

Clay took back his pad and turned to the counter, leaving her to stare at his broad back. His neck, though covered with bandages, burned under her gaze.

"Son, this here is my granddaughter," the old man said. "She ain't meant no harm. She's about as sweet as honey and would never have a cross word for nobody what didn't deserve it."

Clay turned, took off his hat, and nodded. The girl's face, if it was possible, turned even brighter red after her grandfather's speech.

"Grandpa, why do you insist on embarrassing me? Mister, I am truly sorry for my verbal indiscretion. Please accept my apology." She smiled, and it was like all the lanterns in the store lit up.

Ma had taught him to treat women with respect and kindness, and her smile was melting his heart in a way he had never felt before. He wrote on his pad, **apology accepted,** and a smile that hadn't crossed his face for many days exposed strong, white teeth.

He wrote again on his pad, **I don't know your name.**

She smiled again and said, "My name is Andrea Lynn Killganan. You may call me Lynn."

The old man laughed and said, "Yessir, her ma's named Andrea, and danged if every time someone said Andrea, they both answered. So when she wuz about five years old, she says, 'I want everyone to call me Lynn—my name is Lynn.' So since then, she's been Lynn."

"Please don't tell my grandpa anything you don't want

everyone to know," Lynn said, but her smile took the bite out of the words. "Now it's your turn, sir. What is your name?"

Clay didn't know why he did it, but he wrote his full name for her. **Clayton Joseph Barlow, but you can call me Clay.**

"Clayton, that's a nice name. Well, Mr. Clayton Joseph Barlow, I feel I must do more than just apologize. Would you like to come to supper this evening?"

The old man's eyebrows rose at the invitation. Then he shook his head and chuckled. "Yeah, boy, why don't you do that. I'm sure the whole family would love to meet you."

Clay felt surrounded. He wanted to see this girl again, but he couldn't talk. He couldn't carry on a conversation. Would he ever be able to? He thought a moment more. Would he ever get rid of this pad? Coming to a decision, he wrote, **I'd be pleased to.**

Lynn smiled and said, "Good. Supper is usually at six. Please be on time. Father doesn't like to start dinner late. I shall see you then. Oh, I almost forgot." Lynn spoke to her grandfather now: "Your daughter would like for you to bring home some coal oil."

The old man chuckled, turned his head slightly, and said, "I'll tell you he doesn't." Then he said to his granddaughter, "Tell your ma, I'll be bringin' it when I close up."

She looked at her grandfather with mock seriousness for a moment, then leaned over the counter and gave him a peck on the cheek. "Be on time. Don't upset Father again. I feel you are often late on purpose." She gave a small curtsy to Clay, then whirled around and left the store, an enticing smell of lilacs lingering in the air. The tinkling of the bell trailed behind her, as if sad she had left.

"She's a pistol, ain't she?" the old man said, pride in his voice. "She got her humor from her ma. It sure didn't come from her pa. Reckon I never figured what my girl saw in that man. Don't get me wrong. He loves her and provides a good life for them, but I reckon he'd make a lemon taste sweet. Anyway, like she said, if you want to make a good impression with him, be on time." The old man's eyes twinkled as he said, "And I reckon you aim to make a good impression on at least one person in that house."

This had all happened too fast for Clay. One minute he was buying supplies, and the next minute, a beautiful young woman had entered his life and temporarily dimmed his mission. But dinner wouldn't hurt . . . would it?

Clay felt a smile playing at his mouth. He wrote on his pad, **I'll need a suit.**

8

Clay stepped out of the general store into the bright afternoon sun. It was almost mid-May, and the temperature was warming up.

His arms were full. He carried the rifle with a few extra rounds of ammunition in his vest pockets. Under his left arm he had a wrapped package—his suit. He'd never bought himself clothes before.

On the building across the street, a sign was fastened above the door: Ma Nelson's Home Cooking. A couple of horses stood three-legged at the hitchin' rail. His stomach was letting him know it was dinnertime. His neck was itching under the bandage. His red bandana covered most of the white bandage.

Clay crossed the street and walked into Ma Nelson's place. There were five tables with four chairs each. The tables were covered with red-and-white checkered cotton tablecloths. Though they had been washed clean, faint stains from past meals dotted the tablecloths. Two cowboys sat at one table, and a couple of townies, one in a suit, sat at another. He picked a corner table facing the room and the front door, and placed his Winchester on the table and his package of clothes in a chair.

A middle-aged lady came from the back. Her graying hair, pulled back in a bun, framed a full red face. "Coffee?"

He shook his head, pointed to his throat, and wrote on his pad, **Sorry ma'am, can't talk, water and whatever you've got for lunch.**

"Sure thing, that'll be meatloaf, potatoes, and beans. I guess you figured by now, I'm Ma Nelson. You need anything, you just wave at me."

The cowboys had paid him little mind. They were busy reducing their steak to dog bones, but the townies were glancing at him and talking, occasionally giggling. Finally, the one in the suit looked over at him, grinned, then said, "Howdy."

Clay ignored him. He'd been around enough to know when a town tough was set on making himself look good by demeaning someone else.

Suit repeated, "I said howdy."

The other townie laughed. The two cowboys turned to look at Suit, then at Clay. They both shook their heads and went back to eating.

Suit stood and started walking over to Clay's table. "I don't like it when I'm not answered."

Clay looked him up and down, then reached out to the Winchester and eared the hammer back. The metallic clicking of the hammer as it went into full cock stopped Suit in his tracks. Clay rested his hand on the Winchester, but didn't pick it up.

Suit said, "Another time." He turned and went back to his seat. No more giggling came from the townies' table. Each flipped two bits on the table and walked out.

After they left, Clay lowered the hammer on the Winchester as Ma Nelson was bringing his food and water into the dining room.

"I swear. Those boys are going to get themselves killed yet. Enjoy your dinner." She smiled, leaned over, and said, "Thanks for running them out of here. They're bad for business."

Clay smiled back and dug into his lunch. It was nice to be eating solid food. His neck was still sore and his jaw hurt some. It hurt when he swallowed, but not enough to stop him from enjoying the meatloaf and potatoes. He washed them down with water and placed two bits on the table. It was nice to see a friendly face. He picked up his rifle and package and headed for the door.

The cowboys had finished eating and were sipping their coffee as he went out. They looked up and nodded.

Clay went to the stable to check on his horses and gear. He pulled his last seventy-five dollars out of the panniers and headed for the bank.

Brackett Bank was not a large building. When you walked in, you almost ran into the teller's cage. There was barely enough room to open and close the door. Two teller windows greeted the customers, and a gate allowed access to the back office. The safe sat just behind the teller's cage. There was an office door to the right of the safe.

Clay went to the teller's window, laid his writing pad on the counter, and wrote, **I would like to transfer five hundred dollars here from the Uvalde Bank. My name is Clayton Joseph Barlow. I can't talk.**

The teller read the note. "Just a moment, sir. I'll have to request this through Mr. Killganan. I'll be right back." He turned and entered the back office.

Moments later, a man in his mid-years, of average height, and with no hair came walking from the office.

"Mr. Barlow? I'm Elmer Killganan. I'll be happy to take care of this for you. When will you need the money?"

Clay wrote on his pad, **How soon can the transfer be done?**

"Well," Killganan said and cleared his throat, "transfers are normally done within two or three business days."

I'd like it Monday, Clay wrote.

"That might be a bit soon."

What is your transfer fee? Clay wrote. It is so frustrating not to be able to talk, Clay thought.

"Well, uh, the fee is our standard five percent."

I would think for a twenty-five-dollar profit, you could have the transfer by Monday, especially if you send the wire now, he wrote.

"I think you misunderstand me. We can do it in one day, but it is just normal business to take two to three business days."

Will it be here Monday? Clay wrote again.

"Well, yes. I think we can do that. Would Monday afternoon, say around two o'clock, be satisfactory?"

Yes, thank you, Clay wrote for the final time. He shook hands with the banker, then turned and left the bank. Are all bankers pompous? he thought. He'll be surprised when I show up for dinner tonight. With the thought of dinner with Lynn, a smile broke across his face. For a moment, his duty slipped into a distant second. Slowly, it pushed back to the forefront. I've got to get my voice back, he thought. Writing everything down on a pad of paper takes much too long.

He looked around, realized that he was just standing in front of the bank, and turned back down the street to Fort Clark.

When he arrived, the fort was a beehive. A large contingent of cavalry was preparing to depart. Captain Dixon walked out of the infirmary.

"Good," Captain Dixon said, "I wanted to see you before we left. The Apaches have made several strikes between here and the border. Colonel Mackenzie is going after them. We shouldn't be gone more than a few days. I want you to stay in the infirmary until we get back. I'll check your throat then. Got to go." Dixon walked over to the orderly who was holding his horse, mounted, and moved to his position in the troop.

Clay doffed his hat to Dixon and, seeing the colonel, to him as well. The men were impressive. Clay had heard a great deal about the Buffalo Soldiers. These men looked like they could take on any number of Apaches who might be for them. He looked around at those seeing the soldiers off. He could plainly see the worry on the faces of the wives. Must be hard for them to have to wait, he thought.

CLAY LOOKED at himself in the half-mirror. He'd never worn a suit before. The gray eyes staring back at him looked older than he remembered. He could see some worry lines around his mouth. He combed his black hair back with his fingers and rubbed the pronounced dimple in his chin. His ma loved his dimple. He didn't mind it until he started shaving. It had become difficult to shave. He rubbed his square jaw where the knife had lodged. It wasn't nearly as sore as it had been. His face still looked young, though he already towered over most folks. Many still considered him a boy. He felt like a boy in a man's body, but he had a man's job to do and he was prepared to do it.

He adjusted his tie and wiped his boots on the back of his black pants. Time to go. He should have gotten some type of hideout gun like Hayes had. That would at least give him a bit of comfort. For now, he had no weapon except the rifle. Clay considered for a moment whether or not he should take it. Of course he should. This was still Indian and bandit country. He slipped some extra cartridges in his coat pocket, picked up the Winchester, and walked outside. Shadows were growing as the sun drifted lower in the west. The green of the oak leaves took on a purple cast from the red sunset. When he crossed the creek, no squirrel came out to bark at him. The squirrels were already in their holes with their tails wrapped around their noses, not taking any chance of becoming roaming owl fodder.

The old man from the store was waiting for him as he entered Brackett. "Reckon no one told you where to go. Thought I'd just be your guide. By the by, don't think I ever introduced myself. My name's Jeremiah T. Brennan. Most folks call me JT."

Clay stopped, handed JT his rifle, and pulled out his pad and pencil. He wrote, **How about if I call you Mr. Brennan?**

The old man chuckled and said, "That's just fine."

Clay put his pad and pencil up and took back his rifle. The house they were approaching was near the creek. It was made from limestone with a cedar shake roof. Nice house, Clay thought. It faced toward the north, toward town. A wide, tall covered porch extended the full length of the front of the house. A two-person swing hung on the east end of the porch. A short, glistening white picket fence circled the house.

"I've got to warn you, Clay," Brennan said, "Lynn's pa is a real stuffed shirt. I will say he loves and takes care of his family, but he is truly a pain to be around. I have yet to see what my daughter sees in the man. But she loves him, so I put up with him." Brennan laughed again and said, "Or he puts up with me. Here we are, can't put it off any longer."

Clay smiled as he opened the gate for Brennan. He followed him across the walk to the house and up the three steps to the porch. The old man pulled the door open and called into the house, "I'm here. We can start eating." He turned, winked at Clay and whispered, "Drives Elmer crazy."

Lynn and her mother, looking like sisters, came to the door. They both bestowed a kiss on JT's cheek. "Hello, Papa," Andrea said.

"Hi, Grandpa, are you trying to upset Father? It doesn't take much from you."

"Lynn!" her mother said.

JT looked his daughter over. "Andrea, you're looking as beautiful as your ma. You look mighty nice too, Lynn. Expectin' someone special?"

"Grandpa, shame on you!" Lynn said, her cheeks coloring. She turned her attention to Clay. "Clayton, I'd like to introduce my mother, Andrea Killganan. Mother, this is Clayton Joseph Barlow."

Clay had removed his hat when he entered the house. He handed his rifle to JT and bowed slightly, taking the extended hand in his huge right hand, his smile apologetic.

"It is very nice to meet you, Mr. Barlow. I am happy Lynn invited you to supper. It is always nice to entertain new guests."

Clay nodded and smiled again. With his hat under his arm, he pulled out his notepad. **It is my pleasure, ma'am. Thank you for having me. Please call me Clay.** He extended the pad to Mrs. Killganan.

She read it and, with a tender smile, said, "Thank you, Clay. I hope you're prepared to write a lot tonight, for I have many questions. May I take your hat?" She took Clay and JT's hats and hung them on the hat tree next to the front door.

Lynn took the Winchester from JT. "Clayton, is it all right if I leave your rifle here next to the hats?"

Clay nodded.

"Please, Clay, let me show you to the dining room," Lynn's mother said. She took Clay's arm and walked with him into the dining room.

Lynn and JT moved ahead.

Clay was momentarily startled, but quickly returned the smile to his face. The Suit he'd had trouble with at Ma Nelson's was sitting comfortably to Mr. Killganan's left. JT moved quickly to sit next to the Suit, causing Mr. Killganan's obvious consternation.

Mrs. Killganan smiled. "Clay, may I introduce you to my husband, Elmer Killganan."

Killganan rose and extended his hand, and with a tight smile, said, "Yes, Andrea, Mr. Barlow and I met in the bank today."

Clay shook the hand, smiled, and nodded to Killganan.

"And this gentlemen"—the word gentleman was pronounced cooly by Mrs. Killganan, because the Suit did not stand—"is

James Davis. Everyone calls him Cotton. I'm sure you can see why."

The man's hair was so blonde it was almost white. Clay put out his hand, and Davis reluctantly took it. "Come, Clay, you'll sit over here, next to me and Lynn." She guided him behind Davis and JT.

They reached the end of the table, and Clay pulled the chair out for her and gave her a small nod.

She looked somewhat surprised, but appreciative. "Why, thank you, Clay."

He then stepped around to the side of the table where Lynn was about to pull out her own chair. He placed a firm hand on the chair, looked into those deep purple eyes, and slowly pulled the chair out for her. She smiled straight into his eyes, then gave a small curtsy and sat down. Clay slid Lynn to the table, moved to his chair, and sat.

None of the other three men had missed the show. JT was grinning. Both Killganan and Davis were frowning. Davis had remained seated throughout the episode. As his daughter was seated, Killganan sat down, his chair dragging noisily across the wooden floor when he pulled up to the table.

I'm sure glad Ma taught me manners. She told me they'd come in handy someday.

Clay picked up his pencil and started to write. **I'm sorry this is necessary. I want to thank you for the supper invitation. You have a beautiful home.** He first passed the pad to Mrs. Killganan, and then to Lynn. She read it and passed it to her father.

Killganan read the note. "Mr. Barlow, may I call you Clay?"

Clay nodded.

"Clay, it's our pleasure. What you see around you is Mrs. Killganan's doing. She has a talent for decorating."

Mrs. Killganan beamed at her husband. "Thank you, Elmer. Clay, I'm glad you like it. I enjoy the effort and the results. Now, tell me about yourself. How is it that you come to be here?"

Clay wrote on the pad. **It's a long story.**

Mrs. Killganan looked at his note. "Why, Clay, we have all evening. I'm sure we are all interested. Isn't that right, Cotton?"

She hadn't missed the animosity that had passed between the two young men.

"I reckon. Though I'd rather hear about Lynn's day."

Lynn laughed and said, "Cotton, my days are so much alike, I'm sure it wouldn't be near as interesting as Clayton's." She laid her hand on Clay's arm. "We'd love to hear about you."

Though she left her hand on his arm only momentarily, Clay could still feel the warmth through his suit jacket. He marveled at the feeling. It was as if her hand were still there.

Between eating and writing, the evening passed quickly. Cotton spoke seldom, obviously irritated that Clay was receiving all of the attention from those at the table.

Sadness, tears, and occasional gasps from the ladies, accompanied Clay's writing out of his story. He left out the gruesome details of his parents' murder for the sake of the ladies. Though they were genteel women, they were familiar with this country and easily pieced together the awfulness that he had discovered. Mr. Killganan sat quietly, eating slowly, listening as Mrs. Killganan read, out loud, each of Clay's descriptions.

Clay was thankful that she was reading his notes. Some of the questions he could answer with just a nod or the shake of his head. It allowed him to enjoy the food that had been set before him.

Mr. Killganan directed an appreciative glance at Clay when he explained his arrangement with Adam Hewitt for the running of the ranch.

Clay also explained how Mr. Tropf had allowed him to accompany the freight train.

Mr. Killganan commented that Mr. Tropf was a good businessman.

When he explained how he had received his neck injury,

Cotton barked a harsh laugh. "Reckon he sure fooled you. You're lucky to be alive."

Clay turned his icy gaze to Cotton, whom he had ignored through most of the evening. He held Cotton's stare, until Cotton coughed and looked away.

"Cotton, that is an awful thing to say," Lynn snapped, coming quickly to Clay's defense.

JT winked at Clay, turned to Cotton, and said, "You reckon you could've done better?"

Cotton turned red. "I woulda sure searched him better. I wouldn't have missed that knife."

JT laughed. "Cotton, yore bones would be out there feedin' the buzzards right now. Hayes is a known man. He'd a had you when he first saw you." JT laughed again and went back to eating.

Cotton's face turned a more brilliant red.

Mrs. Killganan broke the tension quickly. "Clay, what does Dr. Dixon say about your throat?"

Clay hated not being able to talk. Everything took longer when he had to write it down. He wrote, **Dr. Dixon says that he doesn't know if I will get my voice back, but he thinks there's a good chance when all of the swelling goes down.** He handed the pad to Mrs. Killganan.

As she read it, Lynn's eyes filled with tears. "Oh, Clay, I do hope you get it back. It must be so frustrating to you, having to write everything down." She picked up her napkin and dabbed at the corners of her eyes.

He turned to her. He wished he could tell her how much her understanding meant to him. It was, for a moment, as if they were the only two in the room. Then Mr. Killganan cleared his throat. Clay felt embarrassed for Lynn. He glanced at Cotton. The young man's face was filled with hurt and jealousy. Reckon I'd better be on the lookout for him, Clay thought. He wanted to turn the attention from himself and Lynn. He wrote on his pad, **How long have you folks lived in Brackett?**

"We moved here to start the bank," Mr. Killganan said. "It's been five years now. September, and Lynn will be off to Macon, Georgia, for school."

"Father, you know I don't want to go to school back East. I want to stay in Texas. I can learn just as much here as I can in Georgia."

"Lynn," her father said, "we have spoken of this before. There are no girl schools here that I would deem appropriate for you to attend. I want you to broaden your education and return to help me run the bank."

"Father, you know I enjoy working with you in the bank. But I will not go so far away for my schooling. There is a new school starting this year in Thorp Springs. I believe it is the Addran College. It is a christian school that will allow both men and women to attend. That is where I want to go."

Mrs. Killganan, with her soft, persuasive voice, brought calm back to the dining table. "My dears, can't we discuss this later? There is sufficient time to work this out before school starts."

Mr. Killganan smiled at his wife. "Of course, my dear. Shall we have coffee?"

Lynn smiled at her mother's peace-keeping efforts as well and said, "Yes, Mother."

Clay laughed inside. *Mr. Killganan, you don't stand a chance.* He glanced around the table. Lynn was smiling as if only she knew what the results of this argument would be. Her father looked as if he felt he had won another argument. Cotton looked lost, but JT appeared supremely pleased. Mrs. Killganan was in complete control.

Mrs. Killganan and Lynn served the coffee. Clay had lemonade. Every so often, Clay would steal a glance at the black-haired girl. He had never seen such a beauty.

Clay had a rest from writing as Mr. Killganan discussed his day. Killganan talked about how good Lynn was with numbers, not Clay's strongest suit. It said a lot that Killganan wanted to bring her into his business to work at the bank. He even mentioned her taking it over in the future. Clay enjoyed being a part of this family conversation. It reminded him of home. With the thought of home, his demeanor darkened, thrusting his immediate goal back to mind. He would bring those men to justice, or die trying.

"Clay," he heard Lynn saying, "are you all right?" Again, her hand was resting on his left forearm.

He came back from the dark place and smiled at her. He wrote, **I've really enjoyed this evening.**

She smiled back at him. "I have too. Maybe we can do it again."

Mrs. Killganan said softly, "Lynn, would you like to invite Clay to your birthday party?"

Lynn smiled, and her violet eyes shimmered in the lamplight. "Would you come, Clay? It'll be great fun. You could meet my friends."

Clay tore his eyes from her face and wrote on his pad, **When is it? I'll be leaving soon.**

"It's day after tomorrow, May nineteenth. I'll be seventeen. Oh, and maybe you'd like to go to church with us tomorrow?"

Clay thought for a moment. He should stay in Brackett until Colonel Mackenzie and Doctor Dixon returned. Colonel Mackenzie had said that they should be back either the nineteenth or the twentieth, so he would still be here.

Before he could answer, Mrs. Killganan said, "Oh my, look at the time. Cotton, shouldn't you be getting home? Your folks will be wondering where you are."

Cotton Davis jumped like he had been stung by a scorpion and stood up. "Why, uh, I guess, ma'am." He looked at Mr. Killganan as if he might get a reprieve.

No reprieve came. Mr. Killganan glanced up at Cotton. "Goodnight, Cotton."

Mrs. Killganan rose from her chair. "Let me show you out,

Cotton. It was so nice to have you visit for supper. Please tell your mother that we must get together soon." She continued talking, guiding the young man to the front door, out and down the porch steps.

She returned quickly and seated herself. "Did I miss anything?"

"Andrea, you're as sweet as your mama, and just as controlling," JT said.

Mrs. Killganan turned to JT with feigned shock. "Papa, why would you say such a mean thing to your only daughter?"

He lifted an old, wrinkled hand and affectionately patted her arm.

She smiled into his eyes, and then turned to Lynn. "Did I miss anything?"

"No, ma'am. I'm waiting for Clay's answer."

Clay wrote on his pad, **I'd like to come to your birthday party and go to church with you tomorrow.** He slid the pad over to Lynn.

She read it and said to no one in particular, "He said yes, to both." She then turned to him. "The party will be at three in the afternoon, on the front porch and under the big oak in the front yard. I'll plan on you being here. Church will be at nine tomorrow morning."

"Papa," Mrs. Killganan said, "isn't it time for you to be headed home?"

"Now don't you be trying to manage your old papa, girl. But yep, it is getting late. Thanks for a mighty fine dinner. Elmer, I enjoyed it, which don't happen too often."

Lynn jumped up and ran around the table to give her grandpa a kiss. "Goodnight, Grandpa. Love you."

He hugged her and cleared his throat. "It's good that you do. Night, Clay. Reckon you can find your way to Fort Clark."

Clay smiled at the old man and saluted with a forefinger. He turned the page on his pad and wrote, **I should be going. Thank** you folks for a fine dinner and great company. I'll see you all in the morning.

He handed the pad to Mr. Killganan. "It was our pleasure, Clay. Tomorrow it is."

"Not so fast, young man," Mrs. Killganan said. "Why don't you two young people go out to the swing? It's a beautiful night. I'll bring you both a piece of cobbler."

Clay and Mr. Killganan looked around with surprise. Clay didn't need much urging. He stood up and held the chair for Lynn. She took his arm, smiled up at him, and they walked outside to the swing.

Clay could hear Mr. Killganan say to his wife, "What the blazes are you doing?"

A soft voice answered, "Nothing, dear."

Lynn sat first in the swing. The swing was built for two people, but Clay was a big man. Because of his size, their arms touched as they sat.

Clay could think of nothing to say. Then he laughed to himself—he couldn't say anything even if he could think of something. He lightly propelled the swing, and it drifted forward and back in the nighttime breeze. The fragrance of the honey-suckle floated in the night air. He could smell her hair, the lilac scent intoxicating.

"Isn't this lovely?" she said. "I think this is the best birthday present I've ever had."

He got out his pad. In the faint light escaping through the front windows, he wrote, **Your birthday is Monday.**

She read it and laughed, the sound like tinkling bells, then said, "It doesn't matter, silly. It's still my best birthday present."

Mrs. Killganan brought out two bowls of her peach cobbler. "Don't stay out too late, Lynn. Your father expects you at the bank in the morning."

Clay took the cobbler in one hand. Mrs. Killganan took his

other hand. "It was very nice meeting you, Clay. Don't be a stranger." With that, she walked back into the house.

Clay found himself hoping this evening would never end. He was happier than he had been since his folks died. He couldn't describe it, but he felt like he'd found another home. Mr. Killganan hadn't been as bad as he had expected.

The peach cobbler was delicious, but it couldn't take his mind from the girl sitting next to him. He reminded himself that he had plans that couldn't involve her, shouldn't involve her. If things were different, he might even think about taking her back to the homeplace. But there was too much death ahead of him. If she really knew what he planned, she would probably have nothing to do with him.

He turned to look at her, and she gazed up into his eyes. She leaned toward him expectantly. He stood up.

A surprised look crossed Lynn's face. "Is something wrong? Did I do something wrong?" Tears were welling up in her eyes.

He set the bowl on the swing and took out his pad. **Sorry, Lynn. I've got to be going. I've really enjoyed this evening. I'll see you tomorrow at nine.** Clay reached out and touched her cheek, then spun around and marched out of the yard. He didn't want to hurt her, but he had some pretty rough things to do, and she was going off to college. She had a bright future ahead of her. His future could include a six-foot plot of real estate. He couldn't ruin her life.

He was halfway back to the fort when he realized he had left his rifle. He shook his head with disgust. If this was what happened when you got to thinking about a girl, then he was going to be a dead man. He had to keep his focus, keep his mind on the work ahead. He couldn't let anything, not even a lovely, smart, sweet-smelling girl—

The rapid footsteps closed on him quickly. He spun, just in time to count three attackers, and Clay wasn't armed. He was even without a knife. He had left the Boker at the general store.

As the three closed on him, he could see they wore sacks over their heads with cutouts for their eyes. He felt the rush of anger flowing over him. He'd done nothing to these men. He'd give them what they were looking to dish out.

The three men were running at full tilt, intent on tackling him and then beating him to death. When they were almost on top of him, he knelt and drove his fist, with all the might of his massive shoulders and arm, into the first man's groin. He felt the contact and knew from this point on he would be fighting only two men. As the second one came in and jumped at him, he ducked lower, until the man's hips were sliding over his left shoulder. Grasping the man's thighs, he stood and thrust upward as high as he could, lifting his assailant to over eight feet. The man's momentum carried him over, then he fell almost straight down, landing on the point of his right shoulder. There was an audible snap. The man screamed and lay writhing on the ground.

The third man had slowed and was circling him, now cautious, realizing that he was alone. Clay saw the glint of steel in the man's right hand. Surprised, he saw how the man was holding the knife, like he was going to make an overhand stab. This was no knife fighter. Clay circled him, watching and waiting. The man raised the knife over his head and lunged forward. Clay thought back to all the lessons that Pa and Slim had given him. He remembered them telling him that if he was ever in a knife fight to make up his mind he was going to get cut, so it wouldn't be a surprise. He also remembered how he had been taught to handle an attack such as this. But his opponent gave him such an opportunity, he couldn't resist. As the man's momentum carried him forward, Clay aimed a kick right between the man's legs, striking with all of the stored power in his body.

The man cried out. His hand released the knife as he fell to the ground, moaning and crying in pain. "I think you've killed me," the man said between moans.

"Isn't that what you planned to do to me?" Clay picked up the big bowie knife, reached down, and yanked Cotton's sack from his head.

"I think I'm dying," Cotton said.

"You'll live, although you and your friend might walk a little funny for a while."

Clay walked over to the one he had hit in the groin with his fist. He yanked the man's mask off. It was the same one who had been with Cotton in Ma Nelson's. He was doubled over in pain. He looked up at Clay. "Mister, please don't hurt me no more. I swear, I think you've ruined me for life."

Clay stepped to the remaining man of the trio. He pulled the sack from his head. He didn't recognize him. The young man was holding his right arm. He was obviously in excruciating pain. "You broke my shoulder. That's my right shoulder, my ropin' shoulder." The man's arm was just hanging in the grip of his left hand.

Running steps could be heard from Fort Clark and from Brackett. Clay waited for the arrivals. The guards from Fort Clark showed up first. They both knew Clay. The corporal spoke up. "Looks like you were a mite busy, Clay. Thought you could use our help, but guess I was wrong. Is this all of them? I count three."

"That's all," Clay said.

"You want I should hold them till the marshal gets here? I can toss 'em in the stockade."

"No, I don't need them arrested. Thanks, though."

"Okay, looks like they all might need to see a doctor. 'Specially this one, appears he has a broken shoulder."

The people of Brackett came running up. Of all people, JT was in the lead. "Thought you might've been jumped. Had a good idea who might be behind it. Cotton." He gave the three a disgusted look, then turned back to Clay. "You all right, Son?"

"Yes, sir. I'm just fine."

JT laughed and said, "Boy, I guess you are. You realize you're talking?"

The question stopped Clay for a moment. He felt his throat as if it could give him an answer. "Well, sir, I guess I am." He grinned at JT in the starlight. "I should thank these boys."

The town marshal showed up next with some of the townspeople. "What's going on here?"

JT responded to the marshal's inquiry. "Marshal, I'll tell you what's going on. Your son, Cotton, and these two other no accounts decided they'd jump a wounded man. They got their comeuppance, I'd say."

Great, Clay thought, I've just beat up the marshal's son.

"Here's his knife, Marshal." Clay handed over Cotton's bowie knife. The marshal looked at it for a moment, then looked over at his son holding himself and moaning.

"What's your name, Son?"

"Clay Barlow, Marshal."

"You any kin to Bill Barlow of New Braunfels?"

"My pa."

"A good man. Sorry to hear about your ma and pa. Good folks."

"Thank you. I think the one over there has a broken shoulder. He'll be needing a doctor."

"They can wait. You want to press charges?"

"No, sir. To be honest, I've more important things to do than wait around for court."

"Understand. You're free to go about your business." The marshal turned to the other three. "Get up, you bushwhackers. Consider yourself lucky I don't throw all three of you in jail. Cotton, you get home right now. Shad, you know where the doctor is. Go see him. Maybe he can fix up your arm."

Several of the townspeople had gathered around. Clay could see Mr. Killganan there, his face hard, his arm around Lynn.

Shock enveloped Lynn's face, made more stark by the

starlight. Her wide eyes looked black as she stared at him. Seeing me for the first time, Clay thought. Guess that mean's no birthday party.

JT threw his arm around Clay's shoulders. "Rest up, Son. You've earned it. Glad you're talking. When you can think about it, that'll be a big relief for you. I'll see you tomorrow."

Clay nodded, took one last look at Lynn and walked back to Fort Clark.

Clay rolled out of bed early. The sun was just starting to peek over the eastern horizon. He washed up, shaved with the straight razor he had picked up at the general store, and got dressed. His neck and jaw were feeling better, but still sore. His throat felt raw. Must be from the talking last night, he thought.

He stomped his boots on and walked out on the porch. The infirmary faced east, toward the parade ground. He sat in one of the chairs to watch the sunrise. *Ma always loved to watch the sunrise.* He couldn't think of his ma without the picture of the way he had last seen her returning to his mind. When that happened, he could feel the bile rising in his throat, accompanied by anger. *How could anyone be so brutal to a woman?*

"Howdy, Son."

Clay jerked with surprise. The marshal was standing in front of the porch, looking up at him. *I didn't even hear him. I've got to stop this, or I'll be left dead somewhere.*

"Morning, Marshal. What brings you out here?"

"Mind if I join you?" The marshal stepped up on the porch and pulled up a chair next to Clay.

The fort was coming to life. Clay could see activity across the parade ground at the stables. He could hear the boot steps echoing on the plank floors of the infirmary.

"Welcome, Marshal. Have a seat. Mighty impressive sunrise this morning."

"Clay, I'll get right to the point. You did what you had to do last night. Those boys, including my son, were intent on doing you harm. I realize that.

"I heard murmuring last night from some of the parents about getting even. I put a damper on it, but I can't be around to protect you all the time."

"Marshal, I can take care of myself."

"I know, Clay. But we've had enough excitement in Brackett for a while."

"Marshal, you just need to control your town. That's what they pay you for."

"Boy, I know you're Bill Barlow's son, but don't tell me what I need to do. I know my duty. Now, I know you're headed west, after the killers. I'm just asking you leave now, today."

Clay looked down at his boots—they could use some polish. He looked directly at the marshal, the muscles in his face tight. "Marshal, I've never been posted out of town. I know my pa never was. I'm law-abiding. I didn't start that fight, and I have no wish to be in another, here. I think you're being mighty unfair.

Now it was the marshal's turn to look away. For a moment, he watched the cavalry men exercising their horses. He turned back to Clay. "You're not being posted out of town. Understand, I like you, boy. You come from good stock. I'm just asking. I don't do much asking, Son."

"Captain Dixon told me to stay here until the troops get back so he can examine my neck. He said they'll be back either Monday or Tuesday. I've got business at the bank, but it's closed today. I'll take care of that tomorrow. I do have to pick up some things at the general store, but I think Mr. Brennan will open it for me."

"When's your business with the bank?"

"I'm supposed to be there at two on Monday. But I've also been invited to the Killganans' for Lynn's birthday and to church today. Don't know if I'm still invited to either, but if I am, I'd like to attend."

"Two days. I'm afraid trouble might erupt in that time. You need to leave today."

"Tell me again, Marshal. Are you posting me out of town?"

"I told you, no."

"Are you arresting me?"

"I'm not arresting you, right now."

"Then, Marshal, I have plans. Those plans require me to remain in Brackett for two more days. If you're not posting me out of town or arresting me, I'm staying until after the party."

The marshal stood and walked around Clay to the porch steps. He took off his hat and wiped the sweat band. He wiped his graying hair back with his other hand and put his hat back on. He walked down the porch steps and moved toward town until he was even with Clay, where he turned to look at him. "I've asked you nicely, boy. That's something I don't usually do. The doctor said that Shad will never have full use of his right arm, and I don't know if those other two boys will ever have kids. Don't hurt any more of my citizens, or I'll be coming for you, and I won't be asking."

Clay watched the marshal amble back to Brackett. *I don't want any trouble with the law, but I'm in the right here. Anyway, I've got to stay for the bank. I wish Pa was here to tell me what to do.* He stood and walked back into the infirmary to get his coat. He had time to get something to eat before church. Maybe he could wake Mr. Brennan and take him to breakfast.

He slipped his black suit coat on. With his black pants and black hat, he couldn't decide whether he looked more like a preacher, a gunfighter, or an undertaker. He just hoped that Lynn would still want him to go to church with her. But most of all, he hoped no one started anything. He sure didn't want trouble, not with the law.

The walk from Fort Clark to Brackett was uneventful. This early, there weren't many people on the street. The fort was busier than Brackett. He knocked on the door of the general store. No answer. *I know Mr. Brennan said he lived behind the store.* He knocked louder this time. He waited. He was about to knock again when he heard rustling from inside the store.

"Hold your blasted horses. Ain't you got the sense God gave a mule? This here is Sunday. I ain't open on Sunday."

"Mr. Brennan, it's Clay Barlow."

Now footsteps approached the door, and he could hear a key being inserted into the lock. Brennan unlocked and opened the door. "Come on in, Son. Don't just stand there. I want to lock this place up so nobody else has a dad-blamed idea to knock."

"Sorry, Mr. Brennan. I just thought that you might have my supplies ready."

"I do, I do. I think you'll like your guns. The gunsmith fixed 'em up real good. He said he even worked the triggers a bit. Hope you like 'em."

Brennan pulled the gunbelt out from under the counter. The two Model 3s were in the holsters. Clay slipped his coat off, laid it on the counter, and swung the gunbelt around his waist. It felt good to have guns on again. His rifle was fine, but the gunbelt was comfortable. It felt like an old friend. He slipped the Model 3 from his right holster. It slid out smoothly. The gun felt natural. Without the finger ring on the trigger guard, it fit perfectly into his hand. He dropped it back into the holster, waited a moment, and drew.

"Whew. Clay, like I said yesterday, you are fast. Don't know if I've ever seen a man that fast. Just a word of caution. Be careful.

There're some men that if they find out how fast you are, they'll be looking for you."

"Mr. Brennan, I'm not looking for trouble, except with those killers."

"I know, Son. But with that speed, I have a feelin' it'll be lookin' for you. Now try the crossdraw."

Clay pulled the Model 3 from the crossdraw holster with his right hand. It felt just as natural as the first one. He tried the trigger a couple of times, being careful not to let the hammer fall on an empty chamber. "These are mighty nice, Mr. Brennan. I hate to lose my Remingtons, but these two feel even better."

"Yeah, and you won't be packing cylinders with powder or trusting caps to fire when the hammer hits 'em. Those Smith & Wessons are good handguns. They'll last you for many a year.

"Tell me, Clay, you don't use your left hand?"

"No, sir."

"Just a suggestion, Son. I'd be practicing with that left hand. Cross draw might be right for you, but if you can shoot with both hands, you'll have an edge. Never know when an edge will come in handy."

Clay nodded. "Thanks for the advice. You got a box of ammunition handy? I need to load these guns. If you don't mind, I'll leave the rest of the stuff till tomorrow. You up for some breakfast? Thought I'd eat something before I go see your granddaughter."

"You bet. Let me get a shirt on and I'll be right out. Don't worry about the rest of your gear. It can stay here as long as you want."

JT disappeared in the back, after grabbing a box of bullets out of Clay's bag of purchases and tossing them on the counter. Clay loaded both revolvers with five rounds each, leaving the empty cylinder under the hammer. He had just finished putting the remaining cartridges on his gunbelt when JT walked back in.

The two left the store and walked over to Ma Nelson's place.

There were a few more people on the streets now. Clay felt as if everyone was staring at him. He mentioned it to Brennan.

"Don't worry, boy. Most of these people are looking in admiration fer what you did. Cotton and his cronies have been running roughshod over this town. They don't give the younger boys a moment's rest. They're getting old enough, now, to be giving some of the adults trouble. Yessir, the majority of those folks are grateful."

They walked into Ma Nelson's eatery. It looked like most of the men in Brackett were there. Brennan and Clay headed for the only open table. Halfway to the table, a big man stood up in their path. "Howdy, JT. This must be Clay Barlow."

Clay stopped, not knowing what to expect. JT said, "Durned tootin' it is. You can thank this boy for slowing up Cotton and his bunch."

"That's just what I aim to do. Thought I was gonna have to come into town and take them on myself, the way they treated my boy. He's too young—no way he could defend himself."

"I'm Sean Thomas. I ranch south of here. Just wanted you to know I'm much obliged. You ever need anything, just look me up."

"Thanks, Mr. Thomas. I appreciate you saying that." The two men shook hands. Clay and Brennan moved on to their table. Clay sat down facing the front door.

Ma Nelson was out of the kitchen before they were seated. She had two cups in one hand and a big pot of coffee in the other. "How 'bout some coffee? You two look like you could go for some breakfast. JT, you want your regular?"

Brennan nodded. "That'd be perfect, Emma. But I need that coffee bad. If you'd stop jawin' and start pourin', I'd be a happy man."

"You keep your sass to yourself, JT Brennan. You'll get your coffee when I'm good and ready." She poured Brennan a cup and said to Clay, "If I remember correctly, you don't drink coffee. How about some milk or water?"

"Milk would be fine, ma'am, and I'd like five eggs, some bacon, and a whole passel of biscuits."

"A man after my own heart. I love hearty eaters. It'll be right out. And you, JT, you keep a civil tongue in your mouth."

"Hey, Emma, how 'bout some more coffee 'fore you leave."

Emma sloshed more coffee into JT's cup, making him jerk his hand away. "Now, I've to get this boy his breakfast. After all that righteous exertion last night, I imagine he's plenty hungry."

Laughter filtered across the room. Then the hum of conversation started up again. Clay looked around and saw nothing but friendly faces. *Guess none of these folks are upset with me. So what did the marshal mean?*

"Mr. Brennan, at dinner last night, Lynn asked me to go to church with her today. But last night, after the fight, she didn't look too happy with me. You reckon she still wants me to go with her?"

Brennan poured some of his coffee into his saucer, blew on it for a moment, tilted the saucer to his mouth and, with a loud slurping sound, sucked the cooled coffee from the saucer. "Son, you got to understand women, and when you do, you can explain 'em to me." He chuckled and turned to one of the men at the adjoining table. "Ain't that right, Ben?"

The other man looked up from his breakfast. "I've been married to my Helen for twenty years. Reckon I don't know much more about the way a woman's mind works than I did before we were married."

"Yessir," Brennan said, "there's no explainin' them. But let me just tell you, Clay, Lynn likes you. She may not have liked the violence she saw last night, but she likes you. You just be patient with her. She'll come around. Why, I bet she's looking forward to taking you to church to save you from the violent path you're headed down."

Ma Nelson came out with a glass of milk, two loaded plates of food, and a big basket of biscuits. "JT, why don't you do something useful with your mouth and wrap it around one of my tasty biscuits before they float off the plate? Clay, don't take his advice about women. The only way he got his sweet wife was because she had her hat set for him, though heaven knows why that good woman could be so blind."

"Emma, don't talk like that in front of the boy. He needs to respect his elders," JT said.

"Humph." She headed back to the kitchen.

"There goes a fine woman, Clay. If I was twenty years younger, she wouldn't know what hit her."

Clay laughed and said, "Looks like she likes you just like you are."

JT shook his head. "I'm too old to break in another woman. Anyway, reckon I was married to the best. Just can't see myself doing it again."

"Mr. Brennan," Clay said, switching back to the original subject, "I used to go to church with my ma and pa, when we could. It's nothing new to me."

"Don't matter, Son. My Lynn loves to help people. I reckon you're foremost in her mind. So, like I said, be patient. If she likes you, and she does, she'll make it work out."

Conversation died as the two men dug into their breakfast. Clay made the eggs, bacon, and several of the biscuits disappear within a few minutes. He broke one of the hot biscuits open and smeared fresh butter, from the butter dish on the table, onto the biscuit. Then he took a little of the peach jam and added it to the rim of the biscuit. He bit off the edge of the biscuit with the jam on it and leaned back in his chair. A look of pure ecstasy relaxed his face. He closed his eyes. The tension, for a few moments, evaporated. He was back in his ma's kitchen eating one of her hot biscuits, fresh jam, and just-made out-of-the-churn butter.

The door of Ma Nelson's eatery slammed as a couple of her

customers left. Clay snapped out of his reverie. JT was looking at him with a sad, knowing look on his face. He quickly looked away, then down, and put more jam on his biscuit. The mood broken, he was embarrassed that he had been so easy to read.

JT leaned forward and said in a low, soft voice, "It's okay, Son. I could see you leave for a moment. It's good to remember the good times. Don't feel embarrassed by it. I know your ma would be pleased you had her on your mind."

Clay nodded and cleared his throat. He finished the biscuit, drank the last sip of milk, and stood. "I've got to be going if I'm going to be on time for church." He reached into his pocket and pulled out a dollar and laid it on the table. "This'll cover breakfast. Thanks for the advice. Reckon I'll see you later."

Ma Nelson came back in as he was leaving.

"Mighty fine meal, ma'am. Thank you."

She smiled at him. "You have a good day, Clay."

LYNN CAME WALKING out of the house as he was opening the gate. "Clay, I didn't know if you would come. Do you still want to go to church with me?"

"I said I would. Although I'll admit, when I saw your face last night I didn't think you'd ever want to see me again."

"Clay, it was so violent. You broke Shad's shoulder. The other two you, well you, uh, you hurt them."

"They attacked me. Cotton had a bowie knife. If he'd known how to use it, I might not be talking to you today."

"I know. Cotton is a bully. But you hurt them so bad."

Clay could feel himself starting to get angry. What did she expect him to do?

"Lynn, would you rather I just stood there and let them have their way with me?"

"No. Of course not. And I am glad you aren't hurt. With everything happening, I haven't said anything, but I am so glad you have your voice back."

He smiled at that. "Yes, I am too. Captain Dixon said that it was a toss-up whether or not I'd get it back. It's such a relief. Guess I have Cotton to thank for that."

She laughed her musical laugh and said, "I don't think he wants any more of your attention." She went on, "I don't think he'll be walking too well for a while." Her violet eyes twinkled in her blushing face.

"Why, good morning, Clay," Mrs. Killganan said as she stepped out the door her husband was holding open for her.

"Good morning, Mrs. Killganan, Mr. Killganan," Clay said as Killganan followed his wife out the door.

"Good morning, Clay. You're joining us for church?"

"Yes, sir, if that's all right."

"That's fine. You have your voice back. Congratulations."

"Thank you, sir. I sure am relieved."

The May day was perfect as they strolled to the church. Killganan introduced Clay to several of the other folks. Most were friendly. Some were a little cool, but he could handle that. They moved into the church. The windows were open, and a warm breeze moved through the congregation.

There was singing, a prayer by one of the deacons, and then the preacher came to the pulpit. He opened his bible and looked out across the congregation, his eyes resting on Clay for a moment, before moving on.

"Brothers and Sisters," the preacher began, "last night, violence came to our good town. The evil was already here, in the form of three thugs who have seen fit to terrorize the youth of our town. Yes, Mrs. Wilson, I am talking about your son, Shad, one of the criminals."

Shad's mother stood up in the pew, pushed herself past others sitting there, and marched out of the church.

The preacher continued as she was walking out, "Last night,

justice descended in the form of this young man sitting with the Killganans."

Clay glanced at Lynn. She was so small sitting next to him, like his ma, but she was beaming with happiness. She glanced up and smiled at him, melting his heart.

"In the thirty-first verse of Numbers, the Lord says to Moses, 'Avenge the children of Israel.' That's what Mr. Barlow has done. He has avenged our children of the bullies of Brackett. I, for one, want to say thank you."

He continued his sermon in the same vein, calling upon the citizens of Brackett to surround and support Clay, and thank him for doing something that the marshal had not done.

The church service finished. The minister was standing at the door shaking hands with his congregation as they left the church. When Clay came to the minister, the man grasped his hand. "Thank you. I hope the Lord prepares a way before you that your burdens may be light."

"Thanks, Reverend," Clay said.

"Oh, Clay," Lynn said, "I'm so proud of you."

He felt the warmth and gratitude of not only Lynn, but of many of the citizens of Brackett. Many of the families waited in the churchyard to shake his hand and thank him.

Mr. and Mrs. Killganan had gone home ahead of him and Lynn. They strolled back to her home, enjoying one another's company and the warmth of the day. *This day couldn't be more perfect.* They reached the house, and Clay reached down with his left hand to open the gate for Lynn.

"Barlow!"

Clay stopped. He looked at Lynn and saw the fear in her eyes. He slowly turned to see Cotton coming down the street toward him, with a gun on his hip. He pushed the gate open and told Lynn, "Get inside, now."

She ran into the house, and Clay started moving out into the middle of the street. He didn't want any stray bullets going into the Killganan house.

"Cotton, you don't have to do this."

"I'm gonna kill you, Barlow. You come into this town and think you can run roughshod over everybody. I'm here to tell you, that ain't gonna happen."

Clay brushed his jacket away from his gun and slowly removed the hammer thong holding his six-gun in the holster. Fifty yards separated the two men. Clay started walking toward Cotton.

Cotton had been stepping in long strides when Clay first saw him, but when Clay started walking to meet him, his steps shortened.

"Cotton, what are you doing, Son?" The marshal had come out of an alleyway and was even with Cotton, next to the general store. He was carrying a shotgun.

Cotton kept his eyes on Clay. "Pa, you stay out of this. I mean it. This is something I aim to do."

"Son, that boy will kill you. I knowd his pa. He was one of the fastest men I ever did see, and he's taught his son. You don't stand a chance. But if you should kill him, you'll be an outlaw and you'll have to fight me. Is that what you want? You want to gunfight your pa?"

Clay kept his eyes on Cotton, occasionally glancing at Marshal Davis. He could see people inside the homes watching, and waiting. Time seemed to slow. Clay didn't want to kill Cotton, but if Cotton started to draw, Clay knew he would kill him. Like Pa had taught him, third button and don't stop shooting till your man is dead. It had to be like that. There was never time to try to wing a person. Clay kept walking.

"I don't want to gunfight with you, Pa."

"Then don't draw on Barlow. That'll settle the whole thing.

"Barlow, you willing to call this off?"

"I am. I don't want to hurt anyone, Marshal. But if I have to, I will." Clay kept walking.

The sun was warm on the streets of Brackett. Faces stared out the windows along Main Street. A couple of chickens pecked around the big oak, chasing grasshoppers. A quail called from a thicket north of town. Squirrels scampered and barked in the trees along the creek.

Clay kept walking.

They were within twenty feet of each other. Clay could see the sweat running down Cotton's face. The dark stains under his arms were heavy with sweat. Cotton had stopped. Clay watched his eyes. *Pa always said the eyes were dead giveaways when a man was going to draw. He was scared. He had to draw now.* The opportunity was gone.

Now Clay was within ten feet of Cotton. He kept walking. The fear was clear in Cotton's face. Clay could see Cotton's desire to draw was intense, but his body wouldn't let him do it. They were too close. There was no chance of survival at this range.

Clay stopped three feet from Cotton. "Drop your gunbelt, Cotton."

There it was. He really wanted to do it. But it passed. Cotton's hands were shaking. Empty eyes stared at Clay. Cotton reached for his gunbelt buckle, released it, and let the belt and gun fall into the dusty street.

"I would've killed you, Cotton. I hope you believe that. I don't want to, but I would. I'm gonna be in town one more day. I don't want to see you again while I'm here. Just one more day, and then I'll be gone."

Clay looked into those vacant eyes. "Do you understand me, Cotton?"

Cotton looked down, and said, "Yeah, I understand."

"Good, now pick up your gunbelt and take it over to your pa. Don't go for that gun. I'll be watching."

Cotton looked up for a moment, then bent over and carefully

picked up the gunbelt, keeping his hand away from the gun. He carried it over to his pa and handed it to him.

The marshal glanced at Clay, then put his arm around his living son and walked him back to his office. Clay watched them disappear inside. He left his six-gun loose in his holster and turned back to the fort. Lynn and her parents came out on the porch as he passed. He said nothing, nor did they. One more day, he thought.

10

Clay stepped out of Ma Nelson's into the bright, West Texas sunlight. He was going to miss Ma's cooking and her independent spirit. The steak she had set before him for dinner today was as big as a plate. It and the beans would stick to his ribs for quite a while. He looked south and could see increased activity at Fort Clark. Colonel Mackenzie was returning.

After checking north—he was learning to be more alert—he crossed the street to the general store. The little bell tinkled as he walked through the front door. The sound reminded him of Lynn, her smile, her eyes. He'd see her later in the day. Today was her seventeenth birthday.

"Howdy, Clay," JT said from behind the counter. "Got all your gear right here. You're welcome to check it."

"No, thanks, Mr. Brennan, just let me know how much I owe you."

"Reckon that'll come to an even twenty dollars."

Clay peeled twenty dollars off and laid the money on the counter. The old man had packed his supplies into the new saddlebags.

"Oh, I forgot, I'll need a new slicker. That's something else Hayes owes me for, when I catch him."

"Reckon that man's built up quite a debt. You think you'll see him again?"

"Yep. I figure he headed over to San Felipe del Rio to be with the rest of the gang. They know by now that I'm after them. Doubt that they're too worried." Clay grinned. "I'm just a boy."

The old man chuckled and said, "Son, if they knew what they were up against, they'd keep goin' to El Paso, or maybe California." A frown crossed JT's face. "You take a word of advice from an old man. Be careful and keep your eyes open. If you see one, the others are probably going to be around somewhere. Don't let 'em slip up on you. You're just one man, so stay alert."

"Yes, sir, I sure will. I've learned a whole bunch in this last month. Pa always said if you wanted to stay alive, you had to continuously be learning. That's what I aim to do.

"Could you gimme another two hundred rounds of that .44 American for my revolvers?"

"That's a lot of firepower, Son. You already have two hundred rounds in your saddlebags."

"I plan on doing some practicing along the way. Also, do you have a left-handed holster that'll fit this gunbelt? I want to start working on this left hand."

"Well, let me see." JT shuffled under the counter for a bit and pulled out a perfect match. "Think that'll work for you?"

Clay looked it over, took off his gunbelt, slid the crossdraw holster off, and slipped the left-handed holster on. He put the gunbelt back on, pulled the Model 3 from the crossdraw holster and dropped it into the left-handed holster. He tried drawing several times. "Feels mighty awkward."

"Keep trying, Son. A man with your coordination will have it down in no time. You want this crossdraw holster?"

"Yep. I'm gonna hang on to that until I'm comfortable drawing with my left hand." Clay switched the holsters back, slid the

Model 3 into the crossdraw, and put the left-handed holster in the saddlebags.

He paid for the holster and ammunition. "Mr. Brennan, I thought of two more things. I need a pocket watch. The killers took Pa's. If you've got something, not too expensive, I'd like to have it."

JT rustled through a drawer. "Here you are, Clay. Took this on trade for some supplies. It seems to run good and is pretty solid."

Clay took it for a moment and looked it over. The metal housing had a pewter cast to it. He pushed the release and the top sprang open. Nice big numbers. "I'll take it. The other thing's a little harder. I'd like to get Lynn something for her birthday, but I don't have the slightest idea what to get a girl. Could you help?"

"It just so happens," JT said, "I can. Lynn's had her eye on this here piece of ribbon for some time. Thought her ma would get it for her, but she didn't."

Clay looked at it for a moment. The ribbon was almost exactly the color of Lynn's eyes. She'd be mighty pretty wearing it in her hair. "I'll take it."

JT folded it over gently and handed it to Clay. Clay slipped it into his vest pocket. "Thank you," Clay said. "How much do I owe you?"

"Give me two dollars for the watch and two bits for the ribbon."

Clay tossed two dollars and twenty-five cents on the counter, then picked up the saddlebags and slicker and threw them over his left shoulder. "Guess I'll be headin' out."

He felt an emptiness. He had come to like this old man, and here he was moving on. *I'd better get used to feeling like this. Don't know when I'll be able to settle down.*

JT walked him to the door. "I'll admit I'm gonna miss you, Son. Wish you were settlin' down around here. You've made some friends. People respect you. Lynn has become downright attached to you. She's gonna miss you."

"Yes, sir, and I'll miss her." He felt the boy coming out in him, and tamped it down. "You going to be at her party?"

"Wouldn't miss it. A granddaughter turns seventeen only once. Reckon I'll see you there."

The two men shook hands. Clay stepped out the door and heard the tinkling of the bell for the last time. *This sure is a lonely business.*

He turned north up the street, and crossed over. After walking up the boardwalk past a couple of buildings, he entered the bank.

"Good afternoon, Mr. Barlow," the teller said. "I'll get Mr. Killganan."

Elmer Killganan came into the front of the bank from his office. He opened the gate between the teller's cage and the front with his left hand and offered his right to Clay. "Good afternoon, Clay. Glad to see you. Let's go back to my office."

Clay shook Killganan's hand and walked straight back toward his office. Killganan followed, closing the door behind him. Killganan motioned for him to have a seat in front of his desk. "How are you, Clay?"

"I'm fine, Mr. Killganan."

Killganan sat in his desk chair and pulled it up to the desk. "I want you to know I admire the way you handled the confrontation with Cotton. I'd hate to see the boy killed. I think there is still hope for him. He can be quite a nice lad."

"Yes, sir. I guess I haven't seen that side of him."

"No, you haven't. Let's get to business. Your wire came in this morning." Killganan opened a desk drawer and took out a stack of bills wrapped in a piece of paper. He took the paper and slid it across to Clay. "This is a receipt showing you received the five hundred dollars minus the five percent transfer fee."

Clay looked it over, signed it, and slid the paper back across the desk.

Killganan added his signature, then put it back in the desk

drawer. He then counted out four hundred seventy-five dollars. "That's a lot of money, Clay."

"Yes, sir, it is. But Hayes stole just about everything I had with me, so I have to replace all that gear. When Pa was living, of course, he took care of all the money, he and Ma. I never realized how expensive living is." He smiled and said, "Guess I'm figuring it out."

"Life is expensive," Killganan said. "Just a word of advice. If you don't have it working for you, money goes through your hands quickly. I understand you still have money left in the bank in Uvalde. Don't just let it sit there. Find a way to make it work for you."

"Thank you, Mr. Killganan. Pa told me the same thing. I have a couple of ideas.

"If you don't mind." Clay slid off his boots and put two hundred in each boot and pocketed the remaining seventy-five. "Reckon that's about the safest place I know to carry it."

"That's smart, Clay. I'm glad to see you're thinking. Now, Lynn is expecting you at her party."

"I plan on going. I'll go by the livery and get my horses and gear, then I'll be by."

"One thing, Clay. Lynn thinks a great deal of you. She's my only daughter. Don't break her heart."

Clay was surprised at Killganan's frankness. But JT had said that this man loved his family. Clay had seen it manifested before with the care in which Killganan treated his wife and daughter. "No, sir. That's not my intention at all. But I do have to leave. I have a job to do, and Mr. Killganan, I won't rest until the murderers of my folks are brought to justice."

"I understand. Just treat her kindly."

Clay stood. This time, he thrust his hand out to Killganan. "It's a pleasure meeting you, sir."

Killganan shook hands with him. "Thank you. I'll see you at the party."

Clay stepped back into the bright sunshine, pulled out his watch, and checked the time. He had about twenty minutes to make the party. Plenty of time to go to the livery and pick up his horses. They were probably restless and ready to move on.

He walked into the stables as the smithy came from the back.

"Ready to settle up and pick up my gear," Clay said.

"Gear's in the office. Nothing to settle, Mister. You paid me plenty when you brought 'em in. I noticed that's a mighty used saddle you have there."

"Reckon I could use another one to ride. I was using the old one to hang the panniers on."

"Got a couple you might like." The blacksmith took him over to a rail where several saddles were hanging.

Clay looked them over. "How much for this one?"

The smithy scratched his beard and rubbed the saddle. "This is a mighty fine saddle, good strong leather, as you can see, used enough so it won't be squeakin' on you. I'm not really looking to sell it, but I'd be willing to part with it for only sixty dollars."

Clay looked at the man in feigned disbelief. "Mister, I may be young, but I'm not that young, and I don't see any gold inlay. I'll buy your saddle—in fact, I'll give twenty-five dollars as it sits."

The smithy looked aghast at Clay. "Why, Son, that's highway robbery. I couldn't think of going that low. I'd just be giving it away. Tell you what I'll do, I'll let you have it for fifty dollars, even though you're taking money out of my children's mouths."

Clay shook his head in amazement. He looked out the double doors of the stable toward the general store, looked back at the saddle, and rubbed the seat and cantle. "Mister, this seat's so thin I'll probably have saddle sores within an hour of forking it. I'm tired of dickering with you. I'll give you thirty-seven dollars and fifty cents. That's more than it's worth, but I think you ought to be able to make a profit."

The blacksmith's face looked like he'd dropped a red-hot horseshoe down the front of his pants. He shook his head, kicked at the dirt, patted the saddle again, and spit. "Boy, don't you know a man's got to make a living? I've got mouths to feed. My family depends on me. Why, I know for a fact this saddle has only been ridden by one other man. He was old and frail. He was so light this here saddle likely didn't even know he was there. You'll be able to ride for days without any discomfort. But, I'll make you one last offer, though it pains me to be giving this saddle away." The blacksmith turned and spit again, for emphasis. "I'll let you steal it from me, and this is my last and final offer, for forty dollars. Not a cent less."

Clay immediately stuck his hand out. "You've got a deal, as long as you'll throw in that nice blanket hanging over there."

The blacksmith turned and looked at the red checkered horse blanket, shook his head, and reluctantly took Clay's hand. "Boy, you're as hard a trader as a Tonkawa."

Clay shook the man's hand and grinned. "That's who taught me."

The blacksmith laughed. "Boy, I ain't had so much fun in a coon's age. Let me help you with your gear." He turned back to the office. When he came out, he had the two panniers in one hand and Clay's old saddle and blanket in the other.

Clay grabbed the red checkered blanket and laid it over the sorrel's back, smoothed it out, and tossed the new saddle on top of it. He was cinching the saddle up while the blacksmith saddled the buckskin and fastened the panniers.

Clay said to the blacksmith over the saddle, "I'm going to need a scabbard for my rifle."

The blacksmith nodded. "I've got work to do today. Don't have time to spend the rest of my day bargaining. I've got one I'll let you have for five dollars. Is that fair enough for you?"

Clay laughed out loud. "Yes, sir, that'll be just fine."

The blacksmith brought the scabbard, and Clay fastened it to the saddle on the sorrel. He secured the saddlebags and slicker behind the saddle and mounted.

The blacksmith handed him the reins to the buckskin. "Good luck to you."

Clay turned the horses out of the stable and walked them into the street. He rode toward the Killganans' house. The marshal stepped out of the alleyway alongside the stable.

"Marshal," Clay said, pulling the horses up, "what can I do for you?"

The marshal glanced up and down the street. He scratched his sideburns, and after waiting a few moments, he finally looked back up to Clay. "I just wanted to thank you for not shooting my boy. He's got a lot to learn. I'm glad he has more time to learn it."

Clay rested his arm on the horn and tilted his black hat to the back of his head. "Marshal, believe me, it was my pleasure. I've no desire for a gunfight, nor to kill a man. I've got to do what I must, but after that, I'm thinkin' I'd like to go back to the homeplace and settle down. That's sounding better every day."

The marshal nodded. Frown wrinkles played across his forehead. "Hope you can, Son. But I've got a feelin' about you. You've got the makings of a lawman. What with having no desire to build a reputation, you'd make a good one. Good luck to you."

The two men nodded to each other, and Clay rode on toward the Killganan place.

The party was going full swing when he pulled up to the hitching rail. The musicians were already tuned up, and the fiddlers and caller were swinging along to "Cotton-Eye Joe." The yard was just big enough to accommodate the dancers at one end. Several couples were kicking up their heels and enjoying the lively square dance, while others stood and clapped to the rhythm.

Clay stepped from the saddle and tied his horses to the hitching rail. Lynn was radiant. He had never seen a girl or woman as pretty as her, except maybe his ma. Lynn was talking to a girl he didn't know, which wasn't a surprise, he thought. He didn't know much of anybody in this town. She saw Clay, smiled and waved, then came running down the porch steps. She thought better of her public display and slowed to a quick walk.

He took his hat off when she approached. "Happy birthday," he said.

"Thank you, kind sir. Oh, I'm glad you could come, Clay. Put your hat back on, silly." Lynn looked at the loaded horses. "You're leaving?"

"Reckon I have to, Lynn. You know what I've got to do. But let's not talk about that. You're about as pretty as a fresh spring day." He pulled the ribbon from his vest. "Sorry it ain't wrapped. Happy birthday."

"Oh, Clay, it's so lovely." Then she grinned at him and said, "Grandpa told you, didn't he?"

"I guess I'm caught. He did. I wanted something you really liked, and he said this was it."

"He was so right. Thank you for the ribbon, but most of all, thank you for thinking about me." She pinned the ribbon in her hair and put her arm in his. "Come, Mother wants to talk to you."

They walked up the porch to where Mrs. Killganan was standing, smiling. She was almost as lovely as her daughter. "Good afternoon, Clay. I see you are about to leave us."

Clay removed his hat again. "Yes, ma'am. I'll be going to the fort and then pulling out. I'll camp somewhere between here and San Felipe del Rio."

"Lynn, honey, would you go to the kitchen and get your father a cup of coffee and take it to him? You know how parties don't agree with him. I'm sure he's in the study reading."

"Yes, Mother." Lynn flashed a smile at Clay that made him feel warm inside. "I'll be back in a few minutes." And she was gone.

"Clay, I wanted to take a few moments to talk to you, alone. You know that Lynn has strong feelings for you." It wasn't a question.

"Yes, ma'am, I do. I'm pretty sure I feel the same way about her. I can't be positive, 'cause I've never felt this way before."

Mrs. Killganan smiled a knowing, sad smile. "I know you do. Mr. Killganan and I like you, Clay. You could have killed Cotton yesterday, but you exercised restraint. I admire that. Come back, Clay. That will make us all happy, especially Lynn."

Clay felt that warm feeling inside that he had always felt around his mother. It caused an ache he feared might never go away. Mrs. Killganan was a kind person.

"I'll remember that, ma'am. If I don't see him, tell Mr. Killganan I appreciate his hospitality. It's mighty nice to be in your home."

Lynn opened the door and stepped out on the porch. "Father wants to see you, Mother." She laughed quietly. "I think he wants to know how long my party is going to last."

Mrs. Killganan turned to go, but looked back over her shoulder and said, "Remember what I said, Clay."

Lynn took Clay's arm and pulled him toward the swing. They sat down and watched the party. Another square dance was playing, and Clay could see Mr. Brennan swinging a girl Lynn's age.

He looked back to Lynn when she said, "Clay, what's going to happen to us?"

Her being so direct caught him off guard. "I don't know. I want to come back. I'd really like to come back, but I don't know what's going to happen."

"Clay, you know I care about you."

"I feel the same about you, Lynn. I just don't know what will happen. I'll promise you this much: If I'm able to come back, I will."

"Clay, that's all I need to hear. I'll be going to school this fall at Addran. Pa will give in. If I'm not here, that's where I'll be. I'll be waiting for you."

These were new feelings for Clay. He wanted to stay, but he

knew he must go. He held Lynn's hands for a moment. "I must go."

"I know. I'll miss you. Please be careful."

Lynn's grandfather walked up onto the porch as Clay stood.

"You leavin'?" JT said.

"Yes, sir, I've got to head to the fort, and then west."

The Killganans had come out on the porch. The party was going strong. Clay could feel the warmth of Lynn standing next to him.

"You take care, Son," JT said. "We'll be looking for you."

"Good luck, Clay," Mr. Killganan said.

"Return safely, and God bless you," Mrs. Killganan said.

"Thank you, folks. It's been a real pleasure meeting you. I'll be seeing you." Clay shook hands with the two men, and Mrs. Killganan stood on her toes to kiss him on the cheek.

Lynn said, too brightly, "I'll walk you out."

The two of them walked from the porch to the horses. The time passed quickly.

"Don't forget me, Clay. Please take care of yourself." Lynn, like her mother, stood on her toes and kissed Clay on the cheek.

"I'll never forget you. I'll be back." He untied the two horses and mounted the sorrel. He looked down, for a moment, into Lynn's face. Tears were running down her soft cheeks. Her face cast indelibly in his memory, he turned his horses toward the fort.

11

C lay stopped at the creek flowing out of the springs and watered the horses. After they had drunk their fill, he crossed the creek and rode into the fort. It was a beehive of activity. There were extra horses at the stables. Tents had been pitched on the parade ground, and Indians were camped there. The troops had made it back. It must have been successful, because everyone was laughing and joking in the rough way of soldiers around the world.

He pulled up at the infirmary, tied the horses, and went in. Captain Dixon spotted him immediately and walked over to him. "Looks like you are doing much better," he said as he grasped Clay by the chin and turned his head first to the left and then to the right. He continued to examine his neck for a few moments longer. Then he asked, "How's your throat feeling?"

Clay smiled and said, "It's feeling real good, Captain."

Dixon, surprised and pleased, said, "Well, look at you, talking and everything. You have to be my prize patient. I honestly didn't know if you would regain your voice. Congratulations. You're feeling okay?"

"Yes, sir, my neck and throat are feeling great. I've still got some soreness, but it isn't bad at all. Looks like things went well for you."

"Clay, you wouldn't believe it. Colonel Mackenzie took our men, following the Black Seminole scouts, into Mexico. Those scouts led us straight to Costilietos's camp. He's one of the main chiefs of the Lipan Apache. We hit them, and hit them hard. We captured Costilietos himself, forty or fifty prisoners, and a large number of horses and firearms—total success. We have only a few wounded. It was very successful.

"I heard," Captain Dixon said, changing the subject, "you were attacked by three ruffians, and yesterday, you almost had a gunfight. You need to join the frontier army, where it's safe."

Clay grinned. "Can't help if everyone wants to pick on a little guy like me."

"Yeah, I understand you put the three attackers down—impressive. I also heard that you've been seeing the banker's daughter."

"Yes, sir, I have. A really nice girl. I plan on seeing her again."

The captain's eyebrows went up. "Ahh, like that. Good for you. Are you going to stay here or go after those killers?"

"I've made a commitment, Captain Dixon. Reckon I'm sticking to it."

Dixon nodded. "I figured you would. Well, you're well enough to go. Your neck will continue to get better. Just try not to get into any more fights till that neck is healed. By the way, the colonel said he wanted to see you as soon as you got back to the post. I think he's in his office now."

"I'd like to see him and thank him for his hospitality. And, Captain Dixon, thank you. I wouldn't be walking around if it wasn't for you. I owe you."

"Think nothing of it—

"Captain Dixon," an orderly called, "we need you over here right now."

"Gotta go, Clay. Good luck to you."

"And you." They shook hands quickly, and Dixon was off to his patient.

Clay walked over to the bed he had been using for the past week and picked up his rifle. He walked back outside and slid the rifle into the scabbard. He left the horses tied and walked to headquarters.

The office was a madhouse. He went to the sergeant's desk. "Sergeant, Clay Barlow to see Colonel Mackenzie."

"Wait here." The sergeant knocked on the closed office door.

"Come."

"Colonel Mackenzie, Clay Barlow is here to see you."

"Send him in, Sergeant. See that we're not disturbed."

"Yes, sir. Mr. Barlow, you can come in." The sergeant closed the door behind Clay.

Clay walked over to the colonel's desk. "Good to see you, sir."

Colonel Mackenzie had gotten up from behind his desk. He looked at Clay with a startled expression. "Son, the last time I saw you, you were writing your words on a piece of paper. Sounds like things are looking up."

"Yes, sir, they surely are."

There were two chairs in front of his desk. Mackenzie took one and offered the other to Clay.

"I hear you had a successful mission," Clay said.

"We did. I give all the credit to the Seminole scouts. They got my buffalo soldiers right on top of the Kickapoo and then the Lipan. Those Indians never knew what hit 'em. That reminds me, I have a gift for you."

He got up and walked over to the gun case, where a shotgun sat among the rifles. He pulled it out of the gun case and said, "This look familiar to you?"

Clay stood and walked over to the colonel. "Sir, that's my Roper. I can't believe it."

"That's not all." The colonel pulled a deerskin bag out of the gun case and handed it to Clay.

Clay opened the bag. There must have been twenty-five or thirty Roper shotgun shells. "Colonel, I don't know how to thank you. This shotgun was given to me. I really hated that Hayes got it, almost as bad as I hated to lose my horse."

"You're very welcome. It is a miracle we found it. We didn't find your horse. I fear the Indians had already eaten it." The colonel quickly continued when he saw Clay wince. "Though it is possible that Hayes got away."

"I understand, Colonel. I know the Indians love horse meat. I just hate to think of such a good horse being eaten. But I'm mighty thankful for the return of the shotgun."

"Son, I feel sure Hayes is one of the murderers you won't have to worry about." The colonel walked over to his desk, picked up a cigar out of his humidor, and offered one to Clay.

"No, thank you."

"Helps me think," the colonel said around the cigar as he was lighting it. Puffs of smoke rose in the room. "When do you expect to be leaving?"

"Captain Dixon said I was free to go. I'll be leaving as soon as I walk out of your office."

The colonel stepped over to his bookshelf and pulled out a book. He handed it to Clay. "I think this will do you more good than me. Anyway, I have another one."

Clay took the book. It was Blackstone's *Commentaries*. "Colonel, I don't know how to thank you."

The colonel smiled around his cigar, took a puff, and pulled it from his mouth. "Son, you continue to read and learn. We need men like you in this country."

A knock on the door sounded, and the sergeant stepped into the room. "Sorry, sir, but the major said this can't wait."

"Tell him just a moment.

"Clay, I hate to interrupt this, but duty calls. It's been nice knowing you. I wish you good luck in your endeavor. If I can ever be of help, let me know."

"Thank you, sir. Congratulations again, and thanks for Blackstone and my shotgun."

The colonel laughed and clapped Clay on the shoulder. Clay slipped out of his office as the major stepped in and the door closed. He walked outside and over to the infirmary, dropping the book into his saddlebags. He checked the shotgun to make sure everything was working, took four shells from the bag, and loaded it. With the shotgun and bag of shells in one hand, he stepped up into the saddle. Clay hung the bag over the saddle horn, then leaned over and unfastened the buckskin's reins from the hitching post.

He rode west, between the infirmary and one of the troops barracks. Once outside of the fort, he stopped the sorrel and looked back. A lot had happened in the days that he had been here in Brackett. Again, he was leaving security and friendship. He looked toward Brackett and Lynn. *Will I survive? Will I be back? Will Lynn still feel the same way when I come back?*

Clay took one last look and turned his mount toward the setting sun. It was reflecting red and golds from the Las Moras Hills to the north. The few puffy evening clouds were gold rimmed, the sun behind them. He could feel the sorrel's muscles quiver.

"You boys have been cooped up for days. How about a run?"

Clay bumped the sorrel in the flanks and yelled. The horse jumped forward so fast that the pull from the buckskin almost yanked him out of the saddle. Both horses wanted to stretch their muscles, and they were soon running side by side. The wind felt fresh, exciting. This was no time to be sad or somber. Life was here and now. They ran for a couple of miles before he slowed them to a walk. Fort Clark and Brackett had disappeared below the hills, and he was again alone in the wild. He could feel the freedom and loved it. It should still be daylight when he reached Maverick Creek. He'd cross Zoquete Creek first. That was about halfway between Brackett and Maverick

Creek. He picked the horses up into a fast walk and relaxed in the saddle.

It was dark when he reached the creek. The stars were out. A sliver of moon was peeking over the Eastern hills, turning the sage and mesquite into silver skeletons and lighting the plains with a cool white light.

He found a camping spot under the trees. Clay quickly dropped the panniers from the buckskin and took the saddles off the horses. He gave them a rubdown with dry leaves. After the rubdown was complete, he took both horses down to water. It was a still night. He could hear the racket from the turkeys up the creek, going to roost in the trees. As always, they were making a tremendous fuss. They would settle down soon and be his alert system for up the creek. No one could be stealthy on the dry leaves and get past the turkeys without an immense amount of clucking. If they were frightened off their roost, nothing was louder than turkeys flying through the trees at night.

A lone coyote serenaded the pale moon. At the first sound of the coyote, the horses' heads jerked up from the water. Clay talked to them in a soft, confident voice. He calmed the beasts, and once they had finished drinking, Clay brought them back up to the camp. He retrieved the ropes from the panniers and staked the horses on the good grass.

Once he had taken care of the horses, he made himself a bed under one of the big oak trees. This would be a cold camp tonight, no fire. He had some jerky in his saddlebags. He had filled his canteen at the creek while he was watering the horses. Jerky and water. Not bad. He'd be asleep in no time. If anything tried to slip up on him, in these dry leaves, either he'd hear them or the horses would let him know. He reached into his saddlebags for the jerky and felt a sack he didn't recognize. He pulled it out. Inside was a big steak sandwich and a piece of birthday cake. Lynn. When did she do it? He couldn't remember being away from her, except when she went into the house. She probably had someone else put it in his saddlebags. However she did it, he was going to have a banquet tonight, and he was grateful.

He unwrapped the sandwich and bit into the juicy steak. He loved cold steak almost as much as when it was cooked fresh. It had a tangy taste that set his taste buds to celebrating. The bread was covered with fresh butter, and fresh-cut, early tomatoes were sliced thick, between the bread. Clay leaned back and enjoyed his feast.

After finishing the sandwich, he unwrapped the big piece of cake. He immediately decided he'd save half of it for breakfast. He got out his Boker and sliced the cake in half. The cake had a thick, creamy icing over chocolate. His ma seldom made anything chocolate, since it was so expensive. Sometimes, when they visited his French grandparents in D'Hanis, his grandma would fix chocolate cake. This was a real treat. He had taken his second bite when he saw the horses' heads snap up and heard the rustling in the leaves. He slid his Model 3 out of the holster and waited. Nothing. Then, there it was again. The horses went back to feeding, and he went back to eating. It was nothing more than an armadillo rooting in the leaves for ants or grubs.

Clay finished up half of the cake, folded up the sandwich wrapper, and put it into his saddlebags. He took a long drink of water and smoothed out a place on the ground after moving a few sticks out of the way. He had taken a pair of moccasins out of one of the panniers. He pulled his boots off and slipped the moccasins on. He adjusted his saddle and lay his head back. A few of the stars were visible through the oaks. A light breeze had started up. He had the shotgun close, with a Model 3 in hand. The last thing that passed through his tired mind was a thought about that tasty cake.

~

CLAY AWOKE when a stray beam of sunshine made it through the oaks and struck him in the eyes. He glanced over at the horses. They were indulging in a little breakfast for themselves, the tasty grass shoots coming up between the leaves. He put his hat on, stretched, then pulled on his boots, followed by his gunbelt.

The horses needed water. He led them down to the creek and let them drink their fill. After they were finished, he staked them back out on a fresh patch of grass. His breakfast consisted of the chocolate cake he'd saved and water. A breakfast fit for a king.

Clay saddled the buckskin and then put the old saddle on the sorrel. He'd give the sorrel a break today and ride the buckskin. Once the panniers were tied on the sorrel, he slipped his moccasins into the saddlebags and stretched again, feeling the muscles in his broad chest and back. He rolled up the two ropes and slid them back in the panniers. With the shotgun in his left hand, Clay mounted the buckskin.

The buckskin was feeling sassy this morning and provided Clay a little workout with a few crow-hops around the clearing. The sorrel watched with a disinterested stare. Once settled down, Clay rode the buckskin over to the sorrel, picked up the reins, and headed west. Before he broke out of the trees along the creek, he pulled the horses up. Pa had taught him to never ride out into an open area without looking it over. He'd never seen anything of real danger, but he knew there could always be bandits or Indians waiting. Yet again, today was no different than so many that had come before. It was all clear. He'd be in San Felipe del Rio in just a few more hours.

Clay started to move the buckskin out when, from the corner of his eye, he caught a flash. He froze. There it was again. It was a little north of where the road would take him. There was a rocky outcropping seventy-five or so yards north of the road. He estimated about seven hundred yards from him. Several big boulders were behind the outcropping, interspersed with large patches of prickly pear and a mesquite thicket. There was only one reason for someone to be up there. They had to be looking for a traveler along the road. Could whoever it was be looking for him? Was it the Pinder Gang lying in wait? How did they know he was after them if Hayes had been picked off by Indians?

He surveyed the terrain south of the road. There was a deep ravine that ran west from Maverick Creek. It had mesquite and a few scattered oaks along its banks. He could move through the ravine, get past the ambusher, and slip up behind him using the mesquite thicket.

Clay backed the horses deep into the oaks along Maverick Creek. He dismounted and took his moccasins from the saddle-bags, then slipped off his boots and replaced them with the moccasins. He tied the horses' reins with loose slipknots. If he was killed or injured, he wanted them to be able to get loose and fend for themselves. He tied his boots across his saddle and slipped the shotgun from his slicker, then opened the sack hanging from the saddle horn and took out a handful of shells. Clay slipped the shells into his pockets, took a long drink of water from his canteen, and hung it back on the buckskin's saddle. He eased up to the edge of the trees, got his bearings, and slipped back.

Now was the time. He and Running Wolf had stalked each other many times. He had slipped up on deer so close he could reach out and touch them. This time, it was a man he was stalking. With the shotgun in his left hand, he removed the leather hammer thong from the Smith & Wesson New Model 3 in his right holster. He left the thong in place on the crossdraw holster, just in case he fell. When that was done, he wheeled around and started trotting to the ravine. Once in the ravine, Clay began his long-legged run. He covered distance quickly, knowing that the ravine walls shielded him from view of whoever might be on the rock outcropping. He had run for ten minutes when he came to the big oak he had marked. He eased out of the ravine, scanned the area to make sure there were no other threats—it was Indian country, after all—and slipped through the mesquites.

He had come out of the ravine well behind the outcropping and out of view of anyone who was watching from there. He had been slipping through the mesquite and acacia, slowly making his way to the outcropping, when he came to the road. This would be the only opportunity for the man or men to see him. He lay in between two patches of prickly pear and examined the hillside. No movement. A horned toad was keeping him company from under the prickly pear on his left. It turned its little horned head to watch him with curiosity, the gray-tan body well camouflaged among the rocks.

Clay took one last look, then was up and running across the road. Reaching the other side, he fell to the ground and lay still, watching the outcropping. There was no movement. He eased to his feet, checked his right holster to make sure the revolver was still there, and slipped the hammer thong off the crossdraw. From tree to tree, prickly pear to prickly pear, he slipped. No noise came from his moccasins. He was a silent shadow drifting among the trees. He thanked the Tonkawas and Running Wolf for teaching him this skill.

Movement up ahead. He saw the switch of a tail. He froze and waited. There, no more than twenty-five yards in front of him, were two horses. So more than one man, he thought. His breathing slowed. His senses intensified. He moved forward, step, pause, look, step, pause, look. Now he was close to the horses, and he could hear voices ahead. He eased to the side, where the horses could see him. He was within arm's reach. They both saw him at the same time and jerked their heads up, their eyes wide. He moved slowly and let his hand run up the neck of the one nearest. They watched him, tense, for a moment more, then went back to tearing and chewing what little grass they could find on the hillside.

He could hear what the men were saying. "This is the third

day we've been out here. That boy ain't comin'. Gideon don't know what he's talking about. If Hayes put a knife through his throat, he ain't nowhere but dead. I'm ready to head back to town and have a drink."

The other man cursed and said, "You ain't been with us long. You go against my brother and he'll kill you quicker than one of them Apaches."

Clay could see them now. They were no more than fifteen feet in front of him, sitting on the ledge, screened from the road by some scrubby mesquite, watching for any travelers from the east.

The man on the left wore a slouch hat, a shirt that looked like it hadn't seen water since before Adam, and bib overalls with patches on both knees. He was of average height but wide shoulders. A gunbelt with a crossdraw holster cinched his overalls at his waist.

The man with the Sharps was small, no more than five and a half feet tall, with narrow shoulders. He wore a wide-brimmed, low-crowned gray hat that had seen better days. His scruffy beard continued from dirty hair peeking out from under his hat. While Clay was watching him, he turned to spit. His eyes looked like saucers when he saw Clay. Spittle ran out of his mouth onto his already-dirty beard.

Clay stood like a stone, almost six feet, towering over the two men, a shotgun staring at them. The muzzle looked like a cannon.

"Howdy, boys," Clay said. "Enjoying the scenery?"

The other man spun around and reached for the Colt in his crossdraw holster, but the hammer thong held it snug.

Clay swung the muzzle of the Roper on Slouch Hat and eared the hammer back in one smooth motion. "You might want to rethink that decision."

Clay had recognized both men from the wanted posters. The man in the slouch hat was Harly Pinder, the youngest of the remaining Pinder boys. The sharpshooter was Milo Reese. He was the one, according to Hayes, who had shot his pa.

Harly slowly moved his hand away from his Colt. He sneered at Clay and said, "What do ya want, boy?"

Clay continued to smile, although he was seething inside. This was part of the crowd that had changed his life forever. He'd never killed a man, but right now, it wouldn't be hard. "Why, Harly, I want you and Milo."

Clay could see the stunned look on both men's faces. They still had no idea who he was.

Milo spoke up, his lower jaw quivering. "Whatcha want us fer? We ain't done you no harm. Why, I don't even know ya."

Clay watched the little man. The quivering jaw, beady eyes, buck teeth, and scrawny face reminded him of a cornered rat. This was one of the lowest type of men. He took people's lives from a distance. A man without the courage to confront his prey. To top it off, he did it for money.

"You might know my pa, Bill Barlow? Does that ring a bell for you?"

Clay could see the fear and desperation in both men's eyes.

Harly said, "I ain't kilt yore pa and I sure ain't kilt yore ma. That tweren't me. This here scrawny little feller, he killed your pa. Shot him dead, he did."

"Harly, don't ya say that." The little man was almost crying. Every word that left his mouth was a whine. "I just did it 'cause his brother"—he jerked his thumb at Harly—"made me. I wouldn't have done it no other way. I had nuthin' agin your pa."

Listening to Milo almost made Clay physically ill. His ma and pa were dead, and this sniveling little creature was whining for his life. "Harly, I never said anything about my ma. You two drop your sidearms."

"Listen, boy—" Harly started.

The roar of the shotgun reverberated out of the rocks and through the hills. The ground between the two men exploded.

Both men jumped back. Harly had backed up close to the edge of the outcropping. His boot heel caught a mesquite root, and he started flailing with his arms to catch his balance, but he was too late. He sailed out into space. For a moment it looked like he was motionless in the air, then he tumbled, head over feet, to the rocks waiting twenty feet below. His body hit the rocks with a sickening thud.

Clay swung the muzzle of the shotgun toward Milo. "Move over to that boulder."

Milo, with the blast of the shotgun, had ripped off his gunbelt and thrown it on the ground.

"Don't shoot me, Mister. Please, I don't wanna die."

Clay used the shotgun to motion toward the boulder. The little man moved quickly to the boulder. "Now I want you to kneel down with your hands stretched out, above you, and on the boulder."

"Please." The word was almost like a wail.

"Shut up. If you turn around, I've another load here for you."

Clay moved to the edge of the outcropping and peered over. Twenty feet below lay the crumpled body of Harly. It looked like he'd hit the rocks headfirst. His neck was twisted in an awkward direction. The thigh bone of one leg was sticking through the skin.

Clay looked at him for only a moment, then switched his gaze to Milo. His stomach was turning over something fierce. He had killed a man. Though he had known it would happen, Slim's words came to mind, "You never forget." He wanted to forget. He wanted that picture out of his mind. But he knew that Slim was right. He would never forget Harly, nor would he forget any other men who might die because of him. He picked up both guns and slid them behind his gunbelt. All the time, he kept an eye on Milo. He felt sure there was no danger of Milo doing anything, except maybe running. But remembering Hayes, he knew no man would ever get the drop on him again because he'd failed to search him. "Pull your boots and shirt off."

Milo didn't stop to answer. He jerked off his shirt and leaned against the boulder to yank his boots off.

"Toss your boots over here and lay down on your belly, your hands extended out in front of you."

Milo tossed his boots to Clay, and dropped to the rocky ground without a complaint. Clay picked up each boot and checked inside—no hidden guns or knives. He walked over to Milo, and with the shotgun muzzle on the back of Milo's head, he searched him thoroughly.

Clay eased over to the Sharps and picked it up. As filthy as Milo was, the Sharps was just the opposite. It was in immaculate condition. He looked at the weapon with loathing. This was the instrument that had dealt such a horrible blow to his family. If Pa hadn't been shot by this rifle, he and Slim may have been able to fight off the Pinder Gang. But you couldn't blame a rifle, Clay thought.

"Like hell you can't," he said. He shucked the round out of the Sharps, lifted it by the barrel with one hand, and with all the might in his young, strong shoulders, swung it against the rock. The stock shattered, and the action bent. Milo lay quivering on the ground. Clay ignored him and looked at what he held in his hand. This rifle would never bring pain and suffering to another family. He threw it out over the outcropping. It sailed as far as the energy could take it and dropped, a mangled piece of metal.

He turned back to Milo. "Milo." The man jerked at the mention of his name, "It's your turn."

12

Clay was riding Milo's horse, and Milo was leading Harly's with Harly across the saddle. Milo had calmed down since he figured out he wasn't going to get shot. But every word out of his mouth was still a high-pitched whine.

"Mr. Barlow, sir, you ruined my beautiful rifle. That was one of the truest shooting rifles I've ever owned."

"Shut up, Milo."

The men moved to the east to pick up Clay's horses. Clay had reloaded the spent shell from the Roper. "Keep walking, Milo. Go to the acacia near the big oak."

Milo turned off the road and walked toward the horses waiting along Maverick Creek. "Why did you kill my parents, Milo?"

"I only shot your pa, Mr. Barlow. I only did that because Gideon would've killed me if I didn't. I sure didn't want to. I ain't had nothin' to do with your ma."

"Milo, do you know what a man's liable to do when you kill his parents?"

Clay could see Milo start shaking again. *How could this be the deadly sharpshooter Milo Reese? This guy was afraid of his own shadow.*

"Who did?"

"Mr. Barlow, sir, if I was to tell you, Gideon would kill me fer sure."

"Hold up a minute."

Milo stopped, halting Harly's horse, and turned to look up at Clay. "Gideon won't get the chance, Milo, if you don't start talking."

The frightened man stared into the deadly maw of the 12 gauge shotgun. "I, I wasn't there until later. I waited on the ridge. Then rode down. I rode down way after Gideon hurt your ma. I ain't had nothing to do with that."

"Then tell me every detail of what happened as far as you know. Keep moving. You can walk and talk."

Milo moved out toward the acacia and detailed the killings. His story coincided pretty well with the one he had heard from Hayes.

By the time he finished talking, they had reached the creek. The horses were where Clay had left them. "Okay, Milo, go sit under the big oak, and don't make a move."

Milo moved over to the oak that Clay indicated and sat down. Fear still etched his every feature, but he had calmed down. He watched Clay with cautious eyes.

Clay walked over to his horses and gave them a quick check. He took off his moccasins, slipped them into his saddlebags, and pulled on his boots. "You boys thirsty? Milo, come over here. We're going to take the horses to water before we head to San Felipe."

Milo got up, walked over, and took his horse and Harly's. Clay slid the Roper into the scabbard and made sure his Model 3 was loose in the holster. "Don't get any ideas, Milo. If you do, they'll be your last. You do what I say, and you'll be resting in a nice safe jail, instead of draped over your saddle like Harly."

Milo glanced at him and looked away. "No, sir, you're the boss."

They walked the horses down to the creek, where the animals drank deeply of the cool water. When the horses were finished, they led them back up the bank. Clay mounted the buckskin and signaled Milo to mount his horse. Once Milo was mounted, Clay rode over next to him and shook out a small loop from his lasso. He flipped it over Milo's neck and took a couple of turns around the buckskin's saddle horn.

"That ain't necessary, Mr. Barlow. What if my horse gits skittish? I could end up with a broken neck."

"Start moving, Milo, and shut up. I'm not here for conversation."

WHEN THEY RODE into San Felipe del Rio, the sun had just reached its zenith and was starting down. It wasn't much of a town. Riding in, Clay had noticed the verdant fields of wheat and vegetables. Someone had invested a lot of work and money to redirect the water from the San Felipe Springs to irrigate their fields.

San Felipe was fortunate to have the sweet water from San Felipe Springs. Nearby, the Rio Bravo flowed, not nearly so pure. Even with the springs and the agriculture development, it was a sleepy little town, but it looked like everyone had turned out for the parade. Clay spotted the marshal's office and pulled up in front. The marshal stood there with his thumbs hooked into his gunbelt.

Clay dismounted, tied up his horses at the hitching rail, then motioned for Milo to toss him the reins of his two horses and tied those. He yanked, none too gently, on Milo's rope. "Get down, Milo." He turned to the marshal. "Howdy, Marshal, I'm Clay Barlow. I could use your help."

"Reckon you've got some explainin' to do, boy," the marshal said.

Clay took a closer look at the marshal. Run over boots, dirty pants, and a dirty shirt and vest to go along with the pants. Hopefully the man was better at marshaling than at hygiene. "Be glad to. First, I'd like to get this man in your jail and turn him over to you."

The marshal eyed him for a moment, then said, "We'll see. Bring him on in."

Clay removed the rope from Milo's neck and tied it back on his saddle. He motioned Milo in ahead of him. People had gathered around the horses and were looking at Harly. One of the men grabbed Harly by the hair and lifted his head up. Still holding the man's head where others could see, he said, "Why, Marshal, this here is Harly Pinder. He's deader than a dried catfish. His brother's not gonna be too happy about this, not too happy at all."

The marshal stopped so quick Milo almost ran into him. "Let me see."

The man turned Harly's head so that the marshal could get a good look. "Well, I'll be fried." He turned back to Clay. "Boy, you know who this is?" Without waiting for an answer, he said, "This here is Harly Pinder. His brother is Gideon Pinder. You're gonna be in a heap of trouble when he finds out."

"I know who he is, Marshal. He and this little rat tried to ambush me on my way from Brackett. Now can we get this man in jail?"

"Go on in," the marshal said. The man holding up Harly's head dropped it and walked toward the saloon.

Clay pointed Milo to the two-cell jail. The marshal locked the door behind him. Milo moved over to the bunk and sat down, relief covering his face. There was a single chair in front of the desk. Clay sat down, and the marshal sat behind his desk and leaned back in his chair. He crossed his arms and appraised Clay for a few moments.

"Okay, boy, start explaining."

Clay pulled out the wanted poster from inside his vest and handed it to the marshal. The marshal looked over the poster with Milo's picture on it. He looked at Milo then back at the picture, then back at Milo. "I reckon you got you Milo Reese all right. What do you want me to do with him?"

Clay was surprised at the comment. "Marshal, this man killed my pa, and he's wanted. That's his poster. There's also a reward on him. I'll take that reward, and you can have the prisoner. He's implicated Birch Hayes, Zeke Martin, and the three Pinder brothers in the murder of my folks and our ranch hand, Slim. It sounds like you know at least the Pinders. I expect you to arrest them and hold them for trial."

"Now, boy—"

Clay could feel his anger rising. This man with a badge acted like he had no desire to see justice done. He remembered Pa talking about these kind of lawmen. They were just biding their time and taking their paycheck. "Marshal, my name is Clay Barlow. You can call me Clay or you can call me Barlow, but drop the boy."

The marshal was taken aback for a moment. He was about to say something when the office door swung open.

"Clay, looks like you've been busy."

Clay turned around to see Jake and another man standing in the doorway. He grinned at Jake. "I figured you to be halfway to El Paso by now." Clay stood and shook Jake's hand.

The men ignored the marshal, still sitting behind his desk.

"Clay, I'd like you to meet Major John B. Jones. Major, this is Clay Barlow, Bill Barlow's son. I was telling you about him."

The two men shook hands. "Clay, I'm glad to meet you. I am very sorry to hear about your family. Your pa was a fine man. He had a reputation as a man to ride the river with. He'll be sorely missed. Your ma, I heard, was a very pretty and kind lady. It is a major loss, when such upstanding citizens are murdered."

"Thank you, Major. I appreciate your kindness."

Major Jones said, "I assume Marshal Taylor is helping you in your endeavors?"

"No, sir, not much."

"Now see here—" the marshal began, rising from his chair.

"Sit down, Taylor," the major said. "I want to hear this young man out."

Jake pulled up two chairs from the corner of the office and moved them over to where they were on each side of Clay. He and the major sat.

"Clay," Major Jones said, "tell us what's going on."

Clay told the three of them everything that had happened since leaving the wagon train, with the exception of Lynn and the fights with Cotton Davis. He showed them all of the posters. The major interrupted occasionally to ask a question. Marshal Taylor never uttered a word. When Milo was mentioned, the major turned a cold stare on the man in the cell. Milo fidgeted and finally got up to look out the cell window.

"I believe that's everything. Harly Pinder is strung across the saddle outside. Seems the marshal might know of the Pinders."

The major turned his stare on Marshal Taylor. "Do you know this Pinder Gang, Marshal?"

Now it was the marshal's turn to squirm. "Reckon I know of them, Major Jones. I've heard they come into town on occasion. Don't know that I'd know them if I seen them."

"Marshal, here's what you're going to do. You will wire Austin, advising them you hold Milo Reese in custody. As soon as you receive authorization, you will pay Mr. Barlow the reward. If any of the Pinder Gang comes into San Felipe, you will arrest them and hold them for transport. Am I being clear enough for you?"

"Well, Major, that reward could take a while, and I don't rightly know the Pinders by sight."

Major Jones slid the posters in front of Marshal Taylor. "There's pictures of these men. It's very simple. If you see them, arrest them."

The marshal nodded. It was hot in the office, but he was the only one sweating.

"Now, take care of the body on the horse outside. As far as the horses, those men tried to kill this young man. I'd say he has a right to the horses and the equipment on them, wouldn't you agree?"

"Well, Major, that might fall under city property."

"Were these men taken in San Felipe?"

"No, bu—"

"No buts." The major turned to Clay. "Clay, do you want the horses and gear?"

"No, sir. I'm fine."

He turned back to the marshal.

"In that case, the city of San Felipe will pay to Clay Barlow a fair sum for said horses and gear. Now, does that sound fair to you, Marshal?"

"I reckon, Major. I'll have to get the approval of the mayor."

"That won't be a problem, will it, Marshal?"

"No, sir."

"I would expect that the wheels of justice will turn quickly in this case. I would expect Clay to receive the money from the city today, before I leave. Clear?"

"Yes, Major."

"Good, you'll find us at the eatery. Please bring his money there." Major Jones looked first at Clay and then the marshal. "Are we done?"

Clay couldn't contain his grin. "Yes, sir, Major. I'm more than done."

The marshal nodded and said, "Reckon that takes care of it."

"Fine." The major shook hands with Marshal Taylor, then turned to Clay and Jake. "Shall we be going?"

Clay closed the door behind them as the three men stepped into the bright afternoon sunlight; by the middle of May in Texas, it was getting hot.

Music could be heard coming from the Mexican cantina at one end of the street, competing with a tinny piano banging away in the saloon across the street from the marshal's office. Next to the saloon, an eatery, of sorts, was doing a less than booming business.

"How about we grab some grub?" Major Jones said. "I've eaten at the place across the street. It's not bad."

Clay heard his stomach growl. "Major, that's a fine idea, but I've got to take care of my animals first."

"We'll see you there," the major said.

Clay turned, untied the horses, and led them past the general store to the livery stable. He stopped at the trough outside the stable and let the horses drink. An elderly man sat in a chair, leaning back against the front of the stable, his hat pulled down over his eyes. With his left index finger and thumb, the man grasped the corner of his hat brim and slid it to the back of his head. "They look a mite thirsty," he said.

"Been a while since they had a drink. I'd like to stable 'em for a few days and make sure they're fed good, including oats."

"I can do that. The oats'll cost you a little more. You the feller what brought in Pinder and Reese?"

"How much you charge?"

"You got two horses. Stable, water, feed, oats—you want 'em let out into the corral for a while every day?"

"Yep, that sounds good."

"I figger that'll run you forty cents a day. I'll take good care of 'em."

Clay thought for a second. That was a really good deal the old man was giving him. Pa always said if you paid a man a little more than he asked, you could usually count on good service. "Tell you what I'll do, I could be needing either one or both anytime, could be late at night. Make it fifty cents a day and you've got a deal."

The old man pushed up out of the chair, walked over to Clay, and took the horses' reins. He favored his right leg. "You drive a hard bargain, young feller, but I reckon I can handle that. When your horses stop drinking, They'll get a good rubdown and I'll toss 'em some feed and a few oats."

"Mister, I usually rub down my own horses."

"Son, you just leave it to me. They'll like me faster if I'm the one doing the rubbing. If you want, I'll put yore gear in the office, and you can pick up what you need later."

"Thanks," Clay said. "Reckon I could use some food."

"Well, go on. People call me Rud. If you don't see me, just give a yell, and I'll come hoppin'."

"I'm Clay. Thanks again." Clay turned and headed back up the street to the eatery. He surveyed San Felipe as he walked. There wasn't much going on here. It made Brackett look like a thriving city, although someone had put in a bank. Other than the bank, there was the Mexican cantina, the stables, and the general store next to the stables. The bank, saloon, and eatery were across the street from the store. Just on the other side of the general store was the marshal's office and a ladies' clothing store. Houses were located north of the commercial buildings.

He reached the eatery and walked in. Major Jones and Jake were seated facing the door, drinking coffee. "Come on over and sit," Jake said. "You've had a busy day. Major, we better get some food out here. I could hear Clay's stomach from down at the stables."

Clay grinned and took a seat at the table and ordered lunch.

"So how's your neck feeling?" Jake said.

"How'd you hear about that?"

"Word gets around."

"Fine. It gets better every day."

The food came out. Clay had a big plate of fried chicken with pinto beans and fresh sliced tomatoes. When he was walking up, he had seen the big garden at the side of the restaurant.

Silence surrounded the men as they ate. Clay finished and leaned back in his chair. This felt good. A good meal and good men. These were men with the bark on. They held the door for women and took no guff off other men.

"I'll tell you, Jake," Clay said, "I know now what you meant when you said I needed to get some experience under my belt. I searched Hayes, and missed that knife. I never even thought of the possibility of there being one down his back."

"Many a man woulda missed it," Jake said. He pulled out his plug and took a bite off it, offering it to the major, who turned him down. "But I'll just bet anyone around, you won't make that mistake again."

"No, I don't reckon I will."

"Clay, what are your plans?" the major asked.

"Well, sir, I've still got four more killers to catch up with. I aim to do it. I don't care how long it takes."

The major persisted, "I understand. But after you catch these men, what are your plans?"

"Major, I don't rightly know. I still have Pa's ranch. I've met a really nice girl in Brackett. I'm contemplating settling down and ranching the land I grew up on." Clay turned the question back on Major Jones. "Why do you ask?"

"You ever thought of joining the Rangers?"

Clay looked at Jake for a moment, then gazed out the window at the dusty San Felipe street. He turned back to Major Jones. "No, sir, I really haven't. First place, there are no Rangers to join. Second, I don't see myself as Ranger material. I'm still mighty young, for something like that."

"Stop and think, Clay," Major Jones said. "You captured Hayes when he was trying to escape from the army."

Clay started to respond, and Major Jones held up his hand.

"I know he got away, but anyone could have made that

mistake. You survived a knife in the neck. Darn few men could have done that. You spotted an ambush. Most any other man would be lying out on the prairie with a bullet through him. You didn't try to slip away, but you attacked. You captured both men."

Major Jones took a sip of his coffee and continued. "Son, that's Ranger material. You may be young, but you're already seasoned, and you'll continue to learn. You're still after the rest of Pinder's gang. You might get killed, but that's not stopping you. Also, we heard about what happened in Brackett, with those three toughs jumping you and then the marshal's son bracing you the next day. We also heard how that turned out. I dare say, you could've killed him, but you didn't. That's what I want as a Ranger, a man who thinks.

"Now, as far as there not being any Rangers right now, you're right. But I'm on a recruiting circuit. I found Jake and I need his help. Fortunately, there was another scout, a good man, here in San Felipe who could take over Jake's job. So Jake will be riding with me as we recruit men to fill the Frontier Battalion of the Texas Rangers.

"This is an important election year. Richard Coke is going to be elected, and that will be the end of this miserable, carpet-bagging government we've had for the past ten years. One of the first things that Governor Coke will do is reinstate the Rangers. Our state has suffered much from the Indians since the war began and since we've had the useless state police. We will now put down the Indian problem for good and deal, as need be, with the bandit problem that exists in Texas."

Major Jones took another sip of his coffee. "I've said a lot here, Clay, so that you understand the important role the Rangers will play in cleaning up our state. I'd like you to be a part of it." With that, Major Jones leaned back in his chair and finished off his coffee.

Clay thought for a moment before he responded. *This is a real honor. But what about Lynn? How would she feel about this? I'd be gone a lot.*

"Major Jones, joining the Rangers is a big commitment. I'm only seventeen. I still have the Pinder Gang to catch. I've got a girl to think about. I'm sorry, but right now, I can't accept your offer. I thank you for it. But, I can't accept."

Major Jones nodded. "I understand. You've got a mighty full plate. But I want you to know that this offer will stand. I don't know exactly what the date will be that the Rangers will be commissioned, but it will happen. If you decide to join us, come see me."

The three men were about to leave when the door opened and in walked the marshal.

Major Jones nodded to him and said, "Afternoon, Marshal Taylor, do you have something for Mr. Barlow?"

"Afternoon, Major, matter of fact, I do. I spoke with the mayor and he authorized me to pay Mr. Barlow for the two horses and gear belonging to Pinder and Reese. You've got to understand that we're a small town, and we don't have the finances of Uvalde, San Antonio, or Austin."

The major nodded.

"Reckon, counting the horses, tack, and weapons, the mayor said we can pay Mr. Barlow one hundred and fifty dollars."

The major shook his head in disgust. "Why, man, one good horse is worth that, and those outlaws had excellent horse flesh." He turned to Clay. "Are you satisfied with that paltry amount?"

Clay hadn't expected anything. He was pleased with the windfall, but he didn't show it. "I guess that'll have to do, Major."

The marshal handed the envelope to Clay, tipped his hat, and started to leave.

"Marshal," Major Jones called, "how much is the reward on Reese?"

The marshal had reached the door. "The reward's one hundred dollars, Major. We should have it tomorrow."

"Then I expect that you'll get it to Mr. Barlow as soon as you receive authorization. Am I correct?"

"Reckon I will."

"Good. Marshal, we'll be leaving today. But I would consider it a favor if you would see that Mr. Barlow is given every assistance possible in the apprehension of the Pinder Gang."

"It'll be my pleasure, Major."

But it was clear the idea of helping Clay was anything but a pleasure for Marshal Taylor.

"Thank you for that. Have a good day."

Marshal Taylor turned and retreated as quickly as possible.

After the marshal was gone, Jake laughed. "Major, you sure lit a fire under that *hombre's* blanket. I figger he planned on selling those horses and gear, and also collecting the reward on Reese, if he didn't plan on letting him go."

"I'm sure you're right, Jake.

"Clay, I'd like to stay, but Jake and I have a lot of miles to cover over these next few months. You're going to be on your own here, so be careful. Think before you act, but then act swiftly and decisively. I have faith in you, and I look forward to seeing you next year."

Once outside, the three men turned right past the saloon and headed for the stables.

"Clay," Jake said, "I wish I could stay and help you. But we've got a lot of riding to do. You watch yourself. Gideon Pinder's the leader, but Quint is a sneaky son of a gun. You wanna keep yore eye on him. I don't need to tell you about Birch Hayes. He's slick, and he's as fast with a gun as he is with a knife. You're after a dangerous bunch. You just keep a keen eye peeled."

They had just about reached the stables. The old man was back in his chair in front of the building.

Jake nodded at the man in the chair. "You can trust that old man. His name is Rud Campbell. Before he got that leg shot up, he and I did some Rangerin' together. Not many people around here know that. But he is one tough old codger, and he can shoot the eyes out of a gnat at fifty paces. You need help, you ask him."

The old man slid his hat back and appraised the three men. "Howdy, Jake, Major. I reckon you'll be wanting your horses and gear. Looks like you've got some ridin' in mind."

Jake worked up a spit and hit the lizard sitting next to the stable door. The lizard shook his head and dashed back inside the barn.

"Don't ya torment my lizard, Jake," the old man said. "He's about the only thing I can trust in this town."

"Rud," Jake said, "I want ya to take good care of Clay. He's a friend."

Rud perked up. "Well, I reckon any friend of yours and Major Jones is a friend of mine. Let me git yore gear."

The men saddled their horses and slung their gear to the saddles. They led the horses outside and mounted up. Everything having been said, they turned the horses north and rode out of town.

"Son, reckon you'll be looking for a place to stay. If you want to sleep in the hay in the back of the barn, you're welcome. There's a hotel up past the saloon. But it's noisy, and I don't trust the owner. If you don't mind eating Mex food, which I happen to like, there's Maria's boarding house, down past the cantina."

"I like Mexican food."

"Good, then Maria's is the place for you. Maria Lopez owns it. She's got clean, safe rooms. You can leave your things in your room, and they'll be there when you get back. That's more than I can say for the hotel, and the food is great. You'll get plenty of tortillas, but ain't nothing wrong with that."

"Thanks, Mr. Campbell."

"Ain't no Mr. Campbell around here. Just call me Rud. Now, if you want, you can leave whatever things you want here, and I'll lock 'em up in the office. They'll be safe there. I sleep in the back of the office with a loaded shotgun."

"Reckon I'll just take my Roper and saddlebags. That's all I'll need for now. See you later."

The sun was drawing low in the west when Clay walked out of the barn toward Maria's boarding house. Jake had left. Alone again. His thoughts turned to Lynn, back in Brackett.

I wonder if she's even thinking of me? I like the idea of being a Ranger, but how will she feel? How would any woman feel about her man being gone so much? Will I be successful with the Pinder Gang? I wonder if they've heard about Harly?

Clay's mind ran on as he walked across the dusty street of San Felipe, his long shadow copying each step he made. *Tonight, a good rest. Tomorrow, I'll continue my search for the Pinders.*

The small room was still dark when Clay opened his eyes. He lay still. His senses, keen for the new area, went to work. He could hear pans rattling in the kitchen. He was in bed at Maria's.

He swung his long legs out of the bed and slid the Smith & Wesson back into its holster. He had slept well. Maybe too well, his pa might say. *Would I have awakened if someone had tried to slip into the room? There are no horses to warn me. Caution. That's how I stay alive.*

Clay slipped his trousers and socks on. His boots were next, and then his gunbelt. He double-checked that the hammer thong was removed from the hammer, and drew three times. *I've got to find time to practice with that left-handed holster.*

He poured water from the pitcher into the wash basin, then paused and checked the window, making sure the curtain was closed. Clay fished a match from his vest hanging over the chair back and lit the kerosene lamp. He pulled a straight razor from his saddlebags and stropped it a few times on his crossdraw holster. He needed a shave. It had been a couple of days, and the black stubble irritated him. Pa was always clean-shaven. He aimed to be like his pa.

When he was finished, he put the razor back in his bags and pulled out a clean shirt. It was red-and-black checkered. He'd gotten it, with a few other clothes, at the Brackett General Store. His thoughts turned back to the tinkling bell and Lynn. *Wonder what she's doing now? Still asleep? Maybe she's up, getting ready for the day.*

He pushed her from his mind, put his vest on over the shirt, wet his hair from the basin, and combed it back with his fingers. He picked up his hat, brushed it off, curled the brim, and positioned it on his head.

Enticing smells came from the kitchen. He headed to the dining room. Maria's boarding house was a rambling adobe. She had at least five bedrooms, kitchen, and a combination dining and sitting room. A huge table was covered with food. A veranda ran the front of the house, with several rocking chairs inviting her guests.

Maria walked in from the kitchen as Clay came into the dining room. "*Buenos Dias, Señor.* I trust you bring a big hunger with you this morning."

"Yes, ma'am. You'll never find me without that."

Maria looked him up and down. "*Si.* I think it would take much food to fill that handsome body."

Clay blushed. He'd never had a woman be so frank with him. He didn't know what to say, so he grinned at her, pulled out a chair, and sat down.

"Señor, if I was twenty years younger, I would make sure you would be looking at me and not the food." She laughed. "But I am old now, and the young hombres no longer look at me. Although, they do love my food. Now, you eat."

Clay picked up the egg platter and shoved five eggs onto his plate, grabbed some tortillas, and then some beans. He picked up the big bowl of salsa fresca and ladled the salsa over his beans and eggs.

Maria came back into the room as two Mexicans entered. They talked for a moment, and the two men sat across from Clay. "Coffee, Señor?" Maria asked.

"No, thanks, Maria. If you've got some water back there, I'd go for that."

"Ahh, no coffee? The señor doesn't want to stunt his growth." She followed the statement with a big belly laugh at her own joke and poured coffee for the two other men.

Clay grinned and stuffed more egg in his mouth. The two Mexicans chuckled and watched appreciatively as Maria's ample body swished back into the kitchen.

"You're not from around here, Señor," the bigger of the two men said.

"No," Clay said. "You?"

"Close," the man said. "We work for a *ranchero* a few miles on the other side of the Rio Bravo. Some days, when we are off, we come to San Felipe to enjoy Maria's cooking, and perhaps to have a leetle fun in the cantina. We go back today."

The smaller man looked up from his breakfast and said in a sharp tone, "How is it that you are staying at Maria's and not at the *gringo* hotel?"

Clay took a closer look at the two men. They both carried big, black, round sombreros that they hung from the back of their chairs. The bigger man was clean-shaven. He had the typical build of the range rider, narrow hips and wide shoulders. He was almost as tall as Clay, but heavier in the shoulders and arms, especially the forearms and wrists. The smaller man was completely different. His movements were quick. His mustache was thick above his lips. At each end it turned and grew down almost to his chin. He was a wiry man, and pushy.

"It was recommended to me," Clay said, ignoring the gringo comment. He continued to eat. He had eaten a few more bites of the delicious eggs and tortillas when the smaller man spoke up again.

The man pointed his fork at Clay to emphasize his words. "You didn't answer the second part of my question, Gringo."

Maria came into the dining room as the smaller man finished his statement. "Juan, do not be rude to my guests!" Then they proceeded to argue in Spanish, words flying back and forth like daggers. "Señor, please forgive my rude friend. He did not learn well from his parents."

Clay said, "No problem, Maria. I've met rude people before."

The smaller man laid his fork down gently and stood. "Señor, you are treading on, how do you say, dangerous ground."

Clay looked up at the man. *Just what I need. It's not bad enough I'm chasing four killers, now I have a good chance of alienating the Mexican community.* "Sit down, *amigo*. You haven't finished your breakfast. You wouldn't want to miss Maria's cooking, since that was part of your reason for coming into San Felipe."

The bigger man said something in Spanish and the man sat down, still angry.

"My friend, Juan, has a short cord." The man turned to Maria. "How do you say *fusible* in English?"

"Ahh, fuse," Maria said.

"Yes," the man said to Clay, "my friend has a short fuse."

"I've noticed," Clay said.

"My name," the big man told him, "is Arturo Ignacio Santiago Torres, and my short-tempered friend is Juan Raul Fernandez Medina. Call me Arturo and he is Juan."

Clay extended his hand across the table. "Arturo and Juan. I am Clayton Joseph Barlow. You can call me Clay."

Arturo took Clay's hand immediately. Clay could tell Juan still hadn't cooled down, but after a moment, he shook Clay's hand as well.

The door opened and Rud walked in. He yelled back into the kitchen, "Maria, you leave anything for me?"

She came to the kitchen door. Her face had broken into a big, toothy smile. "Rud, sweetie, there is always a little something for you at my table. Sit down." She turned to walk back into the kitchen, and Rud slapped her lightly on her ample bottom. She giggled and ran into the kitchen.

"How you feeling, boy? I see you've put on the feed bag. You get plenty of sleep last night?" Rud limped over to the chair at the end of table and sat down, his bad leg extending straight out.

"Yes, sir. Like a rock."

"I see you've met Arturo and Juan. Buenos dias, amigos." Rud's Spanish was colored with his Texas drawl.

Juan said to Rud, "You know this man?"

"I darned sure do. Only known him for a day, but he strikes me as a good lad. He brought Harly Pinder in over his saddle, and had Milo Reese with a rope around his neck."

The two men appraised Clay with a new appreciation.

"Those are two bad men," Juan said. "You know they ride with a gang. The leader is *muy malo*, very bad."

"I do," Clay said. "They killed my folks and a good friend. I'm after them."

Arturo asked, "What will you do when you find them?"

"Reckon that's up to them. If I have to, I'll kill 'em."

The two friends looked at each other. Arturo said, "We believe they are rustling our patrón's cattle. If we find them first, we will kill them."

"You have any idea where they are?"

"No, Señor Clay, not yet," Arturo said. "But we will. It is only a matter of time, no? Then we find them and kill them. We do know they have taken our cattle across the Rio Bravo and moved them into the Devils River country. That country is very rough."

Clay thought for a moment. "If I come out to your *ranchero*, do you think your *patrón* would mind you showing me where they last crossed the river? I'm a pretty good tracker."

Juan looked at Arturo. Arturo nodded, "I don't think he would mind at all, Señor."

"Good," Clay said. "When are you going back to the rancho?"

Juan grinned. "We will have a little tequila at the cantina to help wash down Maria's breakfast and head back today. You are welcome to come with us if you like. That is, if you don't mind me calling you gringo."

Clay laughed. "Reckon I can live with that, if you don't mind me calling you Mex."

Arturo threw back his head and roared. "I think he has you, Juan. This will be fun."

Juan grinned. He put his finger and thumb together at the middle of his mustache and ran them across and down each side. "You are a funny man, Señor."

Rud looked at the three of them. "Something going on I don't know about?"

"Almost, Señor Rud, almost," Juan said.

Clay stood. "I'm gonna check on my horses and visit the saloon, if it's open this early. See if I can find anything else out before we leave."

"I'll be along in a bit," Rud said.

"Maria, if it's okay with you, I'll settle up when I come back for my gear."

Maria came out of the kitchen and moved behind Rud, to massage his shoulders. "That will be fine, Señor Clay. I'll be here." She winked at Clay. "Rud, he may also still be here."

"I just might, boy, I just might," Rud said, a big smile on his face.

"Arturo, Juan, I'll see you later."

The two men nodded. Juan waved as he took a sip of his strong coffee. Clay put his hat on and stepped out the door. The morning sun was climbing above the stable roof as Clay crossed the street to check on the horses. He was halfway across the street when the blue roan tied in front of the saloon got his attention.

Clay stopped. Was that Blue? He started walking toward the horse. It stood between two other horses. The horse between Clay and the blue roan moved forward at the rail and exposed the roan's brand. Rocking A W. That was Blue.

Clay checked both guns to make sure the hammer thongs were off. He moved them in the holsters. They were nice and loose. He whistled softly. Blue's head snapped up as he looked toward Clay.

Today was a good day, Clay thought. He had slept well, he'd enjoyed a delicious, sit-down breakfast. The warm breeze slipping through the alleys from the west felt good across his neck and face. He had never drawn on another human being. He could hear his pa saying, "You're ready, just remain cool. Don't get excited. Don't focus solely on your target. Remain conscious of what's happening around you. You can do it."

He stepped up to Blue and rubbed his neck. The horse rubbed his head against Clay's shoulder. Clay scratched him behind his ears, then turned and stepped into the saloon.

He saw Hayes sitting at the back table with another man. Hayes was dealing cards. Clay checked the bartender, fifteen feet to his right, wiping beer mugs behind the bar. Two other men sat at a table in the far corner, to his left, no more than twenty feet, each with a beer.

Hayes looked better than he had the last time he saw him. He'd healed pretty quick.

"Hayes," Clay said, "you killed my family, and you stole my horse and gear."

Birch Hayes, the handsome, educated man who had already killed several men, turned his head to the door. "Hello, boy. You're mighty lucky. Last time I saw you, my knife was stuck in your throat and you were bleeding out. Figured you were dead. That was my favorite knife, well balanced. Did you bring it back to me?"

The man with Hayes let loose a loud, tense laugh. He looked

to Clay, then back to Hayes. The two men in the corner didn't make a move. The bartender laid his hands flat on the bar.

Clay watched Hayes stand and motion his partner up. His partner stood and faced Clay.

"Mister," Clay said, "I don't know who you are. I figure if you're with Hayes, you're probably running with the Pinder Gang. Don't know if you know it, but they killed my ma and pa. I'm only here for Hayes, unless you feel the need to deal yourself in."

The man had a scar on the right side of his face that ran from his ear to the corner of his mouth. The scar was pulsing red.

"You can't take me, boy," Hayes said. "You don't have a chance. I've already killed three men. Tell you what I'll do. You turn around and walk away, and I'll forget all about this."

Clay didn't move. He felt relaxed. It was like emotion had drained out of him. His hands felt loose, ready.

Watch their eyes, he remembered his pa saying.

The two men in the corner sat frozen, their only movement their heads swiveling between Clay and Hayes. Clay noticed the bartender start to edge down the bar. "Mr. Bartender, I wouldn't move another inch. It won't be healthy."

The bartender stopped, his hands still on the top of the bar.

"Hayes, you can start by dropping your gun. Then we'll talk about all your hideout weapons."

Hayes smiled. "Boy, you don't stand a—"

Mid-sentence, Hayes went for his gun. Clay saw his eyes narrow a split second before he drew. *Pa was right.* Now everything seemed to slow. He could see the other man going for his gun and the bartender reaching beneath the bar. His first priority was Hayes. Clay's Smith & Wesson New Model 3 .44 caliber American cleared his holster while Hayes's hand was still moving down to his gun. Clay could see the surprise in the eyes of Hayes, along with the realization that he was a dead man. Hayes's six-gun had just cleared his holster, the barrel starting to rise, when the first .44 American slammed into his third button. He took a step back and, though slower, continued to bring his six-gun to bear. The second .44 slammed into his chest, no more than a half-inch from the first. His gun stopped rising. The third shot formed a half-inch triangle with the other two. Hayes dropped his gun and fell to his knees.

Hayes's partner was bringing his gun to bear on Clay when the first shot hit him in the third button, followed quickly by the second. He fell backward against the table, his gun flew out of his hand, and the bottle sitting on the table catapulted across the room.

Clay watched everything happening as if he were a spectator. He watched the bullets slam into Hayes, then the slight change of direction of the muzzle of his Smith & Wesson to cover the second man. He saw that man fly backward as his two bullets struck right where his pa had taught him to aim. Out of the corner of his eye, he saw the bartender reach under the bar and pull out a 10-gauge double barrel.

He lunged forward and down, having seen the man was right-handed and knowing it would be harder for him to track to the right. As he dove, he holstered his empty revolver and pulled the one from the crossdraw holster. The blast of the shotgun was even more deafening in the bar. The load of shot passed over him. Clay fired. This time, he rushed the shot. The bullet hit the man just below his left collarbone. He heard his pa say, "Stay calm, Son."

The man was trying to bring the shotgun up again when the second bullet hit the third button of his shirt, driving shards of the button into his chest. Clay kept shooting until the man dropped the shotgun and slumped across the bar.

Clay glanced at the two men in the corner. They had their hands up, and their faces were white as fresh snow. He quickly snapped open the top break on the revolver and reloaded. The six-gun slid smoothly into the crossdraw holster, and Clay drew the other one and yanked it open. He was reloading it before the ejected cases hit the floor. Then he dropped it back into the holster and took a deep breath while he watched the door.

Marshal Taylor was the first man through the door. He looked around the smoke-filled room. The acrid black powder made it difficult to clearly make out the two bodies in the back of the room. The bartender was clearly visible, hanging over the bar. His shotgun was on the floor in front of the bar. Several people pushed in behind the marshal. Rud, Arturo, and Juan came in with the group. Marshal Taylor walked to the back of the room and recognized Hayes and his partner.

Clay watched Marshal Taylor kneel down next to Hayes. He took out a four bit piece and laid it on Hayes chest, covering the bullet holes. Then he picked it up and walked over to the other man, knelt down and did the same thing. He shook his head and looked back at Clay. Without saying a word, Marshal Taylor walked over to the bartender and rolled him over. He looked at the man's shoulder and then the three bullet wounds in his chest. Again, he put the now-bloody half dollar over the three holes.

Clay could feel the reaction setting in. He had just gone from never shooting a man to killing three. He took another deep breath. He looked at Rud. The old man nodded and limped over to him. "How you doing, Son?"

Clay spoke low to keep the conversation between him and Rud. "I'm feelin' a little shaky, Rud."

"Well, you just hang on. We'll have you out of here in a few minutes."

Marshal Taylor turned to the men in the corner. "You boys see this?"

Both men started talking at once. "Yes, sir, Marshal, we seen it all."

"Never seen such shootin' in my life."

"Me neither, Marshal. That there Hayes drew first, he—"

"That's right, Marshal, Hayes drew first, but he didn't stand a chance—"

"Who's telling this, me or you?"

"Me, I seen it all."

"Well, I seen it all too."

"Look, Jeb, just shut up," Marshal Taylor said. "Rube, you look to be the most sober, you tell me what happened."

"Marshal, like I was saying, Hayes and that other feller drew first. But they didn't have a snowball's chance. That boy had his first shot going before Hayes even had his gun out of his holster good. Then that young feller blasted Hayes's partner, don't know his name. You know him, Marshal?"

The marshal looked up at the ceiling as if he were asking for patience. "I don't know him, Rube. So, what about Russell?"

"Marshal, the boy told him to stay out of it. But you know, he and Hayes went way back. So he goes under the bar for his greener. Biggest mistake he ever did make. Reckon he'd like to take it back, don't you think?"

"I'm losing my patience, Rube. Just tell me what happened."

"I'm just trying to help, Marshal. Ain't no sense in you gittin' on yore high horse. Though all of this talking is sure making me dry." Rube rubbed his throat and coughed.

"Listening's makin' me pretty dry too, Marshal," Jeb said.

Marshal Taylor said, "Don't reckon Russell will mind if you fellers get you a drink."

Both men started to stand up and head for the bar.

"After you finish the story. Go ahead, Rube."

Both men sat back down, their disappointment obvious. "Like I was saying, Marshal. Russell—dumb, dumb, dumb, Russell—reached beneath the bar for that 10-gauge he likes so much and swings it up over the bar. By that time, this here boy had finished killin' those two, and started shuckin' his other pistol out." Rube stopped for a moment and rubbed his chin, the picture of a man deep in thought. "Yessiree, I reckon he must have seen Russell going for the shotgun. Anyways, he, that's the boy there, he dives forward, and while he's in the air, he puts one into Russell. Must've been cause he was diving, but he hit him in the shoulder or thereabouts. He hit the floor and kept shooting. Why, it all sounded like one shot. Russell's a pretty big feller, but nobody can take that much lead and survive. I reckon the boy shot him five, six times. That's it, Marshal. Now, how about our drinks?"

"Help yourselves, boys."

The two men rushed over to the bar and started rummaging through the bottles.

Marshal Taylor turned to Clay. "You did a heap of killin' here today. You'll need to come down to my office. I'll need a statement from you."

"Reckon not, Marshal," Rud said. "You got all the statement you need from those two. I'll be taking the boy down to Maria's. If you need anything, you can come down there."

The marshal started to object. Arturo and Juan moved to Clay's side. "He'll be with us, *Señor*. I'm sure you won't mind."

Marshal Taylor paused, looked at the four men, and finally said to Clay, "Just don't leave town until I've talked to you."

"Marshal, I'll be leaving today. If you want to talk to me, you best make it soon. Also, I'll be taking that blue roan. That's my horse, saddle, and saddlebags. Hayes stole 'em a while back. I'll be looking through the rest of his gear to see if there's anything else of mine. Plus, he took twenty-five dollars of mine, so I'll be taking whatever money he has."

Clay watched the marshal process everything. It was obvious he didn't like being out of control. But something new for Clay, he saw caution in the marshal's eyes. The man didn't want to tangle with Clay, after what he had seen in the saloon.

"All right, take the horse and whatever money you find. Stop by the office before you leave. I've got the reward money for Milo."

Clay started for the door.

"What about the money, aren't you going to check Hayes?"

"Marshal, if you don't mind, you're going to check everything. Just have the money when I come by to pick up the reward."

Clay walked out of the saloon to Blue. He rubbed the horse's nose and patted his neck. "Good to see you, Blue boy. I thought I lost you for good." The horse nuzzled him and rubbed his head against him. Clay untied Blue, and with Rud, Arturo, and Juan, walked down the street to the livery. He took Blue to water and let him drink. "Rud, can you take Blue for a minute? I'll be right back."

He hurried to the alley to the south of the livery, walked two paces into the alley, and could hold it no longer. He leaned against the livery wall and threw up every bit of the breakfast he had so enjoyed. *I've killed three men today. That makes a total of four men dead. They may have deserved it, but that doesn't make me feel any better.* He dry heaved a couple more times, wiped his mouth, and walked back to the trough. He removed his hat and plunged his head into the horse trough. The cool water felt good. Clay shook his head and combed his hair back with his hand. His thick black hair glistened in the sunlight. He put his hat back on and walked into the stable.

"Arturo and Juan went over to the cantina," Rud said. "We were still at Maria's when we heard the shooting. How'd you know they were there?"

"I saw Blue at the hitching rail."

"You doin' all right, Son?"

"No, not much. I've never killed a man before. It was bad enough with Harly, but I shot three men today, and I've got to live with it."

Rud had pulled the saddle from Blue and was giving him a rubdown. "It's a hard thing. You're right. You'll have to live with it. Just try not to add too many more to those three. The more there are, the harder it is. But, feelin' bad's a good thing. It means you care. When you stop feelin' bad about killing, you've just crossed the line. Whether you carry a badge or not, at that point, you've become a killer. So, don't feel guilty about feelin' bad."

Clay knew Rud was telling the truth. It was the same thing Pa and Slim had told him. But he wasn't done. He still had three more men to apprehend, then he'd be done. What would Lynn think when she heard? Would she have anything to do with a killer? Would she understand, or would she be horrified?

"Rud, you know when Arturo and Juan are leaving for their rancho?"

"I reckon they'll have a couple of drinks and be on their way."

"I'll get my things from Maria's and be right back. I want to be ready when they leave."

14

C lay had settled up with Maria. She'd been sad for him, but happy that he had survived. Maria even fixed him a lunch of beef, beans, and tortillas. It felt good to have something back in his stomach. His saddlebags were over his left shoulder and the Roper in his left hand.

As he walked in front of the cantina, Arturo stepped out. "Señor Clay. We are having one more drink before we leave. Will you join us?"

Clay wanted to be on his way, but he didn't want to insult his new friends. "Thanks for the invite." He turned and entered the cantina.

It was brighter in the cantina than the saloon. More windows allowed a breeze to circulate through the thick-walled adobe building. The breeze and the adobe kept it cooler. A man sat on the end of the bar playing a guitar. There were three young Mexican women circulating around the tables. The music and the brightly dressed young women lent a party-like atmosphere.

A heavy Mexican man stood behind the bar, pouring drinks. "Buenos dias, Señor. Welcome to my humble cantina. What would you like? Would you like a drink or something to eat? *Mi esposa*, my wife, is an excellent cook."

Clay stepped up to the bar next to Juan. Arturo leaned against the bar, facing Clay on his right.

Juan said, "Clay, this is my friend Francisco, and these lovely *chicas*,"—he swept his arm, indicating the three young women —"are his daughters. Francisco, get my friend a tequila."

"Si, Señor Juan," Francisco said.

Clay said. "No, thank you, I don't drink liquor—"

"You don't drink liquor, you don't drink coffee," Juan said. "Maria is right. You want to grow up to be a big gringo."

Clay grinned. "Tell me, Juan, do you think it's working?"

Francisco, Juan, and Arturo roared with laughter.

"Si, Señor," Juan said, looking up at Clay. "I think it is working very well."

Francisco spoke up. "We have some *limón agua fresca*. It is very delicious," Francisco paused and then said, "and it has no alcohol, Señor."

"That'll be great," Clay said.

Francisco brought the lightly sweetened lemon water. Clay reached into his pocket to pay.

Francisco said, "No, Señor Clay. It is on the house. I appreciate what you have done today. None of us want the vermin you have killed today in our town."

"Gracias, Francisco." Clay took a sip. It was very good. It felt calming to his stomach. "When do you reckon you'll be leaving for the ranch?" Clay asked Arturo.

"This is our last drink, and we will be on our way."

The two men tossed down their tequilas. "We go!" Juan shouted. "Adios, Francisco. Adios, mi chicas."

The three girls surrounded Juan, grabbing his arms and pulling him back into the cantina. Arturo and Clay laughed at the smaller man, as he reveled in the attention.

"No, I must go, but I will be back soon."

Clay swung his saddlebags over his shoulder, picked up his shotgun, and the three men headed for the stable.

Rud was again sitting outside in his chair, leaning against the wall, when the men entered the stable. "You boys fixin' to pull out?"

"Si, Señor Rud. We are on our way," Arturo said.

The two Mexicans went to their horses and started saddling up.

Rud stood and limped into the stable with Clay. "You planning on taking all your horses and gear?"

"No, sir, what with getting my stuff back from Hayes, I find myself with an extra saddle, rifle, and saddlebags. I'm only going to take one extra horse, an extra saddle, and the two sets of saddlebags. If you don't mind, I'll leave the panniers, the extra rifle, saddle, and the sorrel with you. In fact, I have no need for three saddles. If I give you the older saddle, how much more cash would I owe you to take care of the sorrel and store the panniers and rifle?"

"Son, you just let me have that saddle, and I'll take care of everything else. That'll be more'n enough."

While Clay saddled Blue, Rud saddled the buckskin. Clay went through his old saddlebags. Most everything was there except the money. Too bad his Remingtons were gone. Hayes had been carrying a Colt, but it was good to have the old LeMat revolver. He pulled it out and checked the loads. Still good. The powder, shot, bullets, mold and handles, along with the caps, were still there.

The men were ready to go. The buckskin carried the extra saddle and saddlebags. Clay had transferred enough supplies to last him for a week or more to the two saddlebags.

They led the horses outside and mounted. "Thanks, Rud," Clay said.

"Be seeing you boys. Don't forget to go by the marshal's office to get your money. You leave it there and it may not be there when you get back."

The men rode the horses up the street toward the marshal's office. They pulled up in front and Clay swung down. "Won't be but a minute," he said and walked in.

"Howdy, Marshal."

The marshal nodded, and without getting up, picked up an envelope on his desk and handed it to Clay. "There's a hundred dollar reward for Milo, plus the money Hayes had, which came to just a little over thirty dollars."

Clay took the envelope, folded it into thirds, and slipped it into his vest pocket. "Thanks, Marshal." He turned to leave.

"You leaving town?"

"Yep." Clay started for the door again.

"For good?"

Clay stopped again and turned to the marshal. "No, sir, I'll be back. I'm hoping to have some more business for your jail."

"Well, you best be careful. That Gideon Pinder and his brother Quint are bad hombres."

"I'll remember that, Marshal." Clay turned and went out the door.

Juan was sitting with a leg thrown across the saddle and his *sombrero* pushed back on his head. "Ready, amigo?"

"More than ready," Clay said. "Let's get out of here."

The three men turned south, down to the Rio Bravo crossing, and galloped out of San Felipe. When they passed the cantina, Juan let out an "Ay, ya, ya" and waved his sombrero at the three pretty little señoritas standing at the door.

Clay laughed. Today had been hard, but it felt good to be leaving a town with friends.

∾

THE TRIP to Rancho Paraiso went by quickly. Within an hour the three men were entering the ranch headquarters. It looked more like a fort than Fort Clark, Clay thought. The *hacienda*, stable, corral, storehouse, and bunkhouse were surrounded by an eight-foot adobe wall. It had a stand along the base of the inside wall allowing men to stand and see over the wall to spot approaching hostiles. He had no idea how long it might have taken them to build it. The entrance could be blocked by closing the eight-foot solid wooden double gate. All of the buildings were thick-walled adobe, cool in the summer, warm in the winter, and built like a fortress. The roof of each building was red clay barrel tiles. The only exposed wood was the thick, rough-cut wooden doors. Whoever had built this was intent on surviving in Apache country.

The gate was guarded by a *vaquero*. "Hola, *Arturo*, Juan, you look too sober to have had much fun."

The guard, Juan, and Arturo laughed at the man's humor as they rode into the compound. They arrived at the hitching rail in front of the hacienda, as an older man with thick black hair, interspersed with white, walked onto the veranda. "Arturo, Juan. You've brought a guest?"

The three men remained mounted. "Si, *Jefe*," Arturo said. "This is Señor Clay Barlow. He has performed the *rancho* a favor and requests one in return."

The older man looked Clay over, then nodded. "I am anxious to hear the favor that has been done for us. Please get down and come inside. Arturo, you and Juan also."

The men dismounted. When they stepped onto the veranda, Arturo turned to Clay. "Señor Clay, it is my honor to introduce you to *Don* Carlos Juan Ortega Valdez. He is the owner of this vast *rancho*. Don Carlos, Señor Clay Barlow."

Clay could feel the power and confidence of the don in his handshake, firm but not hard. His black boots glistened from a recent shine. The tight black pants had silver conchos running down the side of each leg. The last two were unbuttoned to allow the pants to flare over the black boots. He wore a black embroidered short jacket over a white shirt with a full black bow tie. Clay felt out of place in his dusty chaps, boots, and vest.

"Welcome, Señor Clay. Please, come into our humble home."

Juan stepped forward to open the door for the men, and followed them into the hacienda. It was cool inside and surprisingly bright. Desert flowers adorned the side tables of the two wide, comfortable-looking leather chairs with strong, wide wooden arms. There was a long couch with solid arms, covered in a red cowhide. It looked like it could hold five big men.

Don Carlos indicated for Clay to sit in one of the big chairs, and he took the other. "You must be thirsty." He clapped his hands, and a chubby woman dressed in a white blouse and multicolored skirt entered the room.

"Yes, Jefe?" she asked.

"Cool drinks, please. Would lemonade be good for you, Señor Clay?"

"Yes, sir," Clay said. He was still taking in the big room. A huge fireplace took almost all of one wall. You could see through the fireplace to the dining room. He could just see the legs of a massive dining table. Above the fireplace were the horns of a magnificent desert bighorn sheep. The floor was covered with a black bear hide and two longhorn hides.

"Thank you, ma'am," Clay said to the maid when she set his lemonade on the table next to his chair.

She smiled at him, served the others, and left the room.

"Now," Don Carlos said, "please tell me what has transpired and how I might help you."

Arturo spoke up and told the story of the gunfight in San Felipe.

"Impressive, but why were you looking for these men?"

Clay explained about the murder of his parents and Slim, including the capture and loss of Hayes.

Don Carlos sat back in his leather chair, templed his hands, and appeared lost in thought. After a few moments, he again looked at Clay. "You have my sympathies and gratitude, Señor. The man Hayes is known to ride with the Pinder Gang. I am sure Arturo and Juan have told you about our cattle loss to rustlers. I am most certain that it is the Pinder Gang doing the stealing. When we catch them, they will be dealt with. But I do not understand how I may be of help, unless you would like to ride with us to capture them."

"Don Carlos," Clay said, "thank you for the invitation, but that is not what I'm after. I'm a fair to middlin' tracker. I spent many years with the Tonkawa, and they taught me much. What I need—it would save me time—is someone showing me the area where the last cattle were stolen. If I can start with the original theft, I think I can follow them to their hideout."

"Señor, we have tried to track them. We have even crossed the Rio Bravo, but each time, we lose them in the Devils River country. It is very rough."

"Well, sir, if I can track them to their hideout, I can circle back if I need help. But I might be able to take them myself. That's my goal."

Don Carlos hesitated for a moment, then nodded. "Yes, I understand. Before I had heard the story of San Felipe, I would have said you are only a boy and in over your head. But maybe you can pull this off.

"Arturo, Juan, after the horses have been watered, show *Señor* Clay the location of the last theft of my cattle."

Clay stood, along with Arturo and Juan.

"Please, Señor Clay, stay for a few moments. We will have a little food before you go, and you can meet my family. Arturo, Juan, have Nadia fix you something after you take care of the horses."

"Don Carlos, please, just call me Clay, and I'll take care of my own horses."

Arturo spoke up. "It is not necessary. We are glad to take care of them. When you are done, we will be on our way."

"Thanks," Clay said.

The two men nodded to the *don* and left the house.

"It is all right, Clay. Your horses will be taken care of, and you can soon be on your way. Now, you must meet my family."

Don Carlos stood and motioned for Clay to join him. The two men moved into the dining room. Two women and a boy of about fourteen sat in the easy chairs along the wall. All three stood as the men entered the room. Don Carlos smiled as he saw his family.

"Clay, I would like you to meet my lovely wife, *Doña* Alejandra Maria Contreras Dominguez."

The lady extended her hand, and Clay took it. It was soft, her handshake firm. Her face was framed by hair as black as a moonless night, sprinkled, like her husband's, with a few strands of gray. Her full lips spread in a kind smile.

"Hello, Señor Clay. It is a pleasure to meet such a fine young man. I hope you will forgive us, but, through the fireplace, we have had the honor of listening to your story. I am most sorry for the loss of your parents. That must be a hard blow, especially for one so young."

"Thank you, ma'am. It's a pleasure to meet you. Could I ask you all to just call me Clay? Makes me more comfortable."

Doña Alejandra tilted her head. "We would be honored."

Don Carlos continued the introductions. "This beautiful child is my daughter, Diana Margarita Ortega Contreras."

Clay could see the girl's cheeks tint a little redder at her father's words. She gave her father a smile-frown. "Father, you embarrass me, and I am not a child." She gave a small curtsy to Clay and shook his hand.

Clay marveled at the beauty of Diana. Her skin was the smooth, soft golden tan of an early morning sun against the desert. Her long black hair, almost to her waist, was like Doña

Alejandra's without the traces of gray. "Your pa speaks the truth ma'am. You are mighty pretty."

The don laughed, then said, "You will always be a child to me, and see, Clay agrees with me."

Diana lowered her eyes in more pleasure than embarrassment.

"And this rugged young man," the *don* continued, "is my only son, Rafael Antonio Ortega Contreras."

The boy stepped forward and gave Clay a half-bow. His gaze gave away his awe as he grasped Clay's hand. "It is nice to meet you. Before you leave, if you have time, you must tell me the details of the gunfight in San Felipe. You were outnumbered and still killed the *desperadoes*. It must have been a mighty feat."

"I reckon I'm not real proud of it. I had it to do it, but it gives me no pleasure. My pa taught me that a gun is a tool and you use it when you have to. But a man never takes pride in it."

Don Carlos listened to Clay and affirmed his response. "It is true, Rafael. Sometimes it is necessary to kill, but it is never necessary to feel prideful. Only killers feel that way."

The boy bowed his head. "I am sorry, Father. I did not mean to offend our guest."

Clay slapped Rafael on the shoulder. "Why, you didn't offend me. You just had the courage to say right out what so many people want to know."

The family relaxed with Clay's response.

"Shall we move to the table?" Doña Alejandra said. She sat at one end, while the *don* sat at the other, with Diana and Rafael in the middle, facing each other. "You may sit next to Diana, Clay."

"Thank you, ma'am." He held the chair for Diana, then he took a seat on her left, nearer Doña Alejandra.

A light meal was brought out: tortillas, butter, cheese, and something he didn't see often, sliced bananas, pineapple, and an orange fruit he didn't recognize. He had eaten bananas and pineapple before, on special occasions with his grandparents.

Doña Alejandra saw him looking over the fruit. "Have you ever eaten this type of fruit?" she asked.

"Yes, ma'am, I've eaten banana and pineapple on get-togethers with my grandparents, but never the other."

"Then you are in for a treat," she continued. "This is called a mango. We have it shipped in. It grows in our more tropical regions of Mexico. It is very delicious. I do hope you like it."

Clay tried the mango. It was delicious, sweet with a taste of peach and banana and pine. "Ma'am, that's about the best-tasting fruit I've ever had in my mouth."

The don smiled at his wife. Clay felt that pleasing but empty feeling of family. His was gone, thanks to Pinder's gang.

"Do you have a girl, Señor Clay?" The question from Diana pulled him from his reverie.

"Yes, ma'am. At least, I think I do. I'm not sure how she'll feel when she finds out what I did in San Felipe."

"Is she from this country, Clay?" the doña asked.

"Yes, ma'am. She sure is. Lives over in Brackett."

"Then I imagine that she'll understand. There are no police to protect us in this land. We must, sometimes, be judge, jury, and executioner."

"You are so right, Alejandra," Don Carlos said. "People who grow up in this land understand. I doubt that she will have a problem with the justice that you have meted out. Forgive me for saying so, but if she does, she is not right for this land."

"Thanks," Clay said. He had finished and was anxious to be on his way. These were nice folks, but he had a job to do, and he was burning daylight.

It was as if Don Carlos could read his mind. "We would love to have your company, Clay, but I imagine you are anxious to be on your way."

"Yes, sir. I need to find the trail before dark catches me. I hate to be unsociable, because it's very nice meeting you folks. I really appreciate the meal, but I do need to be moving on."

Don Carlos stood, and with him, the family.

Clay turned to Doña Alejandra. "Thank you, ma'am. I appreciate your kindness, and I hope to see you again."

"It was our pleasure, Clay. Please come back to see us when you can."

Diana took his hand in hers as he was leaving. "*Vaya con Dios* —go with God, Clay."

"Thank you," Clay said. "It's been a real pleasure, ma'am."

They all walked him out to the veranda. The horses were at the watering trough by the corral. Arturo and Juan were sitting in the shade, finishing off some beans and tortillas.

Clay turned to Don Carlos. "Thank you, sir. You've got a beautiful home here, and well protected."

The don laughed and said, "Yes, it is not as necessary as it was twenty years ago, but it still brings me comfort. Take care, Clay. If you need any other help, feel free to ask. Your business in San Felipe helped me a great deal. I think the Pinder Gang might be finished in this country, thanks to you. Good luck."

Clay walked over to Rafael. "Maybe I'll see you sometime. Take good care of your folks."

Clay turned and headed for the horses. He checked Blue's saddle, tightened the cinch, and swung up on his back. Arturo and Juan mounted. Leaving again, Clay thought. Wonder if I'll ever see them again. One thing he noticed, the empty feeling wasn't as bad as it had been.

15

The three men turned north out of the ranch headquarters. Clay noticed cattle around the hacienda, and as far as he could see, in all directions. The farther north they rode, the fewer cattle he saw. After they crossed Mezquitosa Creek, no cattle were in sight.

The countryside was cut with washes and canyons. The bottom of the creeks had a few oaks combined with mesquites. Short grass covered the bottoms, but on the sides and tops of the canyons, creosote bush and tar bush competed with the mesquites. Clay looked across the miles of open country, hidden canyons holding water sometimes and distant peaks reaching for the clouds, and felt the immensity of the land. He loved the wildness of it. The sky had turned a brassy-tinted, faint copper-blue as the afternoon warmed. It wouldn't be too many more days before the afternoon temperatures would be intense.

They crossed another, smaller, *arroyo*. Juan said, in a low tone, "This is *Arroyo El Vivora*. It is smaller than *Mezquitosa*. In the bottom, we will find the tracks of our cattle and the rustlers."

They rode down the side of Vivora into the creek bottom. This was a small creek with grass and standing pockets of water.

Clay could see the tracks of many cattle, too many to have gathered here on their own. He spotted the tracks of a horse moving in and out of the cattle, obviously pushing them to the mouth of the creek.

Clay pulled up and turned to Arturo and Juan. "Thanks for your help, amigos. Reckon I'll take it from here."

Arturo looked at the tracks. "You sure you don't want our help?"

Clay shook his head, then said, "No. I appreciate it, but they'll be less likely to spot one than three. Tell Don Carlos thanks. If I get his cattle, I'll send you word."

"Adios, amigo," Juan said. The two men wheeled their horses back to the south, and rode up and out of the canyon.

Clay waited until they were out of sight. Then he dismounted and studied the horse's tracks. All tracks were different. This horse had worn shoes, with the left front worn down past where it should be replaced. The hooves weren't sinking very deep into the ground, indicating a light horse and rider. He walked on a ways, watching for other horse tracks. Sure enough, he found two others and logged them in his memory.

He led the horses over to one of the creek's water holes. While they drank, he pulled off his boots and put on a pair of moccasins. He tied the boots together and tossed them over the saddle of the buckskin. Clay mounted Blue and, with the buckskin in tow, followed the tracks to the creek mouth, where it ran into the Rio Bravo. He found where they turned the cattle north along the river.

The sun was slipping behind the western cliffs along the Rio Bravo. He needed to find a campsite. He had followed the tracks. The men had kept the cattle to the Mexican side, even when the river swung in close and they had to single file the cattle between the river and the bluffs. Arturo and Juan had sketched him out a simple map and shown him where the rustlers had pushed the cattle across the river just above Buey and Jabonillos Creeks. The two creeks ran into the Rio Bravo basin within a hundred yards of each other. Once past Jabonillos, the river basin opened wide and the river shallowed. The rustlers had found a perfect spot to cross the cattle.

Clay crossed Buey Creek and was just coming into Jabonillos when he spotted a perfect campsite. He rode over to the north side of Jabonillos. There was a small grassy flat about thirty feet above the creek bed. The flat backed up against the steep bank that rose another thirty feet or so. That would protect him from anyone slipping up behind him, and the horses would alert him from the other directions. The flat was high enough above the creek so that he didn't have to worry about a flash flood. Heavy rains could happen miles away and push a surge of water down the creek, drowning everything in its path. He had no desire to get caught in a flash flood.

He unsaddled the horses and put his gear close together. He used one saddle as a pillow and leaned the shotgun against the remaining saddle, within arm's reach. He tossed ropes around the horses' necks, removed the bridles, and led them to water on Jabonillos. After they drank their fill, Clay led them back up to the grassy flat and staked them out so they'd have plenty of room, to feed on the rich grass through the night. He checked his boots. Yep, his money was still there. It had substantially increased since his withdrawal of five hundred from the Brackett bank. If he'd known what was going to happen, he wouldn't have taken out so much.

His canteen and water bags were full. He opened his saddlebags and pulled out some jerky and a bag. Maria had packed several tortillas for him. He took out two and leaned back on his saddle. Even at seventeen, he'd spent many a night alone with only the moon and stars for his light, the ground for his bed. This night wouldn't be much different, except for the knowledge that he might kill or be killed tomorrow.

A half-moon rose, sending its light across the countryside.

From where his bed lay, he could look east, out the mouth of Jabonillos Creek, and see the moon's white reflection on the Rio Bravo. He watched the moon rise higher in the eastern sky, its light casting gray shadows across the river bottom.

When he finished the tortillas and jerky, he chased it with a drink from his canteen, removed his gunbelt, and pulled a six-gun from its holster. He slid down so that his head was resting on his saddle and was sound asleep within seconds.

CLAY AWOKE to the comforting sound of the horses munching on the fresh grass. He lay there for a moment, listening to the sounds around him. Cicadas were crying in the mesquite trees. A mockingbird was going through its repertoire, and grasshoppers were serenading one another.

He cracked one eye open. Daylight was slowly chasing night into the past. He felt rested. His young body recuperated quickly. There was no pain or stiffness from his neck. He moved his head from left to right and opened his mouth wide. Still, no discomfort. *I was mighty lucky. That knife could have ended it, right there on Maverick Creek.*

Clay removed his moccasins and slipped his boots on, moving the money inside around so that it was comfortable in his boots. *Hate carrying so much money around. I get back to a bank, I'll get rid of most of it.* He stood and stretched, his long arms spanning more than six feet.

The horses had stopped eating and were watching him. He walked over to Blue and rubbed his nose and neck. The buckskin sidled over and pushed his head toward Clay. "What's the matter, boy? You want to join in on the scratching?" Clay scratched both horses behind the ears, then dug some oats out of his saddlebags and gave them to the horses. After they had eaten, he led them down the embankment to water. Up Jabonillos Arroya, two whitetail deer raised their heads from the water and stared at him. Sensing no threat, they lowered their heads and continued to drink.

He checked the loads in his six-guns, pulled the Roper out of the scabbard and ensured it was fully loaded and then checked the Winchester Yellow Boy. He worked the action levering the round out of the barrel and another in, picked up the ejected round, examined it, and slipped it back into the loading gate. Pa had taught him that if you take care of your weapons, they'll take care of you. He gave them a light wipe-down and returned the long guns to their scabbards and the six-guns to their holsters. Clay saddled the horses. Today, he would ride the buckskin. He pulled some extra rounds for the Winchester from his saddlebags and hung the shotgun shell bag from the saddle horn. He was ready. While he was rummaging through the saddlebags, he pulled out some breakfast—beef jerky and cold tortillas—then stepped into the saddle.

Chewing on the jerky and tortillas, he guided the buckskin and Blue toward the mouth of Jabonillos Arroyo, where it joined the Rio Bravo. He stopped the horses when he had a view of the river and scanned up and down its length. *Wouldn't do to be surprised by Indians, bandits, or the men he was following.* When he was satisfied it was clear, he rode into the sand of the river. The Rio Bravo was wide at this junction with Jabonillos, probably a hundred yards across, mostly sand, with the shallow river coursing through a narrow part. The width of the water was no more than fifteen or twenty yards. *A great place to cross the cattle, especially at night.* He continued following the rustlers' tracks across the Rio Bravo.

Once back into Texas, the rustlers had turned the herd toward the Devils River country. Rain had washed out their tracks, but, with the skills he had learned from the Tonkawa, he could spot scattered scratches on the rocks. He trailed them for several miles. They were driving the cattle hard, pushing them through

rough country covered with short, light brown grass and rocks. The soft green of the mesquite was joined by the darker green of the shorter creosote bush.

He followed them to a cut that angled down to the Devils River Valley. The morning was already warming up. The heat was rising from the rocky country and distorting distant vision. He followed the cut far enough below the rim to ensure he was not silhouetted.

Clay stopped the horses, removed his hat, and wiped his forehead. He wiped his hatband with his hand and slapped the hat back on his head. "What a sight. Pa was right. This Devils River Valley is like a paradise. Come on, boys, let's get down to that pretty water and get you two a drink." The Devils River's clear, cool water was a welcome sight.

Riding down the side of the canyon, he kept his eyes busy, searching canyons running out from the river valley. The river looked out of place in this West Texas desert. Live oak covered the valley bottom. At this point, the valley looked to be a mile wide, the clear blue of the spring-fed river cutting through the green of the valley. Pecan trees and sycamore joined the live oak, with occasional Mexican white oak. Brightly colored red yucca accented the sides of the valley.

Clay's eyes feasted on the beauty of this island valley. He rode the horses up to the rushing river and sat for a moment in the trees, continuing to keep a watchful eye. Then he rode the horses into the clear, cold water. They immediately lowered their heads and began to drink. After they had finished, he rode them a few yards to grass, stepped from the saddle, and pulled his canteen and water bags from the horses. *Reckon I'd rather have this clear water with me than the silty stuff from the Rio Bravo.* He emptied and refilled the canteen and water bottles, then took a long, soothing drink of the cold water. After drinking, he thrust his head deep into the water and let the coolness wash away the heat and sweat.

The short break reenergized him. As he mounted, a bright orange bird with a black face and wings flew to a nearby pecan, giving a high-pitched call. Clay quickly looked around to make sure that the bird hadn't been spooked. He was alone. He'd never seen a bird of that color. He sat for a moment, enjoying the sight of the strange bird, then went back to trailing the cattle.

The rustlers had stayed in the river valley for several miles, until the river started to narrow. Clay could see a rougher stretch ahead and could hear the sound of a waterfall. The tracks started to veer from the valley and turn up a side canyon.

Clay pulled up under a thicket of oak and pecan. He watched the mouth of the canyon and could make out a thin wisp of smoke climbing in the afternoon breeze. When he felt comfortable that he could not be seen from the canyon, he turned toward the Devils River valley wall. Finding a mesquite thicket with scattered grass, he dismounted, took the bag of shotgun shells and the Roper, changed his boots for his moccasins, and left the horses to graze. He slipped into a shallow draw that led up to the valley wall. After traveling a short distance, he turned and examined where his horses were feeding. There was no sign of them. They were well-hidden in the thicket.

Clay slipped along the draw until he came to the valley wall, about a half-mile from the canyon mouth. He had spotted a deer or sheep trail going up the valley wall. Now, he started moving up the trail. It was steep but occasionally leveled out for a short distance. He was hidden from the valley floor by scattered creosote and juniper. He made it to a switchback in the trail, near the top. Several shallow caves lined the trail.

He eased around the switchback, and came face-to-face with a cougar. Clay had been slipping along, his training from living with the Tonkawa effective, never making a sound. He surprised the cougar as much as it had surprised him.

The tawny cat crouched low to the ground. Clay could see the muscles in the cat's shoulders and legs. He whispered, "Mr.

Cougar, neither of us wants to hurt the other. We're just surprised. Why don't you go on your way and I'll go on mine?"

The cat stayed in its crouch, his long, black-tipped tail swishing slowly from side to side, its yellow eyes focused on Clay. The shotgun was ready, but he didn't want to shoot the cat for two reasons. He had no desire to kill the animal. It was beautiful and deadly and deserved to go on living. But he also didn't want to fire and raise an alarm at the rustlers' camp. "Move along, cat. We both have things to do."

The cougar's tail swished twice more. It turned off the trail and leaped up the side of the canyon, disappearing in the juniper. Clay released a sigh of relief. He hadn't realized how tense he was. He took a moment to stretch. He needed to be limber and ready. After scanning around to be sure he was alone, he continued up the trail. Easing over the crest, he moved far enough from the edge so he couldn't be seen from the valley floor, and started jogging across the flat to the canyon edge, where the rustlers were camped below.

Within fifteen minutes he arrived at the crest of the canyon. He dropped to his belly and crawled to the edge, keeping a mesquite in front of him. He eased up next to the trunk of the mesquite and peered over the side of the canyon.

There they were, three men, relaxed around a campfire. The cattle were farther up the canyon, held in by a crude pole fence. A small stream of water flowed down the canyon and into the Devils River. This was a perfect place to hold cattle. They had grass and water, and no one would ever find them here. He lay there for about an hour, watching the activities of the men. None of them seemed anxious to check on the cattle. From where he was, he couldn't identify the men, but he felt certain that none of them were big enough to be Gideon Pinder. If that was the case, Gideon must have hired more men. But more men or not, Clay wanted him, and he wanted him bad. While he was lying under the mesquite, he mapped out an approach down the canyon wall.

Another little-used trail angled down to the canyon floor. It was steep, but should be no problem. There was plenty of cover for his approach. He slipped back away from the canyon wall and ran to where the trail began. He flipped back the loading gate of the Roper, released the hammer thongs on both Model 3s, and slipped over the edge of the canyon wall.

16

C lay arrived at the juniper at the bottom of the canyon, near the camp. He could smell the campfire and hear the men talking. He lay listening for a moment, contemplating the upcoming action. Now was the time. He would have them dead to rights. He was only about thirty feet from the fire. Clay slowly stood behind the juniper. His footsteps making no sound, he stepped from behind the tree. The men kept talking. They hadn't noticed him. But only two men sat at the fire. He snapped his head around, left, right, no sign of the third man. He was committed now.

Clay thumbed the hammer of the Roper back. The audible, metallic click stopped conversation. "Howdy, boys."

The two men turned to look at him. The one with the beard grinned. "Mighty big shotgun you got there, boy. What took you so long?"

Movement from his left caught his eye, and a half-breed stepped from the brush. He had a Winchester trained on Clay. *How do I get myself in these predicaments? Am I ever going to learn?*

"Breed, you got him covered?" the bearded man asked.

Neither of the men at the fire had drawn a weapon.

"Yes, if he moves, he dies," Breed said.

"Good," Beard said, "drop yore weapons, boy. Or I'll have Breed gut shoot you, then we'll drag you into the fire and see how long you last. Nothin' more fun than watchin' a man roast. Drop yore weapons, now!"

This is going to be close. I won't get out of this without getting shot. But if I surrender, I'm dead. Clay eased the shotgun toward the ground. When his hand came even with his holster, he turned loose of the Roper and grabbed the Model 3, diving to his left. He felt the comforting weight of the six-gun in his right hand. The roar of the Winchester echoed through the canyon. Breed worked the Winchester's action fast, but not fast enough. Clay heard the crack and felt the breeze by his ear, as the bullet passed. *He missed —how could he miss?* He watched his shot blossom red on the Breed's chest.

No time for a second shot. The bearded man had dropped his fresh cup of coffee, the scalding liquid spilling all over his lap. If it hadn't been life or death, it would have been funny. He scrambled to get his gun out, but also to get away from the searing heat. Clay immediately switched the muzzle of the Model 3 to the third man. He was standing, and his gun was coming up.

"Drop it," Clay yelled. He knew he had the man dead to rights. The rustler knew it too and heaved his gun into the brush. Clay swung the muzzle back to the bearded man. He was no worry. He had dropped his gun in the dirt and run to the creek and was splashing cold water on his lower waist and legs.

"Don't shoot, Mister, don't shoot. I'm already ruined. I ain't never gonna be good for nothin'."

Clay turned to the other man and signaled him toward the breed. "Go check on your partner."

The man walked over and looked at him for a moment. "He's dead, Mister. You plugged him right in the chest. Why, I never seen such shootin'. Who ever heard of a man drawing with a rifle dead on him? I never, I just never."

Clay motioned him back to the fire. "Where's Gideon Pinder?"

"He's gone to San Felipe," the man replied.

The bearded man was sitting in the creek, moaning.

"Any more of you?"

"No, sir. We're it. I figgered this would be an easy job. Stealing a few cows from a Mex. Never figgered it would come to any shootin'. Why, it ain't even rustlin' if you're stealing from a Mex over the border."

"What's your names?" Clay asked.

"Well, sir, I'm Handy Taylor. The feller sittin' in the creek with his crotch on fire is Zeke Martin. The dead breed is half-Comanche and half-Mex. He goes by the name of Tomas. Don't know any other name for him."

"Zeke, why did Gideon Pinder go into town?"

Zeke had quit moaning, but was still sitting in the creek. "He got word that Harly had been killed. He was some riled up. Reckon he sets a lot of store by his brothers. Heard them talking —seems he took care of them since they was little tykes. His pa was gone drinking, when he weren't working, and his ma was cattin' around. Don't get me wrong, Mister. Gideon's bad clean through, but he shore takes care of his brothers. He was madder'n a wet hen when he heard. Said he was gonna rip the guts out of the so and so that did it. So, who are you?"

"Clay Barlow, Bill Barlow's son."

Clay could see Zeke's eyes grow large with recognition, and his face turned white as a new moon. "Yeah, you heard right, Zeke. I'm Clay Barlow. You're one of the men I'm after. Seems you like to burn people."

"That weren't my idea, Mr. Barlow. No, siree, it weren't me at all."

"Not what I heard. In fact, I heard you like to burn people. You even mentioned gut shooting and burning me, or did I misunderstand you?"

"I was only kidding. I'd never do such a thing."

"You like pecans, Zeke?"

The man looked at Clay. It was obvious he couldn't figure out the boy-man standing in front of him. "Uh . . . yeah. I like pecans."

"Do you like oaks?"

"Mister, I ain't likin' what you seem to have on your mind. Ain't no reason to start talking hanging. I ain't done nothing to deserve such treatment. These are Mex cows. That ain't rustling." Sweat was coursing down the man's white face. "Why, I could even be a help to ya, finding Gideon and his brother."

"Oh, I think you're going to be a big help," Clay said. "Get out of the creek and come over here by the fire so I can keep an eye on you."

"I'm burnt bad. Can I jest sit here for a while?"

"Tell you what I'll do, Zeke. You can sit in that water, and I'll see if I can hit you, from here, with one of these .44s. Your choice." Clay turned the muzzle of his six-gun toward Zeke, and the man scrambled out of the creek.

"Now come over here, take your boots and shirt off, and lay down by the fire, facedown." Clay glanced at Handy. "Move over by him and do the same."

Zeke waddled back to the fire, pulled off his boots and then his shirt. Handy followed suit.

"Toss the boots over here."

Both men tossed their boots to Clay and lay face down on the dirt. He checked the boots for weapons and found none. He moved to the Roper, picked it up, and checked each man. Neither of the men had any hidden weapons.

"Okay, you two, get dressed." Clay watched the two men closely as they pulled their boots on. He turned slightly to Handy, keeping Zeke in view. "What's your story?"

"I tied up with these folks in San Felipe," Handy said. "Thought I might make some travelin' money. Wasn't long before I figured I joined up with some mighty bad *hombres*. Didn't figger they would take kindly with me just riding away. I've been biding my time, waiting for a chance to lay some dust behind me."

"Mister, you have no idea how bad this bunch is," Clay said. "They rode into my pa's ranch, killed him and my ma and our good friend, Slim. This piece of dirt"—Clay indicated Zeke with the muzzle of his revolver—"burned my pa, after they had shot and hanged him. That's the kind of animals you've been riding with."

"Figured pretty close, from hearing them talk. That's why I've been looking for a chance to ride my cayuse out of this country."

Clay thought for a minute. "You ever done any rustling?"

"Well, sir," Handy said, "can't say I haven't slung a wandering loop or two. But nothing major, and that's the gospel truth."

"Ever killed a man?"

"Only for good reason, and they were facing me."

"You wanted anywhere?"

Handy rubbed his chin. "Reckon I don't want to get caught in Mexico, but that's it."

"Okay, here's my deal: You help me drive these cattle to San Felipe, and you're free to go. I'll keep your guns until we get there."

Clay could read relief all over Handy's face. "I'll owe you big, Mister. I'll be glad to help with the cattle, but there's only two of us. We got about five hundred head here. That's quite a few for two men, in this country."

"You're forgetting Zeke. I'd bet he would be glad to help, wouldn't you, Zeke?"

"Yes, sir. I'd be pleased to. I just don't know if I can sit a saddle." Zeke had started to squirm from the pain. It was clear that the heat from the fire was making it more intense.

"I'll tell you what, Zeke, I'll give you another choice. You can trail these cows to San Felipe, or we can ride down to the Devils and find a nice strong pecan tree. Which suits you best?"

"Reckon I'd be glad to help. What's going to happen to me when we get to San Felipe?"

"Why, Zeke, you're going to jail, and then I imagine you'll hang. But that gives you a little longer to live. Now get over there and get your dead partner tied on your horse. You'll ride with him. Handy, pick up those guns and bring them over to me."

The men's horses were saddled, tied out nearby to feed. Handy picked up the guns and laid them at Clay's feet. He got Tomas's horse and his own and led them over near Clay.

Zeke had led his horse to Tomas and hefted the man behind his saddle, tying him in place. Clay pulled a piggin' string off Tomas's saddle, tied all of the guns together, and cinched them up tight across the saddle, behind the horn. He picked up his shotgun and swung up. The other men followed, with Zeke complaining about his burns. Clay wasn't worried about Zeke taking off, not with Tomas tied across his saddle and the burns he had to deal with. Handy seemed like a basically honest cowboy who had managed to get mixed up with the wrong crowd. He was lucky, Clay thought, to be getting out of this situation. He would have ended up at the end of a rope or shot in the back by any one of the Pinder Gang.

The men pushed the cattle out of the canyon and turned them south. An old longhorn cow took the lead and stepped out with a quick step, following Handy. Clay kept a lookout for the mesquite thicket, where Blue and the buckskin were tied. He spotted it soon after they left the canyon and rode up to them. Both horses had been watching the herd. He dismounted from Tomas's horse, untied the guns from the saddle horn and tied them to the buckskin. He stepped into the saddle on the buckskin and slid the Roper back into the scabbard. Clay cleared the mesquites and checked Zeke and Handy. They were both still in position. They probably hadn't even noticed him leave the herd. With Blue and the other horse in tow, he picked up his drag position. No one liked riding drag, with all the dust, but it kept him in a position to watch the other two men.

At the pace the cattle were moving, if they drove straight through, they should push into San Felipe in time for breakfast. He figured they'd pause about midnight and let the stock feed for a while. The cattle were staying fairly bunched together. Maybe they could smell the cougar he had run into earlier.

Clay pulled out of the drag and galloped up to Handy. "Anybody else go with Gideon into San Felipe?"

At a glance, Handy took in the buckskin and Blue. "Yep, he took Quint in with him. Now that's the one you gotta watch. He's fast with a gun and mean as a snake. He's a thinker."

"So there's only two of them?"

"Reckon so. Zeke was telling you straight. Gideon was boilin' mad. He almost killed the breed, but Quint stopped him. The breed was in town when you shot Birch and Shorty. Way he told it, he'd of killed you, but you had folks around you. Way we all figured it, he saved his own skin and dusted it out of town. Been me, reckon I'd probably done the same thing."

Clay mulled over what Handy had told him. Gideon and Quint didn't know him. If he could get the drop on them, he could turn them over to the law and wouldn't have to kill anyone else. He'd rather they be tried and hanged. They'd killed his folks, and they deserved dying. He was just tired of killing. A month ago, he was just a happy-go-lucky kid living the life he loved. Now, he had already killed five men. It sure wasn't anything he was proud of, nor a number he wanted to add to.

"When we get to San Felipe, I'd like to keep the cattle in the river bottom. They'll have grass and water. Don't reckon they'll be inclined to stray far. If we can leave them far enough from town, the Pinders won't even know I'm anywhere around. When we leave the cattle, you're free to go. Just don't alert the Pinders."

"Mister, I've got jerky in my saddlebags and Devils River water in my canteen. When you say go, I'm out of here. I'm gonna cut for San Antone and parts unknown. You don't have to worry about me causing no problems."

"Good. Anything else I need to know about the Pinders?"

"Both right-handed. Quint's sly. You gotta watch him. Gideon, he's just big. Tries to run over everybody. But don't let his size fool you. He's fast with that gun. Probably ain't as fast as you, but fast."

"Thanks," Clay said. "We're going to keep the cattle moving. Stop 'em around midnight and let them feed and rest for a couple of hours. Then we'll push on through to town." Clay wheeled the horses around and rode over to Zeke.

"Mister," Zeke said, "I'm hurtin' mighty bad. These burns make it some terrible to sit in a saddle. We plannin' on stopping soon?"

"People call you Mad Dog, don't they?"

"I don't like that name."

Clay turned in the saddle and stared at Zeke through the gathering darkness. "I don't much care what you like or don't like. I asked you a question."

"Yeah, I've been called that."

"Listen close, Mad Dog. You've got one chance to survive this drive. Do what I tell you. Your job now is to keep these cattle moving to San Felipe. You try to run, I'll catch you. I spent half my growing years with a Tonkawa tribe. They taught me things you don't even want to know. I promise you, when I catch you, I'll hang you. You killed my folks and you burned my pa. I'll make sure your neck doesn't break, and while you're gasping for breath, I'll follow your example and set you on fire. Do you understand me?"

The man stared straight ahead. Clay could smell the fear. "I asked if you understand me."

Zeke turned his head slowly, his shoulders slumped, and he gazed at Clay with a blank stare. "Yeah, I understand."

"What are you going to do?"

"I'm gonna drive these cattle to San Felipe?"

Clay's words were like lashes, cutting through to the soul of Zeke. "Are you going to try to run, when it gets dark?"

"No, sir, Mr. Barlow, I'm sure not."

With Zeke's last words, Clay wheeled the horses around and galloped back to the drag. He had to get away from Zeke. He was afraid if he rode next to him a moment longer, he'd kill him. Before his life changed, he had never felt this pent-up rage. It scared him. It wasn't like anger. When he had been angry before, he was hot and wild. This was different. He felt cold, calculating. He knew what he was capable of, and he didn't like himself. He wanted this feeling to go away and never inhabit his mind and body again.

Clay took a deep breath. He picked up his canteen and let the cool Devils River water run down his throat. It was his first drink since he left the horses, and it was soothing, calming. He took another slow drink of the cool water and then another deep breath. He felt the rage slowly subsiding.

Pa must have known it was deep within me, because he had warned me. "Son," Pa had said, "you come from a long line of fighting Barlows, men who had to kill for their families' or others' survival. Several have been known for bloodthirsty ways. Most were within the law, some not. I'm sorry to say, I have it, and I fear it has been passed on to you. When you feel it, you'll know it. I want you to remember this conversation when it happens, and do your best to control it."

Clay had looked up at his pa and told him he'd never felt anything like that. Now he knew. He also knew that Zeke had no idea how close he had come to dying. Clay forced himself to think of something pleasant. Lynn. *Wonder what she's doing now? Sitting down to supper with her folks? I sure liked her ma, a fine lady. Actually, her pa wasn't bad once I got to know him.* His mind wandered through the days at Brackett and his time with Lynn. It had been a good time. He'd never felt that close to anyone, not even his folks. *But we're awful young. She still has school ahead. Like*

Pa always said, there's a big life out there waiting for you. He continued to think about Lynn and the Rangers, and wondered if she would be in his future.

The night passed quickly. Handy led the cattle out of the Devils River Valley and across the rough country to San Felipe. They had let the cattle rest and graze for a couple of hours around midnight. A few of the cattle had bedded down, and it took some effort to get them up and moving again. But the old longhorn cow started off behind Handy, and the others, though complaining, followed her.

Handy led them into the Rio Bravo river bottom about three miles north and west of San Felipe. It wasn't hard to do, since the cattle had smelled the water and headed for it. The men pulled up in the river bottom and let the cattle scatter along the river. When the cattle had satisfied their thirst, they fed for a short time and bedded down near the river.

Clay followed Zeke up to where Handy was waiting. The rising sun glistened off the polished tips of the cattle's horns.

Clay untied the guns from his saddle horn and handed them to Handy. "Take your guns. You can take a couple extra if you like." Clay had noticed that all the handguns were black powder. "You're welcome to check Zeke's and Tomas's saddlebags for lead and powder, and anything thing else you have a need for."

"Wait, that's my—"

"Shut up, Zeke. Where you're going, you won't be needing any of it. You keep talking and I'll make you walk into town," Clay said.

Handy dismounted and walked over to Tomas's horse. He went through the saddlebags and pulled out some lead and powder. Next, he walked over to Zeke's saddlebags.

Zeke turned to Handy. "Don't you touch—"

Clay had the buckskin standing next to Zeke. He pulled his boot out of the stirrup, and, in one easy motion, his long leg shot out and caught Zeke in the side. Zeke rolled out of the saddle and hit the ground like a sack of oats. The wind gushed out of him like a bellows emptying. Then he started groaning and holding his lower belly and crotch.

"I told you to shut up," Clay said.

"I'm dying here. My skin feels like it's on fire."

"Good. Now you have a small idea of how your victims felt."

The injured man got up, groaning, and started to climb back on his horse.

Clay could feel the rage starting to rise against this man who had caused so much pain. "Nope, you get to walk into town. I think you've earned it."

"I cain't walk. I cain't hardly move. I'm dying here."

"In that case, I imagine you won't make it into town. That'll be a shame. Go ahead, Handy, see what he's got stashed."

Zeke leaned against his horse and watched as Handy went through his saddlebags.

"Well, I'll be," Handy said, "you been holdin' out on us, Zeke?" Handy pulled out three gold double eagles. He started to toss them over to Clay.

"You keep them. Consider it pay for helping me with these cattle."

"Mister, that's two months' pay."

"No matter, you take them. Just stay out of trouble."

Handy pulled some lead, powder, and caps from Zeke's saddlebags and closed them up. He walked around Zeke and mounted his horse. Zeke was still leaning against his horse.

Clay had gotten control of himself. He looked at Zeke. The man looked pathetic. He was leaning against his horse and moaning. Clay thought of his ma's kind heart and all the things she had done for other folks. "Okay, Zeke, mount up. This is your lucky day. But if you give me another reason, I promise you, you'll be walking."

Clay hadn't finished talking before Zeke was back in the

saddle. The man was pale and covered with sweat. *He must have burned himself mighty bad.*

"Handy, you're free to go. Hope you leave the bad side of the law alone."

Handy leaned over and stuck out his hand to Clay. Clay took the hand in his big grip and shook it.

"All you've got's my word," Handy said, "but I plan on going straight from here on. I got a lot luckier yesterday than I deserve. You could have said nothing and just plugged me. I owe you. Hope you have good luck with the Pinders. They're double bad. Adios."

The man swung his horse around and pointed it east, so that he would ride around San Felipe, and galloped into the morning sun.

"By the way, Zeke, what did Pinder do with the horses you took from our ranch?"

"Sold 'em. Ran into a Mex in San Felipe. Last I saw of 'em they were crossing the river."

"Well then, you won't mind me selling yours, will you?" Clay checked his weapons one last time. He loved this country. The sun was stalking the morning sky. It was going to be a hot day in San Felipe. He looked over at Zeke. "Lead the way."

17

C lay and Zeke rode into San Felipe del Rio as the sun climbed midway in the eastern sky. Clay had slipped the hammer thongs from his revolvers and carried the Roper across his saddle. The town was awake and bustling with activity. It appeared the residents wanted to get their shopping done before the blistering afternoon heat set in. It looked like Clay had the attention of everyone in town. The people followed him to the marshal's office. The crowd grew as they neared the office.

They pulled up in front of the hitching rail. Clay motioned Zeke to get down. Zeke eased out of the saddle, his right foot reaching for the ground. He was stiff and slightly stooped as he walked toward the door. Clay stepped down and looked at the faces in the crowd. At least twenty people surrounded the horses. He recognized a friendly face. "Howdy, Rud."

"How you doing, Son? Looks like you been mighty busy. Nasty lookin' feller you got there. He go by the name Mad Dog?"

"Yep, he does. Can you get word to *Don* Carlos that his cattle are in the river bottom, about three miles up the river?"

"Reckon I can. You all right?"

"I will be, as soon as I get rid of this." He indicated Zeke with the muzzle of the shotgun. "Why don't you join us inside?"

"Be glad to," Rud said.

The three men entered the office with Zeke in the lead.

"Zeke, what are you—"

The marshal shut up when he saw Clay with the shotgun muzzle trained on Zeke.

"What's going on here?" the marshal said.

"Marshal, this is Mad Dog Martin. He's running with the Pinder Gang. There's another man hanging off Zeke's horse. His name is Tomas. He tried to shoot me and failed."

The marshal looked at Clay, then at Zeke and back to Clay. "You're racking up quite a tally, Barlow. What's this man done?"

Clay pulled out his dead-or-alive wanted poster on Mad Dog and passed it over to the marshal. "I'm turning him over to you. I'll be in town at least until tomorrow. I expect you want to contact the sheriff who posted that reward and let him know you have Zeke in your jail. I'd also like payment on him by tomorrow. There's also two more horses, guns, and saddles out front. I'd like payment on them tomorrow. To make it easy, I'll take the same amount as before, one hundred and fifty dollars. By the way, Marshal, where's Milo?"

"The sheriff from Uvalde sent a deputy over, picked him up last night. Said he'd hold him as a favor till the Tarrant County Sheriff can pick him up."

"Thanks, Marshal. I'll be seeing Major Jones before long and I'll tell him how you helped me. This man needs to be locked up, and he needs a doctor."

The marshal looked back at Zeke, then turned to Clay and asked, "Did you shoot him?"

Clay laughed and said, "No, seems he got in such a big hurry to get his gun out, he spilled boiling coffee all over himself."

Rud burst out laughing. When he had calmed down, he said,

"Never heard of a man losing a gunfight to a cup of coffee. That's mighty big, mighty big."

"Marshal, he's right," Zeke said. "I need a doctor, bad. I'm in a lotta pain."

The marshal walked to the door. He looked through the crowd, then yelled to no one in particular, "Tell the doctor to get down here, *pronto*. Got a hurt man who needs lookin' after."

"Marshal," Clay asked the man as he returned to his desk, "have you seen the Pinders in town?"

"Yeah, came into town yesterday, probably stayed the night. It'd be my guess they're still here. They were plenty riled when they heard that Harly was kilt. I imagine they'll be lookin' for ya."

Rud shook his head. Clay couldn't hide his disgust. "Didn't you arrest them? You know they killed my folks."

The marshal fidgeted in his chair. "Just had your word. Anyway, they ain't wanted for nothin' in this town. This town's as far as my jurisdiction goes."

Clay walked to the window and looked out. The people were dispersing from around the horses and the dead body. Tomas was probably starting to get a little ripe, with the hot sun beaming down on him. Clay could see a man in a suit, carrying a little black bag, hurrying toward the marshal's office, probably the doc. "Marshal, you have a duty to the citizens of this town to keep them safe. Allowing the Pinders the freedom to walk around sure doesn't fulfill your duty. Have my money ready tomorrow, and don't lose my prisoner. By the way, the body across the horse is starting to get pretty ripe."

Clay wheeled and yanked the door open. The doctor came stumbling into the room, his hand still grasping the outside doorknob. "Sorry, Doc," Clay said. "Didn't realize you were that close." Clay marched out of the office before the doc could say anything. Rud followed.

"What's your plan, Clay?" Rud said.

"My first plan is to take care of these horses, and then get some food in my belly. Then, I reckon I'll go looking for the Pinders."

The two men walked to the livery with Blue and the buckskin in tow. Clay stripped the gear from the buckskin while Rud took care of Blue. They gave the horses a good rubdown and turned them loose into the corral. Both of the horses rolled in the dirt and then headed for the water trough. Clay forked some hay into the feed trough for later, when hunger slipped up on them.

"I've got a boy who works for me around here. I'll send him out to let *Don* Carlos know about his cattle. I imagine you've made a good friend of the *don*. He'll be tickled pink to get those cattle back."

"He treated me right," Clay said. "There was no sense leaving those cattle up the Devils River. *Don* Carlos might have had a hard time getting them across the border, considering the hard feelings around here for Mexicans."

"Reckon you're right, Son." Rud's eyes twinkled when he said, "He's got himself a mighty pretty daughter, don't he?"

"Yes, sir, he certainly has. She'll make some man a fine wife. But it won't be me. You mind stashing my gear in your office, again?"

"I'll take care of it," Rud said. "Those Mexican gals are mighty pretty. Say hi to Maria for me."

Clay picked up his shotgun and headed for Maria's.

THE BREAKFAST RELAXED HIM. He took a few minutes to check and clean his revolvers and shotgun. The Roper was in his left hand, and the two six-guns were loose in their holsters. He looked up the dusty San Felipe street. It wasn't much of a town, as towns go. *I don't know if this town'll make it.* Many border towns popped up, lasted for a few years, and then disappeared.

Clay walked over to the livery. Rud was out front in his chair, leaning back against the barn's front wall, with his rifle across his lap.

"Have a good breakfast?" Rud asked from under his hat. "You might need it. I saw the Pinders, both Gideon and Quint, go into the general store."

"I hear Gideon is fast," Clay said.

"What I've heard to. Supposed to be really fast for a man his size. I imagine he must weigh close to two fifty. He's drifted off to fat quite a bit, but there's still some solid muscle under that fat. So, don't let him fool you. He's a tough man."

Clay considered what Rud had said. "You know anything about Quint?"

"Not much. It's my understanding he's pretty quick with a gun."

Clay looked up the street again. Midday San Felipe was quiet. Most people were trying to find a cool place to escape the heat.

Was this where his short life played out? He'd been lucky, so far. Lucky the knife hadn't cut anything major. Lucky the bartender had missed. Lucky he had spotted Milo. Lucky Tomas had missed. He could feel the noonday sun beating down on him. Sweat was running down his back. *Is it from fear, or am I just hot?* Clay thought that one over for a moment. He had to admit he was afraid, not terrified, but afraid. What had Pa always said, "Nothing wrong with being afraid, as long as you keep on going." He'd also told him that fear subsides when the cause of the fear is engaged. *Well, I reckon it's about to get pretty engaging.*

He checked the Model 3s again. They were loose in their holsters. He decided to leave the shotgun at the livery. He felt as ready as he would ever get. He wiped the sweat from his hands, rubbing them on his trousers.

Thoughts of his ma, lying on the bed covered with her own blood, entered his mind. Then the picture of his pa hanging from the big old oak, his body burned and the bullet hole through his head, leaped to his mind. Clay could feel the rage pushing the fear away. He had chased these men who had done such awful things to his folks. Now, he had an opportunity to bring them to justice. His mind was cool in the hot sun. Now was the time.

"I'll be joining you," Rud said.

"No, I reckon not. This is my fight. I aim to finish it."

The old man nodded. "I surely understand your feelings. I'll just meander up the boardwalk and make sure your back is clear."

"Much obliged, Rud." Clay handed him the Roper. "Mind putting it with my gear?"

Clay turned and started up the street.

"Clay?" Rud said. "I'm sure they're expectin' you. I saw the marshal scurry up the street, shortly after you went into Maria's."

"Thanks, Rud."

Clay continued walking. It was a good day in Texas for justice. *I made a promise to you, Ma. I aim to keep it.* He passed the marshal's office. He caught movement through the window. *If that's a problem, I'll have to leave it to Rud.* He continued his walk. He glanced to each side of the street. He could see faces peering through the windows. A lady had rushed out, holding her skirt up to keep from tripping, and dragged her eight-year-old son out of the street. Another man had walked out of the general store, saw Clay, and trotted to the bank, closing the door behind him.

Clay had almost reached the general store when two men walked out. They had to be the Pinders. They looked like brothers, except one was almost a third again as big as the other. The smaller was Quint, and the huge man was Gideon. Clay stopped, facing them.

Quint stepped off the boardwalk and started moving into the street.

"That's far enough," Clay said.

Quint stopped. "You looking for us, boy?"

"Not any longer."

"What do you want with us?"

Gideon had said nothing. He stood, a giant wearing a black suit with black hat, black vest, and black boots.

"You know what I want. You shot, hanged, and burned my pa, and shot Slim to pieces." Clay looked into the soulless eyes of Gideon Pinder. "And you attacked my ma. Reckon there must be a special place in Hell for a monster like you."

Gideon swelled up like a huge toad. "And he executed the justice of the Lord, Deuteronomy 33:2—I am the sword of justice, boy. You must be prepared to meet your Maker, for today, you shall surely die."

"As much as I would like to kill you both, I'll make you one offer," Clay said. The rage had turned him cold. All he could think about was seeing the two men before him dead in the street. But he could still hear his pa telling him to control the rage or it would take him over. "You two drop your guns, and you'll get a fair trial and a fair hanging."

"Keep thy tongue from evil; do good and seek peace, Psalms 34:13."

"Mister, if you don't drop your guns, the next scripture that comes out of your filthy mouth, I'm gonna send you straight to Hell." Clay had been watching both men.

Clay saw it. Quint's eyes contracted just a fraction before his hand started for his gun. Clay's hand immediately started moving.

When Quint began his draw, Gideon cried out, "Vengeance is mine!" and his hand flashed down to his revolver.

Clay took it all in. He felt like he was one of the onlookers watching from behind the windows. Quint was in a crouch, turned slightly sideways. His dark green vest was unbuttoned and hanging open, exposing the third button on his red shirt. Clay could see Quint's revolver clearly. It had the round barrel of a Colt New Model Army. He knew the caliber, forty-four. He watched the barrel clear the holster, but it would be too late for Quint. He saw, like Hayes, that the man realized he was too slow. Clay could see the fear in his eyes, but determination also. Clay squeezed the trigger when he sensed the barrel was correctly aligned. The first bullet hit a little high, between the second and third button. The bullet that followed drove the third button into Quint's body. Quint was backpedaling, but still trying to level the Colt. Clay could see Quint's eyes start to glaze over as the third bullet struck between the first two. Quint's hand went slack. The Colt fell to the ground, and the man, dead before he hit, followed the Colt.

But all this time, which seemed so long to Clay, was only fractions of a second. He had also followed Gideon's actions. The big man's face was red with anger. Like Handy had told him, for a big man, Gideon was fast. He too was shooting a Colt New Army, and he was just leveling it when Clay's first bullet drove into the middle of his shirt. He didn't budge. Clay eared back the hammer and squeezed the trigger again, then dove to the ground, rolling to his left. The second bullet followed the first into the same hole, as Gideon fired his first shot. Still the man stood like a statue, following Clay with the muzzle of the Colt. Clay saw the smoke from Gideon's Colt. Because he had dove to the ground, Gideon missed.

In his dive, Clay had holstered his empty Model 3 and drew the second one from his crossdraw holster. He was a little slower with this draw. *I should have been practicing with the left-handed holster like JT said.*

Gideon got off his second shot.

Clay felt the slam of the bullet, but now he also felt the comforting weight of the revolver in his hand, and his instinct took over. He squeezed the trigger, once, twice, and watched both shots strike within an inch of each other.

Pinder's legs could no longer hold him up. His knees collapsed and he knelt on the boardwalk. He tried to lift his Colt but couldn't bring it up. The weapon dropped from his hand, and he watched Clay stand. With his fading strength, he motioned Clay over to him.

Cautiously, Clay moved up next to the mountain of a man. When he was sure Pinder had no weapon, he dropped down next to him. *How can this man still be alive?*

Pinder reached for his collar and pulled him close. A grimace of pain crossed his face, only to be replaced by an evil grin. "You got us, kid. If I'd known you were following us, you'd have been dead a long time ago."

Clay still felt the rage. "If takes you to Hell, Pinder. Go quote scriptures to the Devil. This ends it!"

Pinder coughed.

Blood spattered on Clay's vest.

"Wrong, kid. There's one more." Pinder was racked with a spasm. Blood now gushed from the holes in his body and his mouth.

Clay grabbed the big man by his lapels, desperate to know. "Who?"

The light started fading from the black eyes. Pinder summoned his last strength and whispered, "He paid us."

Clay shook the big man. "Tell me, tell me."

Gideon Pinder gave one last gasp. He relaxed in Clay's grasp, his face now frozen in mortal terror as if he had seen into the gates of hell itself.

Clay stood and looked around. No other threats were standing. Two bloody men lay dead in the street of San Felipe. It was his doing. Without thinking, he snapped the Model 3 open. The tinkle of metallic cartridges hitting the boardwalk could be heard like bells in the stillness of the morning. The sound reminded him of the bell in the Brackett General Store, and Lynn, when he first saw her. *Funny I would think of her now.* Pulling cartridges from his gunbelt, he dropped them into the revolver, holstered it, and reloaded the other.

People were emerging from the stores and offices, slowly

gathering around the dead men. Clay felt a hand on his shoulder and turned to look into the old eyes of Rud.

"Relax, Son. It's over. I need to get you to Maria's. You've been shot."

Clay slid the other revolver into its holster and looked down at his right side. He remembered now. Gideon Pinder had been able to get a shot into him. Blood was all over his side and had run down his leg. He raised his eyes from his waist to Rud. "Reckon I've gone and ruined a good shirt and pair of trousers. At least it'll wash off my boots, if I get to it quick."

Clay allowed Rud to take him by the arm. He was starting to feel a little dizzy. They turned together and walked past the marshal's office and the stable, toward Maria's.

"I've got some clean clothes in my panniers, Rud."

"Don't you worry about them clothes, Son. I'll take care of 'em."

Clay looked down the road. *Why, there's the don, Arturo, Juan, and Diana galloping toward me.* He lifted his leg to take the first step onto Maria's porch. But his leg didn't lift. He looked down at it, willing it to move, but it wouldn't. Clay looked over to Rud. Rud was standing there holding his arm. Why was he holding his arm? He felt himself falling into a soft, clean bed. A bed would feel so good. Clay collapsed on the porch.

18

H e opened his eyes. His eyelids felt like they weighed as much as a young calf. Finally, one came open, then the other. He looked around the room. He was in a soft, clean bed. It felt good to lie here, the sun streaming in through the open window, the clean smell of sheets. A light breeze chased the sunlight into the room. A quail called to its brood, and chickens clucked and scratched just outside the window. He could hear a wagon and team moving up the road. *Must be going to the general store. Wait a minute, what am I doing in bed? It's daylight.* He threw back the sheet and started to swing his legs over the side of the bed, but a sharp, intense pain stabbed him in his right side. He relaxed back onto the bed and looked down at himself. A clean, white bandage was wrapped around his waist, and that was the only covering he had on his body. He yanked the sheet back up to cover himself and looked for his clothes. Fresh, clean clothes were laid out on the back of the chair, across the room.

The door opened and Rud walked in. "Well, looky here. Look who's returned to the land of the living. Good to see you, Clay, even though you're still looking a mite peaked. Boy, you sure do fill up a bed."

Clay looked down and could see his feet and ankles sticking out past the sheet. "What am I doing here?"

"I'll tell you what you're doing here, you collapsed yoreself right on Maria's porch. It's a good thing Arturo and Juan had just ridden up. They helped us carry you in here. Son, you may not have your full growth, but you're way too heavy for me and Maria."

"Thirsty," Clay said.

"Maria, bring some water in here for the boy," Rud yelled.

Moments later, Maria came swishing into the room with a pitcher of water and a glass. She poured the glass full, set the pitcher down on the side table next to the bed, and sat on the edge of the bed. Clay slid farther away from her, the sudden movement causing the stabbing pain in his side. "Maria. I don't have any clothes on. Who took my clothes off?"

Maria giggled and said, "Señor Clay, I was married with three sons. You show me nothing new." She leaned forward with the glass to help him drink.

"I can do it," Clay said, and took the glass. The water was cool spring water, and it felt good going down. He emptied the glass. "More."

"You are thirsty, that is good," she said, and poured him another glass.

After he finished, he gave her a sheepish grin. "Thanks. I'm not used to being undressed by a woman." He turned to Rud to change the subject. "How long have I been here?"

"Son, you were hit pretty bad. The doctor didn't know if the bleeding was going to stop. You messed up a pile of Maria's sheets, what with the blood all over them."

Clay turned to Maria. "Sorry."

"It is nothing, Señor Clay. I washed them quickly, and all the blood came out."

"I'll be glad to pay for any damages."

"Do not worry, Señor. I am only glad you are awake. We were very worried."

"As I was saying," Rud said, "you bled for quite a while. It was touch and go. Diana stayed for a couple of days, until her pa made her go home."

Clay had a horrible thought. "Did she see me like this?"

Maria laughed again. "No, Señor Clay. She sat with you, but you were covered, all the time."

"If I could finish my story," Rud said. "Maria finally chased the doctor away and put some stuff on your wounds that stopped the bleeding. You talk about stink. It was a good thing you was asleep, or you wouldn't of let her put it on you. But it worked."

"Thanks, Maria. Sounds like I owe you my life."

"You have a strong soul, Señor. I also believe you were looked after." Maria stopped, looked toward the ceiling, and made the sign of the cross. "Any other person bleeding like that would have died. I don't know how you managed to walk here from the shooting. It is truly a miracle you are alive."

Clay felt drowsiness coming over him. "Reckon I might need to sleep." The last thing he remembered was Maria's brown hand snatching the glass from him.

It was dark when he opened his eyes again. The breeze was cool through the window. The house was quiet, but night sounds slipped into his bedroom. Two coyotes were serenading the hills. He could hear an armadillo snuffling along outside the window, looking for ants and grubs. Placing his hands on the bed, he pushed himself into a sitting position. He felt better. The pain in his side had subsided. It was still there, but now an ache, not stabbing. It felt good to be alive. Clay took a deep breath, wincing only slightly from the pain, and stretched his long arms. He thought of the violence that had happened since he left the homeplace.

The revelation from Gideon disturbed him. Who could it have been who wanted his family dead? Mr. Hewitt came to mind, but he dismissed him quickly. Even though the man had offered to buy the ranch, the families were too close, and Hewitt was a good man. So, who then? He'd have to think on that. He sat in the bed for a few minutes longer, until sleep overcame him. He eased back under the sheets and drifted off.

CLAY WOKE with the rooster crowing and dawn breaking—time for him to get moving. He could hear Maria rustling in the kitchen, and hunger slammed into him. Maria had moved the chair with his clothes closer. He swung his long legs out of bed and stood. He felt fine. A little ache in his side, but not bad. Clay got dressed and started to slip his boots on. All of his money was still in his boots. He pulled them on, tucking his trousers into his socks first. Walking from his room, he found Maria in the kitchen.

"Morning, Maria."

She jumped and turned to him, a big smile lighting her face. "Good morning, Señor Clay. You look good. How do you feel?"

"Like I could eat every piece of food you have in this kitchen."

Maria laughed. "That can be arranged, Señor."

"Maria, since you've seen more of me than I'd like, don't you think it's about time you dropped the Señor?"

Her laughter rang throughout the house. "Si, Clay, you could be right. Now, go sit down and I'll get some eggs whipped up. Would five do for a start?"

"Sounds like a perfect start," Clay said, as he seated himself at the big dining room table.

Maria brought eggs and beans with hot tortillas into the dining room and set them before Clay.

"You have any other guests, Maria?"

"No, Clay, I do not."

"Good, would you mind joining me and telling me what's happened and how long I've been out?"

Maria sat across from Clay, picked up a tortilla, and smeared it with fresh butter. Half of it disappeared into her mouth. She chewed for a moment, and, talking around the tortilla, said, "You have been asleep for five days. When you awoke the first time, you had been sleeping for four days. I am glad to see you up."

"I seem to remember Don Carlos riding up just before I passed out."

"Si, he did. Arturo, Juan, and the little Diana were with him. They helped get you into the bedroom."

Clay looked up from the disappearing eggs on his plate. "They didn't see me undressed?"

Maria laughed again and said, "No, Clay, only me and the doctor. You can rest easy."

Clay grinned at her and said, "Just wonderin'."

"Si, Don Carlos and the little Diana were very worried about you. They had to drive the cattle back to the ranch, but Diana talked her father into letting her stay for two days. She stayed with you all the time. But then she had to leave. When you awoke the first time, Rud rode out and told them. He said they were very happy."

"Good, they're nice folks."

"The don said that he owes you very much, and that you are always welcome at El Paraiso. He also gave me money to take care of your stay, much more than I need."

Clay started to object. Pa had taught him to pay his way.

Maria held up her hand. "No, Clay. He said that this was little enough for what you had done."

Clay ate in silence, enjoying the taste of the food that had been set before him. Maria had brought out some jalapeño jelly that, spread on a tortilla with butter, danced on his tongue.

"It is my turn for questions, Clay. How do you feel?"

"I feel great. Little soreness in my side, but nothing that won't let me ride."

"Perhaps you should wait a few more days before you leave."

"No, I've lain around long enough. Reckon I need to be on my way."

The door opened and Rud walked in. "Well, looky here. Son, you're putting away tortillas like you ain't never had one before. You must be feelin' better."

"I am. I was just telling Maria that I'll be heading back to Brackett today. Putting on the feed bag's made me a new man."

"I imagine there ain't no stoppin' ya." He pulled an envelope out of his vest pocket. "Marshal left this for ya." Rud sat down across from Clay.

Clay opened the envelope. It included the reward for Zeke and the money for the stock and equipment. "I'm kinda surprised. Didn't know if the marshal would pay up or not."

"He ain't the best lawman in the world, that's for sure. But I don't reckon he has a hankerin' to have the Rangers ride out and ask him if he paid you. That Jake and Major Jones are two tough hombres."

"Rud, the major offered me a job as a Ranger. Said they were starting back up next year, once Davis is out of office."

"I'll be durned. That's a right big honor, Son. It surely is. I'll tell ya, though, they'll be gettin' a fine man, and I mean that. Just in the few days I've known you, you've growed a heap."

"Thanks, Rud. I've got to think on it. There's a girl in Brackett. Don't know what'll happen, but I've got to think of her."

"You're a young man, Son. Now this might be the perfect woman for you. But you make sure. Too many young folks, both the girls and boys, get wrapped up in this here love, and before they know it, they're hitched. Then there's kids and scraping for a living for the rest of their lives. Not saying it's wrong. Just saying be sure."

Clay thought of Lynn's black hair and those violet eyes swallowing him up.

"And let me tell you," Rudd continued, "pretty and handsome don't cut it. Sure, it's nice now, but when she's got three or four kids hangin' to her apron and you've got a potbelly, pretty and handsome fly out the window. So you just make sure there's more to it than that. I've said my piece."

"Rud, quit carrying on so," Maria said. "Clay can make up his own mind."

"You're right, that's just an opinion of an old man."

Clay slipped the envelope into his vest pocket and stood. "I've got to be going. Rud, Gideon Pinder told me that somebody hired him to kill my folks."

"I'm sorry to hear that. I was hopin' this was the end of it. Did he say who?"

"No. I've a feelin' that whoever it is only talked to Gideon. But I wanted to take a run at Zeke and see if he heard anything about it."

Rud stood. "That's a good idea. Let's get your gear. We'll drop it off at the livery and head up to the marshal's office. Zeke is still in there." Rud grinned a malicious little grin and said, "I reckon he's survived his coffee spill, though I think he'll not be around anyone of the feminine persuasion for a while."

Clay laughed and headed back to the bedroom with Rud following. Rud said, "Brought your shotgun in—mighty interesting contraption. Also picked up your saddlebags."

Rud grabbed one set, and Clay picked up the other with his left hand, keeping the right free. Rud noticed. The two men walked to the front door, where Maria waited.

"Clay," she said, "I am going to miss you. Stop by anytime you're in this country. I'll always have a place for you." Tears welled up in her eyes, and she grabbed him in a bear hug.

He hugged her for a moment. Then he opened the door. "Thanks, Maria. I'll remember that. You take care of yourself, and if you ever need help, send a message. I'll be here."

The two men dropped the gear in the livery and walked up to the marshal's office. Marshal Taylor was behind his desk when they entered.

He looked up. "You look a sight better than you did a few days ago. Did you get your money?"

"I did, Marshal, thanks. You mind if I talk to your prisoner for a few minutes?"

"What for?"

"I'm not going to kill him, Marshal, at least not yet. I just want to talk to him. In his cell."

"You'll have to leave your guns with me."

Clay unfastened his gunbelt and handed it to the marshal. "Now?"

The marshal unlocked the cell. Zeke Martin had been sitting on the edge of the single cot, inside his cell. He wasn't happy about having Clay in the cell with him.

"Hand me a chair, Marshal?" Clay asked.

The marshal slid a chair across the room and handed it to Clay. He moved it into the cell and sat close to Zeke, facing him.

"I've got a question for you, Zeke. It'd be to your advantage to answer it."

Zeke just stared at Clay.

"Do you know who paid you to kill my folks?"

Zeke shook his head, but said nothing.

"Gideon didn't tell you?"

"Did you really gun down Quint and Gideon, both?"

"Did you ever hear Gideon, maybe when he was drinking, mention a name or anything that would indicate who paid him?"

"I could use a drink."

Clay gave Zeke a threatening look. "Would you like some coffee?"

Zeke looked down at his lap, then back up at Clay. "No, sir, I don't want no more coffee. I'm still sufferin'."

"Think real hard, Zeke." Clay, his eyes narrowing, looked at Zeke's lap.

"I-I might've heard something. We were sitting around the fire, out at the camp. We wuz passin' a bottle around. We'd been hittin' it pretty hard, especially Gideon. He liked to spout those scriptures, but he sure had a taste for the bottle. Anyway, he mentioned something. I don't remember rightly, but I think it was about his good friend the Uvalde banker."

Clay felt like he'd been slapped. Not Mr. Houston. The man had taken Pa's money for years. Not much of it, though. What had Pa said to him? Don't trust banks or bankers. Houston had been really nervous when Clay was in the bank. "You remember anything else?"

Zeke just shook his head.

"You're sure he said, 'Uvalde banker'?"

"I am. I'm sure about that."

"Marshal, let me out of here."

"You find out what you wanted?" the marshal asked, while opening the cell door.

"Maybe. Let's go, Rud." Clay picked up his gunbelt and put it on. "I've got to ride. Thanks, Marshal."

Clay strode out of the marshal's office and stepped out toward the livery, his long legs eating distance.

"Slow down, Clay. Can't keep up with you with this bum leg."

Clay realized he had forgotten Rud. "Sorry. Zeke told me who paid the Pinder Gang."

"Who was it, boy?"

"He said that when Gideon got drunk, he mentioned his friend the banker. The Uvalde banker, Rud. Why would a banker have Ma and Pa killed?"

"Money, Clay. Did your pa owe him any money?"

"No. He maintained an account, but kept very little money in it. Pa always said that banks and bankers couldn't be trusted."

"How about your ranch? Is it worth anything?"

Clay slid to a halt. "That's it. Our ranch. We have a long run of the Frio River, with plenty of good grass. In fact, our neighbor wanted to buy it, but Pa would never sell. I don't know what it's worth now, but it sure is worth a lot more than it used to be, what with all the new folks moving in."

"That's it, Clay. He probably figured with everyone dead, he could buy it up at auction."

Clay continued walking to the livery. Once there, he saddled up Blue.

"Which one you want carryin' the panniers, the sorrel or the buckskin?" Rud asked.

"How about the sorrel, Rud. He's been lazing around here for the past few days."

The horses were saddled and loaded. Clay stepped over to Rud and extended his hand. The old man shook it. "You take good care of yoreself, boy. You're not healed good yet, so don't do any hard work. Look forward to seeing you again."

Clay turned, stepped into the saddle, and gathered the reins for the other two horses. "Thanks, Rud. You've been a big help. Wish you'd let me pay you."

Rud chuckled and started moving to his chair. "Don Carlos done took care of that." He sat down in his chair, leaned back, and as he pulled his hat over his eyes, he said, "Adios."

Clay nudged Blue and pointed him east toward Brackett and Uvalde. "Adios, amigo."

19

The hills of Brackett came into view, shadows lengthening to the east. Clay had ridden hard. He pulled into Brackett and walked the horses toward the livery. He dismounted and tied the animals to the hitching rail at the water trough. All three horses drank deeply. The proprietor stepped out of the barn. "Put 'em up for the night?"

"No, thanks. If you'd let 'em drink for a bit, then rub them down and give them some feed, I'll pick them up in an hour or so."

"Traveling at night ain't the safest way in these parts, bandits and Injuns here about."

"Thanks," Clay said. "I'd be much obliged if you'd put their saddles back on in about an hour. Switch the saddle from the roan to the buckskin. What'll I owe you?"

"Four bits'll do, Mister. They'll be ready."

Clay turned and started walking toward the Killganans' house. He was opening the gate when Mrs. Killganan came to the door. "Clay, it's so good to see you."

He walked up to the porch as she came down the steps and

paused for a moment. "Clay, you look different. Somehow, older. Are you all right?"

He smiled down at her. "Yes, ma'am, I reckon I am. Is Lynn around?"

Her face clouded a bit. "Clay, we heard that you had killed three men. Is that true?"

He felt the pain of her sad, accusing look. "No, ma'am, it's not true."

Clay could see the momentary lightening of her features. He continued before she could say anything. "It's not true, because I killed six men and was responsible for another's death."

He watched the shock gather at her eyes, then her lips tensed and thinned. "Six?"

"Yes, ma'am. Now could I see Lynn?"

For a moment, he thought she was going to refuse his request, but she turned and walked up the steps, not inviting him in. "Lynn, Clay is here."

Time slowed down as he waited. Then, as beautiful as ever, she appeared in the doorway. "Hello, Clay." There was no welcome, no lilting laughter in her voice, only a cool, "Hello, Clay."

"Can I talk to you for a moment?" he asked.

She floated down the steps. Her violet eyes were set off by the dusky light.

"I wanted to see you, before I went back home."

"Yes," she said.

She wasn't looking at him. She was staring at his chest.

"You know I had to kill some bad men. They were the ones who killed my ma and pa."

"Yes. I've heard."

Bright, tinkling, laughing Lynn was gone. In her place was this cold beauty, with no use for him, but it had to be said. It had to be brought out into the open.

"It's over, isn't it?" Clay said.

At last, she looked up at him. He could see sadness in her young eyes, maybe something else.

"Yes, Clay, it's over."

"Because I killed those men."

"Yes, because you killed men. I thought it was three, but I heard you tell Mother, seven. How could you kill seven men, Clay?"

"Lynn, it was them or me. They all had a chance to come in peacefully. They chose not to."

"But, Clay, seven men."

"Maybe you'll understand someday."

He looked at her a moment longer. He could smell her lilac perfume surrounding him, but it made no sense to draw this out.

"Goodbye, Lynn."

"Goodbye, Clay."

He watched her walk up onto the porch, and her steps seemed heavier. Then she was through the door and gone from his life. He turned to leave and thought he could hear a sob from inside the home. Clay closed the gate behind him. Darkness was almost on Brackett. It's appropriate, he thought. His heart heavy, he made his way back to the stable.

The man had just finished saddling the buckskin when he walked up.

"Get your business taken care of?"

"Yes, sir, I surely did."

Clay mounted the buckskin and turned the horses out of town. If he got tired, or his side started hurting, he'd stop, maybe along a creek, and sleep under the stars. The buckskin shied to his left as a man stepped out of the shadows. It was JT.

"Howdy, Clay."

Clay pulled the sorrel up. "How're you doing, Mr. Brennan?"

"A darn sight better than you are, I reckon. You've seen Lynn?"

"Yes, sir, I sure have. Seen her mother too."

"I just imagine that didn't go well. Listen, Son, that girl still cares about you. She's been lambasted by her father since they heard you'd killed three men. He told her he didn't want no killer in his house or his family."

"I understand. But it's not three, it's seven."

"You don't understand a danged thing. You say seven? Seven men who burned your pa and killed your ma? Seven men who were dead set on killing you? Son, you do what you have to do. Sometimes it ain't nice. But you live with it. Did those Smith & Wessons work good for you?"

"Yes, sir, they sure did. I'm much obliged to you. Although I got myself shot. Not bad, but if I'd listened to you and started working on that left-hand draw, I'd maybe not been."

"You all right?"

"I'm fine. It went through my side."

"Listen, give Lynn time. She'll come around. She's still going off to school at that Addran College in Thorp Springs. I'd make it a point to meet up with her, was I you. She'll be leaving here in August."

"Thank you, Mr. Brennan, I'll keep that in mind. I've got to be going. You take care of yourself."

"You too, Clay, you too."

Clay rode out of town toward Uvalde with a heavy heart. He hadn't expected Lynn to react like she had. But, who wants to have anything to do with a gunfighter? *Gunfighter, is that what I am now?*

He wasn't going to push the horses. He had all night. The buckskin stepped out in a ground-covering, long-legged walk. Clay took his mind off Lynn.

How do I handle the banker? He thought about what he would do in Uvalde. The moon had come up and was bathing the road with a pale, somber light. *I'll go to the sheriff. We can see Houston together.*

~

IT WAS STILL DARK when Clay rode into Uvalde. He rode through town to the livery. The barn door was open, and there was a light in the office at the back of the barn. He rubbed the buckskin's neck, dismounted, and looped the horses' reins around the hitching post at the watering trough, leaving them enough slack to drink.

"Who's there?"

Clay could just make out Gabby Johnson standing inside the barn with his shotgun in the crook of his arm.

"Howdy, Mr. Johnson. It's Clay Barlow."

Gabby walked out of the stables. "Clay, you've created quite a stir since I seen you last. Sheriff tells me you been busy cleaning up the Pinder Gang. Heard you got knifed pretty bad. How you doing?"

"Doing fine. I need to put up the horses. Probably won't be a full day, but they deserve some special treatment. They've taken good care of me."

Gabby ambled over and scratched Blue between the ears. "That's what I do, Clay. I'll make these fellers think they're kings. I'll rub 'em down good. They'll like that."

The horses finished drinking. Clay and Gabby led them into the stable and stripped off the saddles and gear. Gabby lit two lanterns in the stable, and took a good look at Clay. The old man squinted in the dim light. "You look different, Clay. You're looking more like your pa every time I see you. You look older."

"Reckon there comes a time to grow up," Clay said. He bent over, picked up a brush off the bench, and started working on the sorrel.

"You don't have to do that. I can take care of it."

"Mr. Johnson, I'm waiting for the sheriff to get up, so I might as well help take care of my horses." He continued brushing down the sorrel. "What time does the sheriff usually start moving around?"

"He should be up right now. He's an early riser, and it'll be daylight most any time. He'll be fixin' coffee pretty soon, then head over to the Hash House to put the feed bag on."

"You mind keeping my things here? I won't be long."

"Heck no. You leave everything. I'll take good care of it."

"How much I owe you for the day?"

"Make it four bits and we'll call it even. I'll take good care of your horses."

Clay finished on the sorrel, slapped him on the rump, and walked over to Blue. He scratched the horse behind his ears, and patted his muscular neck, then started with the brush. Daylight was just breaking, bringing light in through the open back doors of the stable. "Think I'll go check on the sheriff," Clay said.

He passed the bank and his thoughts darkened. *How could a man they'd known for years do such a dirty deed?* Clay could feel the start of the dark rage within him. He took a deep breath and pushed it back down. He could see a light in the sheriff's office. His boots clunked on the dried wood of the boardwalk, as he stepped up to the sheriff's office door. It was early. He knocked.

"Come on in, it ain't locked."

Clay stepped into the sheriff's office. The sheriff was standing at the blackened, potbellied stove, pouring himself a cup of coffee. A look of surprise crossed his face as he recognized Clay. "Coffee?" he asked, indicating the pot of coffee.

"Don't drink it, Sheriff, but thanks."

"I reckon I knew that."

The sheriff put down the pot. Holding his cup in his left hand, he extended his right. "It's good to see you, Clay. Didn't expect you back here this soon. I got a wire from the marshal that you'd killed the Pinder brothers and had been shot in the process. Figured you'd be recovering in San Felipe." Careful with his hot coffee, the sheriff sat down behind his desk. "Have a seat," he said to Clay, indicating the chair in front of his desk. He took a sip of his coffee, then tossed a thumb toward the jail. "Got an acquaintance of yours here in my hotel, Milo Reese. Had a deputy pick him up a few days ago. We're holding him for the Tarrant County Sheriff. Seems Milo shot a city councilman."

Clay looked at the man lying on the bunk in the cell. It seemed like a long time since he had seen him. So much had happened. "You're not going to try him here for the murder of my folks and Slim?"

"No, they have first claim on him. He'll hang for that killing. But rest your mind. If for some reason he gets off, we'll bring him back here, and after a fair trial, we'll hang him. He ain't gettin' out of this."

"Sheriff, have you had much dealing with Houston, the banker?"

The sheriff gave Clay a questioning look. "Not much, other than seeing him around town. We travel in different circles. Why do you ask?"

Clay told the sheriff about Gideon Pinder's dying words.

"You have any idea who he could be talking about?"

"Yes, sir, I surely do. I talked to Zeke Martin. He told me that when Pinder had been drinking, he let slip about his good friend the Uvalde banker."

The sheriff was taking a sip of his coffee when Clay told him. He set the cup down, astonishment across his face. "You sure he said, 'Uvalde banker'?"

"I am."

The sheriff stood up. "Let's go. We can talk on the way." He pulled his gunbelt off the hat rack and strapped it on, adjusting it and removing the hammer thong from the Colt, then grabbed his hat.

Clay followed Sheriff Haskins out the door. The sheriff continued talking. "I know that he's foreclosed a little too quick on several pieces of prime land, when folks found themselves on tough times. One rancher south of here was murdered. I never found out who did it. But Houston bought out the widow for way less than the property was worth. I've been wondering about him, but never had any proof."

"Sheriff, we've got proof now," Clay said.

The sheriff turned down the alley next to the bank. There were stairs going up to an apartment above the bank. "Houston lives over the bank. He's alone. His wife left him a while back. They never had any kids."

The boots of the two men rang hollow in the predawn stillness. The stairway planks groaned and creaked under their weight, as they climbed to banker Houston's apartment. There was a faint light slipping around the curtains of the single side window.

Sheriff Haskins banged on the door. "Open up, Houston, it's the sheriff."

Clay caught a glimpse of Houston when he pulled back a corner of the curtain to look out.

"What do you want, Sheriff? It's awfully early."

"Open the door, Houston. Now."

The door cracked open, but Houston had a chain on it. "What can I do for you, Sheriff?" he said through the crack.

"Houston, if you don't open the door right now, I'm coming through it," the sheriff said.

The door was pushed closed again. Clay could hear the chain being unfastened and the door opened. The sheriff drew his gun, shoved the door hard, and stepped into the room. Clay hadn't drawn, but was ready. The sheriff had shoved the door so hard that it had propelled Houston across the room and slammed him against the wall. He must have just gotten out of bed. He was standing there, against the wall, his pants on, but no shirt to cover up his scrawny, little body. He was pasty-white from working inside his entire life, and his body trembled like he was having a chill.

"What's the meaning of this, Sheriff? I'll have your job for this. You can't barge into an upstanding citizen's house." He looked at Clay, desperation flooding his face.

"Sit down, Houston. You've been mighty hard-hearted, foreclosing on a bunch of folks."

"That's the banking business, Sheriff. If I didn't do it, the bank would go out of business."

"Why'd you hire Pinder to kill the Barlows?"

What little bit of color that remained in Alfonse Houston's face drained away. It reminded Clay of when he had caught the skunk in Ma's henhouse. The only difference was the skunk wanted to fight. This man looked like he was going to throw up.

"I never. Why, I would never have anyone k-killed. I'm not feeling good, Sheriff. I've been ill. Maybe you could come back later?"

The sheriff gave a harsh laugh. "You'd like that, wouldn't you? Not happening, Mister. We've got a witness who says you paid him to kill the Barlows. I've got you, Houston. I'm going to enjoy seeing you dance at the end of a rope. You killed some fine people. You killed a woman. You know what they do to people who harm women in this country? I don't know if I can keep the lynch mob away from you."

The little man's head turned from the sheriff to Clay, back and forth. He was loosing control of his body. His eyes had dilated and were as wide as an owls. A thin stream of drool slipped from the right side of his mouth and slowly made its way down his chin. His whole body was vibrating like a tuning fork. His hands came up to his face. He wiped the drool from his chin.

Clay watched the man disintegrate in front of his eyes. He had never seen anything like this in his short life. *How could such a weak, miserable excuse of a man cause the death of my family?* He felt no anger, no rage, only disgust. He felt unclean just being in this man's presence.

The shell of a man turned to Clay. "I'm sorry. I'm really sorry. I didn't mean for your mother to get killed. I really didn't. They were supposed to kill your pa and leave. I didn't tell them to hurt your mother."

"You piece of trash," Clay said. He shook his head. "You did this and you didn't know. You didn't know you could never have the ranch." Clay reached into his vest pocket and pulled out the paper that had been in his pa's safe with the money. "You'd never have gotten our ranch. When my grandpa gave the land grant to Pa, he put a clause in the contract that he couldn't sell the ranch. He also set it up so that if all of the family died, it would revert back to Grandpa, if he was still alive, and he is. It would never have been yours." Clay, like his pa, never raised his voice, but now he leaned down till his face was inches from Houston's and yelled, "You killed them for nothing!"

The man was trying to read the contract. Clay reached down and yanked it out of his hand. He turned to the sheriff. "I'm done, Sheriff. I can't stand to be around him. My only question is, what will happen to the bank? A lot of folks have money in it, including me."

"Don't worry about it, Clay. The Grahams have been trying to buy Houston out for over a year. They'll jump at the chance. We couldn't ask for better folks to be running the bank."

"Thanks, Sheriff. Mr. and Mrs. Graham are folks I'd trust with my life. In that case, I'm headin' home."

"I'll take care of it, Son. Rest assured, the bank will be fine, and this sorry excuse for a man will hang."

Clay closed the door and headed down the stairs, two at a time. He could hear Houston sobbing behind him. This job was done. He turned to the livery.

Ten minutes later he was mounted on Blue, the sorrel and the buckskin trailing behind. Clay rode north out of Uvalde. The warm morning sun felt good. It melted the fatigue and worry from his young mind and body. The farther away from the banker he got, the cleaner he felt, lighter.

The hill country rose in front of him. In his mind he could

hear the swift, cold, rushing water of the Frio. He'd be home soon. Mr. Hewitt wouldn't mind him staying at the homeplace for a while. Now was the time to rest up and get his strength back. He'd make markers for his folks and Slim, and visit his grandparents. There were decisions to make. Would he go to school to become a lawyer, like Ma and Pa wanted? Or would he take Major Jones up on his offer and join the Rangers? He could even become a bounty hunter. That paid pretty well, and put the criminals behind bars.

What about Lynn, or even Diana? Maybe those chapters were closed—maybe not. All thoughts, all possibilities. For now, decisions could wait until later. He nudged Blue to pick up the pace. *I made you a promise Ma, and like you and Pa taught me, I kept my word.*

AUTHOR'S NOTE

Thank you for reading *Forty-Four Caliber Justice*. I hope you enjoyed it. If you'd like to follow Clay Barlow, check out the sequel, *Law and Justice*.

I would love to hear your comments. You can reach me at don@donaldlrobertson.com.

There will be no graphic sex scenes or offensive language in my books.

Join our readers' group to receive advance notices of new releases, or excerpts from new stories by signing up at:

www.donaldlrobertson.com.

You have my word that your information will remain private and will not be shared.

Thanks again, and as Roy and Dale used to sing:

"Happy trails to you, until we meet again."

BOOKS
Logan Family Series

LOGAN'S WORD

THE SAVAGE VALLEY

CALLUM'S MISSION

FORGOTTEN SEASON

SOUL OF A MOUNTAIN MAN

Clay Barlow - Texas Ranger Justice Series

FORTY-FOUR CALIBER JUSTICE

LAW AND JUSTICE

LONESOME JUSTICE

NOVELLAS AND SHORT STORIES

RUSTLERS IN THE SAGE

THE OLD RANGER

BECAUSE OF A DOG

Made in the USA
Columbia, SC
27 July 2022

64168328R00138